Eric Wilder

Oyster Bay Limbo

Gondwana Press

Edmond, Oklahoma

Other books by Eric Wilder

This book is a work of fiction. Names, characters, places, and incidents either are products of the author's imagination or are used fictitiously. Any resemblance to actual events, locales, or persons, living or dead, is entirely coincidental.

© 2024 by Gary Pittenger

Gondwana Press
1802 Canyon Park Cir. Ste C
Edmond, OK 73013

Front Cover by Gondwana Graphics

ISBN: 978-1-946576-20-0

for Marilyn

"Any sufficiently advanced technology is indistinguishable from magic."
    –Arthur C. Clark

Oyster Bay Limbo

A novel by
Eric Wilder

Chapter 1

Dawn was hours away when John Pierre Saucier banged on Jack Wiesenski's door. J.P. was six feet tall with dark hair and eyes and had the good looks of a movie star and the self-confidence to go with it. He'd spent over twenty years as a deputy with the police department and had wanted to retire for years and start a dog training academy. When his captain fired him, he had no further reasons to procrastinate.

Lucky, J.P.'s chocolate Labrador retriever, waited for Jack to let them in. The footsteps padding toward the door preceded someone opening a crack and peering out.

Seeing it was J.P. and Lucky, Jack, dressed in a blue nightshirt, motioned them to enter, then padded into his little galley as he wiped the sleep from his eyes. Jack was short, probably no taller than five-six or seven. He was wiry, closely shaven, with brown hair buzzed almost to his scalp. From the odd shape of his mouth, It was hard to tell if he was smiling or frowning.

"What the hell, J.P.? It's not even five yet."

J.P. and Lucky followed Jack to the plank table in his little kitchen he called his galley.

"Surely, you didn't forget our duck hunt?" he said.

"I thought you were kidding," Jack said.

"You said you wanted to go," J.P. said.

"You didn't tell me we were leaving in the middle of the night," Jack said.

"We have to set our decoys out and be in the blind before the sun comes up," J.P. said. "You coming or not?"

"My brain doesn't work without coffee. I need a cup," Jack said.

"I have a thermos in the truck," J.P. said. "Where's Chief?"

"I think he thought you were kidding," Jack said.

"Get your clothes on, your shotgun, and let's move it. We don't have much time," J.P. said.

"Hell, J.P.! I don't even have a shotgun."

J.P. shook his head. "This ain't Massachusetts. If you live in Louisiana, you have to hunt ducks. Don't you know anything?"

"I'm a fisherman, not a hunter," Jack said.

Grogan 'Chief' La Tortue entered the front door, followed by his two dogs, Coco, a chihuahua, and Old Joe, a German shepherd.

Chief was an imposing man of American Indian descent. He hadn't bothered combing his shoulder-length gray hair, and it looked like he'd slept in his chinos, moccasins, and blue work shirt. J.P. was at least six inches shorter than the big Atakapa Indian. After propping his shotgun against the wall, Chief went to Jack's coffee pot, finding it empty.

"What the hell?" he said. "You swearing off coffee these days?"

"It's not even five o'clock yet," Jack said. "I'm an early riser. This is ridiculous."

"I have an extra shotgun you can use," J.P. said. "Get your clothes on. Chief and I will start the pot."

Jack grumbled as he disappeared into his bedroom. Dressed in camouflaged fatigues, J.P.'s duck call hung around his neck from a leather strap. Chief found Jack's bottle of Dominican rum and poured some into a mug as the coffee pot began perking.

"I haven't hunted ducks in ten years," Chief said. "Today's the first day of duck season. What's your hurry?"

"Lucky holds the gold medal as the best duck-hunting dog in St. Bernard Parish. The competition is coming up next week. We've barely had a chance to practice with everything happening on the island. The two of us need this hunt," J.P. said.

"Hell, J.P., Coco, and Old Joe are raring to go. Maybe Lucky can teach them a thing or two."

J.P. was grinning as he poured himself a shot of Jack's rum and topped it with the brewing coffee.

"Hope Jack doesn't want to take Oscar," he said. "Bulldogs can't swim."

"That's a fact," Chief said. "Doesn't matter. I doubt we'll get out of the door without him."

Chief and J.P. turned when someone said, "Or us."

3

It was Odette Mouton and her two dogs, Mudbug and Bruiser. Mudbug was small, and Bruiser large. Odette was a former Bourbon Street stripper, short, barely five feet tall, her wind-swept blond hair contrasting with her dark Cajun eyes. She'd hitchhiked to Oyster Island after meeting Jack and Chief at Rockies, a Bourbon Street strip club, and was now part owner of the Oyster Island Dog Training Facility.

"What are you doing here?" J.P. asked.

"I like hunting ducks," Odette said."

"You can't go. There's not enough room in my duck blind."

"Maybe you should have built a bigger blind," Odette said.

"Odette can take my place," Jack said. "I'm not into hunting."

"You're into drinking, aren't you? That's half the fun of a hunting trip," J.P. said.

"I like to drink," Odette said.

"Okay," J.P. said. "The only dog that needs to go is Lucky. The rest can stay here."

"I'll stay with them," Jack said. "You can tell me about the trip when you return."

"Me too," Chief said. "I never liked wasting time sitting in an uncomfortable duck blind."

J.P. was frowning when he glanced at Odette. "I don't know about this," he said.

"You look like twins dressed in matching camouflage fatigues," Jack said. "Get out of here and have fun."

Odette and J.P. grumbled as they loaded their shotguns and ice chests into the back of the island's awaiting all-terrain vehicle. Anticipating the hunting trip, Lucky was the only happy member of the diminished group. J.P. continued grumbling when Odette beat him to the driver's seat.

4

"You don't even know where we're going," he said.

"I take directions," she said.

"Fine. You know where Drusy Lake is on the island's backside?"

"Bruiser, Mudbug, and I have a swimming spot there."

"You never told me that," J.P. said.

"Lots of things I never told you," Odette said.

"You ever hunted ducks?" J.P. asked.

"Since I was about three years old," Odette said. "Cajuns invented duck hunting; my mama could make the best duck gumbo you ever tasted."

"Yum," J.P. said. "Can't remember the last time I had duck gumbo."

"Me either," Odette said. "Isaac has promised to cook us a pot if we bring him some ducks."

Isaac was the chef at the Majestic Hotel and Casino, the main attraction on Oyster Island, the barrier island off the coast of Louisiana, situated about fifty miles from New Orleans in the Gulf of Mexico.

"That shotgun of yours is bigger than you are," J.P. said. "You ever shot it?"

"Trust me when I tell you I can shoot a shotgun as good as you. Don't underestimate me."

"Get your panties out of a wad," J.P. said. "My mama could shoot better than my daddy could. It's different with me because I'm a trained professional."

J.P. grinned when Odette said, "Trained asshole."

Drusy Lake encompassed no more than forty acres, the tops of dead trees protruding from the water. Even in the darkness, Odette could see the shadow of J.P.'s duck blind. She parked the ATV near an open boat with a small motor attached to its backside. Lucky jumped out of the little electric

5

vehicle, headed straight for the boat, and climbed aboard.

"I put out the decoys yesterday," J.P. said. "We just need to get situated in the blind before sunup."

J.P. grabbed the ice chest, and Odette followed him to the little boat. The duck blind was a permanent structure constructed of treated wooden planks. J.P. had covered the frame with grass panels, which looked like a thatch of brush in the swampy lake. He piloted the boat beneath the blind and turned off the little electric motor.

"Did you build this blind?" Odette asked.

"Worked on it over the summer," J.P. said.

J.P.'s head swelled when Odette said, "You did a wonderful job."

"Thanks. At least it's blocking the north wind blowing across the lake."

"Mid-forties isn't bad," Odette said. "We'll forget about the chill in the air when the ducks start arriving."

"In an hour or so," he said. "How about a shot of rum until then?"

Got any coffee in your thermos to go with it?"

"You bet I do. Hot and black," J.P. said.

"Just the way I like it," Odette said.

"I even brought water for Lucky."

"He's a beautiful animal. You're fortunate to have him."

"Getting fired this past year and starting a new career has been tough. Lucky has helped me keep my sanity," J.P. said.

"Dogs are the best," Odette said. "Don't know what I'd do without Mudbug and Bruiser."

Odette cradled the steaming cup in her palms. Letting the warm vapor waft over her face, she waited until he'd laced it with rum before taking a drink.

"Perfect," she said. "Just what I needed to chase the chill away."

"How's your new job?" J.P. asked.

"Beyond my wildest dreams, Eddie has become a better boss than I thought he'd be. He's letting me make tough decisions, and we're both learning as we go."

"I'm glad to hear it," J.P. said. "The training facility is doing well. If things go as planned, we'll have our next big sale soon. There is only one possible fly in the ointment."

"Only one?" Odette said.

J.P. nodded. "Frankie Castellano's lawsuit. If he wins, it's back to square one for all of us," he said. "What else?"

"Eddie's finances. He ate through his profits while the film crew was on the island. He's now into his savings."

Odette laughed when J.P. said, "Does he have enough to weather the storm until business turns around?"

"Eddie has never saved a penny; the severance package the government gave him when they let him go was all the money he had, and that is all but gone."

"How do you know all of this?" J.P. asked.

"I do the books for the Majestic."

"Yeah, but how do you know about Eddie's finances?"

"I got worried when he sold his Porsche 911," Odette said. "He loved that car."

"He told me he wanted something bigger," J.P. said.

"A ten-year-old Chevy sedan? The tires are even worn out," Odette said.

"Shit!" J.P. said. "You just ruined my day. Have you talked to Eddie about it?"

Odette shook her head. "Not yet."

"Why not?"

"We're living on an island ten miles from Chalmette. We can barely find enough people to run the hotel, much less to pay to stay here."

"I grew up sprinkling Louisiana hot sauce on practically everything I eat," J.P. said. "Now, I'm eating antacids like candy. You gave me another reason to buy an extra bottle next time I visit the grocery store."

"I hear that," Odette said. "Our world rests on Eddie's work in the courtroom. He's going broke and hasn't sobered up in six months. I'm scared shitless."

"Feels like we're tightrope walking without a net."

"I know," Odette said. "What else could go wrong?"

"I don't even want to think about it. Let's enjoy this duck hunt and worry about everything else later."

The sun was rising on the eastern horizon, an early morning glow cast upon the lake's calm surface. Odette's expression was perplexed as she stared out at the far bank.

"Hear that?" she asked.

J.P. nodded. They both heard the haunting melody carried on the breeze. It was as if the wind was whispering secrets from the past.

"What the hell?" J.P. said.

Something was moving on the lake's edge. Odette also saw it. Clutching J.P.'s elbow with one hand, she silenced him with the other. The grass panes of the blind camouflaged them from view. Lucky couldn't see the lake for the mats. It didn't matter. A guttural growl emanated from deep in his chest as he lay prone on the wooden planks.

The temperature inside the enclosed duck blind had dropped at least ten degrees as a

8

procession of ethereal figures began emerging from the undergrowth, moving toward the other side. The group looked like a band of spirits dressed in the garb of a past century. They could have been historical reenactors, except they weren't real, their luminescent bodies glowing with a pale light amid the early morning mist rising from the lake.

The dozen or so spirits, their clothes tattered and their hair unkempt, were dressed as sailors from another century. Two men were carrying a wooden chest. The group crossed the lake, their boots skipping across the water like solid ground. When they reached the bank, the person in charge motioned for them to halt.

The imposing man wore black breeches and a flowing silk shirt beneath a black leather vest. His hair was dark, as were his eyes and mustache. The hat of a pirate's captain topped his regal head. The two men carrying the wooden chest set it beside him on the bank. Others in the group began digging a hole in the ground.

Not all of the spirits were men. An attractive woman in a ruby-colored velvet dress stood beside the pirate captain. The woman's skin color, a shade of café au lait, suggested she was of mixed heritage. Her flowing black hair and green eyes seemed to emphasize that conclusion. She had a roll of paper in her hand.

When the sweating sailors had buried the chest, the woman handed the paper and a quill pen to the pirate captain. He made a mark on the form and returned it to the woman.

Odette and J.P. hadn't moved, transfixed by what they were witnessing. So intent were they on watching the eerie scene unfold that they hadn't noticed the flock of ducks that had landed in the water in front of the blind. When Lucky sprang to his feet and began to bark, the ethereal figures melted away. As they did, the ducks flew up and away from the lake.

Lucky was still barking when J.P. said, "What the hell did we just see?"

"I don't know," Odette said. "What I do know is that Isaac's duck gumbo's going to have to wait awhile."

Chapter 2

Eddie Toledo owned and operated the Majestic Hotel and Casino, the Prohibition-Era resort on Oyster Island. He lived on the top floor, and his veranda had the best view of the Gulf of Mexico. Yesterday's rain had finally moved north as the early morning sun peeked through the cloudy sky. Not wanting to go downstairs for breakfast, he nibbled on crackers, his bare feet propped up on the railing surrounding the deck.

Eddie was a forty-something bachelor from New Jersey who'd lived and worked in New Orleans most of his adult life. A respected lawyer, he'd graduated valedictorian from the University of Virginia Law School. He was also the previous Assistant Federal District Attorney in the Big Easy.

Eddie had brown wavy hair, which he'd worn too long for his position with the Department of Justice. He was good-looking and knew it. Gorgeous women were his fatal flaw and why he was now working and living on Oyster Island instead of enjoying the country club life in New Orleans' Garden District.

Following a torrid love affair with the beautiful daughter of southern mob figure Frankie Castellano, Eddie was asked to resign. The situation became even direr when he jilted

Frankie's daughter, leaving her waiting at the altar.

Eddie's suite, in the center of the building and on its highest level, afforded him a fantastic view of the beach. The past few days had been stressful, and he'd gone without much sleep. He was about to nod off in the chair when a cool breeze blowing in from the Gulf caused him to open his eyes.

He went to his apartment to get a sweater. When he returned to the deck, the faint glow of a campfire on the beach cutting through the dim morning haze caught his attention. He decided to investigate and pulled on pants, tennis shoes, and a sweater over his L.S.U. tee shirt.

The three-story Majestic Hotel and Casino had no elevator. It did have lighting and electricity installed courtesy of a film crew filming a vampire movie on the island. The hotel was empty following the departure of the film crew. As Eddie descended the stairs, he felt a ghostly presence. It made him wonder how many people had died in the old hotel and casino and how many spirits resided there. He let the thought pass as he strolled across the covered walkway to shore.

Though the rain had passed, a cold morning mist hung in the air as he shuffled across the sand toward the beach. The odor of salty air and the sound of waves crashing into the shore, a freshly painted red and white Volkswagen camper van was parked in the sand, a fire burning, and no one was there to watch it.

A backpack mounted on an aluminum frame sat near the van. The camper had spread a yellow blanket on the sand in front of the tent, a speargun cocked and loaded lying atop it. As Eddie watched from the ground fog floating up from the sand, someone emerged from the water and walked toward the fire.

The person dressed in a black wetsuit approached him. When they removed their mask, Eddie saw it was a young woman. She pulled off the rubber piece protecting her head from the cold, letting her long black hair cascade to her shoulders.

Consumed by voyeuristic attraction, Eddie remained locked in place as the young woman sat on the blanket and wrestled off her rubber pants to reveal a yellow bikini bottom. When she removed the rubber top, he saw she was naked from the waist up. A branch cracked when he stepped backward. He had little time to react as she dived for the speargun on the towel beside her.

"I see you, and you're about to get skewered. Step into the light."

Eddie complied with the woman's request and said, "Don't shoot me. I surrender."

"Stop right there. You get your eyes full?"

Eddie couldn't help but grin as the woman pointing the menacing speargun at him hadn't bothered covering her half-nude body.

"If I didn't, I have now," he said. "Why don't you put that fish sticker down before you hurt somebody?"

"You'd like that, wouldn't you?" she said.

"I'm not a mad rapist. I'm Eddie Toledo, the owner of the Majestic Hotel. I saw your fire from my window and came to investigate. Can I lower my arms?"

The woman pulled the trigger on the speargun, the spear lodging in the sand beside her. She dropped the weapon and patted the knife sheathed on her waist.

"My knife is sharp as a razor. Make one false move, and I'll cut your balls off."

"Whoa!" Eddie said, lowering his arms. "I'm a good guy. Not here to rape anyone."

The woman took her hand off the knife's hilt. The night was chilly, and goosebumps popped up on her chest and arms. She disappeared into the van, returning dressed in sweatpants and a light blue cotton sweater.

"Who are you?"

"Like I said, I'm Eddie Toledo. And you?"

"Amani LeClair."

"Pleased to meet you, Amani. You have a lovely accent. Where are you from?"

"Jamaica," she said.

Amani's arms were clasped tightly around her chest. "I thought Louisiana was supposed to be warm."

"Not in January," Eddie said. "I'm from New Jersey, though I've lived in New Orleans for the past decade."

"Doing what?" she asked.

"Government prosecutor."

"Figures," she said. "Every lawyer I ever met was kind of kinky."

"Why do you think I'm kinky?" he asked.

"You were standing in the shadows, peeping on me. I'd call that kinky. You a peeping tom?"

"I have my foibles."

Amani smiled and said, "We all do."

Amani had dried her long hair with a towel, and it was beginning to curl tightly.

"Did you see something you like?" she asked.

"I'm sorry," he said. "It isn't often I see a beautiful half-naked girl emerge from the sea."

Amani reached into her duffel bag, tossing him a silver flask she'd fished out.

"You're a ballsy sort, even for a lawyer. Have a drink."

Eddie unscrewed the cap of the flask and took a drink.

"Jamaican rum," he said. "Pretty damn good!"

"You've tasted better?"

"Way better," he said. "Try some of mine."

Eddie fished his flask from his pocket and tossed it to Amani, watching as she took a drink.

"Best rum I've ever tasted," she said. "What Jamaican distillery does it come from?"

"Not Jamaican. It's Dominican Rum."

"No way," Amani said. "Show me the bottle."

"Come back to the hotel with me, and I will," Eddie said.

"I need socks and shoes. Wait for me?"

"You bet," Eddie said.

Eddie waited by the little fire as Amani disappeared into her Volkswagen camping van. She was gone for fifteen minutes. When she returned, a colorful skirt and ruffled blouse had replaced her sweatpants.

Amani was still wearing the sweater and had a potted plant in her arms. The plant's vivid green leaves were attached to a vine that grew up a tall trellis upon which beautiful yellow flowers bloomed.

"I need to water my plant before we go. Mind waiting?"

"Take your time," Eddie said. "I'm in no hurry."

Amani filled a copper pot from the nearby pump to water the flowering vine.

"Your plant is gorgeous. I've never seen anything like it. What is it?"

Amani smiled. "A cerasee vine. It grows everywhere in Jamaica. Locals use the leaves and stems to make cerasee tea. It has medicinal properties. I brought it with me from Jamaica."

"It's lovely, just like you," Eddie said.

Ignoring Eddie's blatant flirtation, Amani said, "I'm starving. Does your hotel have a restaurant?"

"Of course," he said.

"I'll buy your breakfast, and you can show me your bottle of Dominican rum."

"You're on," Eddie said with a smile.

"Shall I drive us?" Amani asked.

"It's not far. Let's walk. Along the way, you can tell me why you're visiting Oyster Island."

"Are visitors discouraged?"

"Course not. It's just that you are off the beaten path. Few people even know about Oyster Island."

"I purchased the Volkswagen camper in New Orleans. The salesman informed me the island has awesome beaches."

"Did he now?" Eddie said.

"He didn't tell me it was too cold to swim without a wetsuit. I had to buy warm clothes."

"In Chalmette?" Eddie asked.

Amani nodded. "A nice town."

Good prosecutors always seem to know when someone is evading the truth. Eddie wasn't just good. He'd been among the best. He decided not to worry about why Amani was on the island.

"I parked the van near the public toilets and bathhouse," she said.

"Good choice," Eddie said. "This was a public beach in the thirties. The WPA drilled a well and installed the bathhouse and toilets. The well still works, and so do the bathrooms. There is no hot water, but the showers work. Are you planning on staying awhile?"

"I'm on no particular timeline."

"Looking for a job?" Eddie asked.

"I have money and not indigent if that's what you mean," Amani said.

"I wasn't suggesting you are," Eddie said. "I'm always looking for help at the Majestic."

"What kind of help?" Amani asked.

"Waitresses, assistant chefs, bartenders, room service, maintenance. The list goes on."

"Doesn't appear you have much of a labor pool on the island," Amani said.

"Right about that," Eddie said. "I'm a desperate man. Do any of the positions I named attract you?"

"I can do all of them, though I'm not looking for a job."

"Perfect," Eddie said. "What's that in your hand?"

"Spanish doubloon," Amani said.

"Find it in the surf?"

"A lucky piece," Amani said.

"Heavy objects float to the beach's surface after a storm," Eddie said. "There's another storm coming tomorrow."

"Maybe a sunken Spanish treasure ship laden with a fortune in gold and emeralds lies in the depths near the island."

"There are rumors," Eddie said. "You know something I don't?"

Amani clutched Eddie's hand. "We only just met," she said. "I can't tell you all of my secrets."

"Nor would I want you to," Eddie said.

Cloudy skies covered the Majestic as Eddie and Amani followed the wooden plankway to the Hotel's front door. Eddie had given Odette the day off to go duck hunting. Meika smiled when Eddie and Amani pulled up stools in the dark little bar and joined her.

"Meika," Eddie said. "This beautiful lady is Amani LeClair. She's visiting the island and is from Jamaica."

Meika was a Cajun beauty with long black hair, dark eyes, and a winsome smile.

"I miss the film crews and thought I was going to be alone again today," she said.

"What you miss is their big tips. Is Isaac in?" Eddie asked.

"You know he is," Meika said. "He told me he was making something special for dinner tonight."

"Like what?" Eddie said.

"He didn't say," Meika said.

As they spoke, a little man came out of the kitchen. "My ears are burning. Somebody talking about me?"

"Guilty as charged," Eddie said. "Amani LeClair, this is Isaac Guillot, the Majestic's incomparable chef."

Isaac was a bald little man no taller than five-six or seven. He looked to be in his mid-sixties but could be much older. His dark eyes had faded, though not his smile. Isaac was smiling when he shook Amani's hand.

"Hope you're staying for dinner. I'm cooking something special," he said.

"What?" Eddie asked.

"Duck gumbo," he said.

"Where'd you get the ducks?" Eddie asked.

"Odette went duck hunting this morning with J.P. and the boys. They should be here any minute with the wild game."

"Sounds wonderful," Amani said. "Right now, I'm more interested in breakfast. In Jamaica, I would order Callaloo with saltfish and fried dumplings."

"I'd love to exchange recipes with you," Isaac said. "Many people's favorite here in Louisiana is eggs Sardou."

"Which is?" Amani asked.

"Poached eggs and creamed spinach on artichoke bottoms with hollandaise sauce. Interested?"

Isaac smiled and nodded when Amani said, "Sounds lovely."

Eddie and Amani were soon feasting on Isaac's egg Sardou.

"How is it?" Isaac asked.

"Wonderful," Amani said. "Eddie is a lucky man to have you as his chef."

"Glad you like it. I'd love to try your callaloo with saltfish and fried dumplings."

Amani beamed Isaac her biggest smile and said, "I'll drop by tomorrow morning and show you. Right now, I have business to attend to."

"Don't go," Eddie said. "You haven't seen my bottle of Dominican rum yet."

"Show me," she said.

Eddie fetched a bottle of rum and topped up their coffee cups.

"I must admit that this is the best rum I've ever tasted," Amani said. "I can't believe it isn't Jamaican."

Odette and J.P. entered the bar as Eddie and Amani discussed Dominican rum. Isaac had a quick question.

"Where are the ducks?" he said.

"No ducks," Odette said. "Sorry."

"Not even a single duck?" Isaac said. "What happened?"

"You won't believe us if we tell you," Odette said.

Odette and J.P. were still dressed in camouflaged fatigues and sat at the bar on Eddie's other side. When Eddie introduced them to Amani, they both did a doubletake.

Neither Odette nor J.P. responded when Amani said, "Pleased. Thanks for your hospitality, Eddie. I have work to do. Perhaps I'll see you later?"

"I certainly hope so," he said.

Meika poured rum for J.P., Odette, and Eddie as they watched Amani leave the bar.

"What's up?" she said. "You look as if you've seen a ghost."

"I think we just did," J.P. said.

Chapter 3

As Isaac served breakfast on the polished oak counter, Odette and J.P. forgot about Amani. Meika topped up their coffee cups with rum as they ate. Isaac gave them a look when Odette placed her fork on her empty plate and dabbed her mouth with a napkin.

"Well?" he said.

"What?" she said.

"I can't believe the two best duck hunters in St. Bernard Parish didn't return with a single duck. There are thousands of ducks in Louisiana now. Surely, you saw at least one."

"Something happened," Odette said.

"Like what?" Isaac said.

"An apparition," J.P. said.

Eddie had turned his back to the conversation as he drank his rum-laced coffee. Hearing J.P.'s pronouncement, he wheeled around on the bar stool.

"You saw a ghost?" he asked.

"More than one," Odette said.

"Tell us about it," Eddie said.

"It was almost dawn," J.P. said. "Odette, Lucky, and I were in the blind. The decoys were set, and the morning fog floated off the lake as the sun rose. I heard something coming through the trees

21

surrounding the lake. Odette heard it, and so did Lucky."

"What?" Meika asked.

"More rum, please," J.P. said.

Meika poured them more rum and said, "Whatever!"

"J.P. isn't exaggerating," Odette said. "Something came toward us through the underbrush."

"Like what?" Isaac asked.

"A band of pirates," Odette said.

"Get out of here!" Isaac said. "There are no pirates in the Gulf of Mexico."

"Maybe not now," Odette said. "There used to be."

"These were ghost pirates," J.P. said. "They were carrying a treasure chest."

"How do you know they were ghosts?" Meika asked.

"Because they walked across the lake like it was solid ground. They dug a hole on the other side of the lake and buried the treasure chest."

Basil Doles had walked in on the conversation. He didn't interrupt as he took a seat at the bar. Meika poured him a cup of coffee.

"Continue with your story," he said.

"There was a woman with the pirates," Odette said. "She wore a red velvet dress and looked exactly like Amani."

"You must be hallucinating," Eddie said.

"Odette wasn't hallucinating, and neither was I," J.P. said. "The woman we saw didn't just look like Amani; she was Amani."

Eddie chuckled and shook his head. "You were a law officer for years. You're suffering from group hysteria."

"Bullshit!" J.P. said. "Odette and I saw what we saw."

"Your brains were compromised when you met Amani. Your memories can't be trusted," Eddie said.

"We saw her," Odette said.

J.P. took a deep breath, drank from his coffee cup, and patted Odette's hand.

"Eddie could be right," he said. "I've seen this syndrome play out for years. I've just never been on this end of the stick."

"You're doubting what we saw?" Odette asked.

"Our brains are powerful organs," J.P. said. "They're fully capable of playing tricks on us."

"My turn to say bullshit!" Odette said. "We saw what we saw. You know we did."

"We saw a woman with dark hair, eyes, and coffee-colored skin. When we met Amani, our brains connected the dots."

"I'm not buying it," Odette said. "Amani is the woman we saw."

Odette and J.P. continued to bicker as Eddie went to the bar to talk with Basil.

Basil was reading the Chalmette newspaper. He dropped it on the bar when Eddie sat on the stool beside him.

J.P. and Odette looked at Basil when he said, "Could one of the pirates have been Jean Lafitte?"

"Don't know," J.P. said. "Maybe. Why do you ask?"

"The Chalmette newspaper ran an article last week about the treasure map I found in the hotel safe."

Eddie grabbed the paper and began reading the article. "I didn't show the map to anyone. Did you?"

"Nope," Basil said.

"Then who did?" Eddie asked.

"Don't know," Basil said. "Can we speak in private?"

"Let's go to your office," Eddie said.

Basil Doles was the son of the wealthiest man in St. Bernard Parish. He'd recently completed his law degree from L.S.U. and was helping Eddie with his lawsuit against Frankie Castellano. He and Heather, his new bride, had lived on the island until recently. They'd bought a starter home in Chalmette, and Basil commuted to the island daily to help Eddie with the lawsuit.

A movie had just been filmed on the island. The studio's construction crew had modernized the complex and fitted it with computers, printers, and phones. The filming crew was gone, and the offices were empty except for Eddie, Odette, and Basil. Eddie followed Basil down the short hallway to the complex.

"What's so important that you need to talk to me privately?" Eddie asked.

"We had a break-in last night," Basil said.

"Was something stolen?"

"Not that I can tell," Basil said.

Eddie gazed around the complex. "Nothing appears out of place. How do you know someone was in here?"

Basil opened his office door, grabbed a sheet of paper from the top of his desk, and showed it to Eddie.

"What is it?" he asked.

"A copy of the treasure map we found in the old safe when the film crew's construction manager opened it for us. It was jammed in the copier when I tried to use it earlier this morning."

Eddie stared at the copy of the map. "Who even knew it was in the safe?"

"You, me, and everyone who read the article," Basil said.

"Then the person who broke in was probably from around here."

24

"Not necessarily. The article was republished on the Internet and has made the rounds on all the major social networks. No telling who read it," Basil said.

"Damn!" Eddie said. "How did they get in?"

"When I got here this morning, the front door was locked. No one has keys to the complex except Odette and us. They must have picked the locks. I guess they found the treasure map in the safe, made a copy, put it back in the safe, and left."

"If they didn't want anyone to know they were here, why didn't they clear the jam?" Eddie said.

Basil grinned and said, "They did. The problem is that two sheets were jammed in the copier. Whoever did this got the first copy without realizing another sheet was also stuck."

"Damn!" Eddie said. "Any ideas?"

"I'm clueless," Basil said.

"I'll talk to J.P. about it. Maybe he'll have some ideas."

"There's something else we need to discuss."

"Like what?"

"I can't keep working for you," Basil said. "Marriage and impending fatherhood have altered my perspectives on life. I need a real job and to move on with a paying job."

Basil nodded when Eddie said, "Heather's pregnant?"

"It's changed my perspectives," Basil said.

"I have money. I can pay you," Eddie said.

Basil raised a hand and shook his head. "No, you don't."

"You know something I don't?" Eddie said.

"Have you talked to Odette lately?" Basil asked.

"Every day. Tell me what she said."

Basil had an empty box beside his desk and was beginning to pack his belongings into it.

25

"Maybe you'd better ask her," Basil said.

"Are you leaving me? We have a hearing in three days."

"Sorry," Basil said.

"You're killing me here."

"Wish I had a choice," Basil said. "I don't."

When Eddie returned to the bar, he found Odette talking with Meika and Isaac.

"How's Heather?" she asked.

"Pregnant," Eddie said.

"Seriously?" she said.

"His asshole is puckered so tight he can hardly breathe."

"He'll make a wonderful papa," Meika said.

Odette slid off her stool. "I'm calling Heather. We need to plan the baby shower."

Isaac said, "Since we have no ducks, we'll have to cook up something else."

"Wait," Odette said. "I'll drive up the road and buy some ducks. Everybody and their brother went hunting today."

"You can't do that," J.P. said.

"Why not?" Odette asked.

"It's illegal. You'll spend the next ten years in a federal prison," J.P. said.

Odette looked at Eddie and said, "Is he making this up?"

"Nope," Eddie said. "The Migratory Bird Treaty Act of 1918 prohibits the capturing, selling, trading, and transporting of protected migratory bird species. Don't even think about it."

"Damn it!" Odette said. "I had my heart set on a bowl of Isaac's duck gumbo."

"It doesn't even sound good to me," Eddie said. "Why is duck gumbo better than gumbo with oysters, crawfish, or shrimp?"

"Have you ever eaten wild game?" J.P. asked.

"Wipe that smarmy smile off of your face," Odette said. "We're talking about food and not some sexual escapade you once fantasized about."

"Odette isn't lying," J.P. said. "Duck gumbo prepared by a Cajun cook is wonderful. You'll never taste anything quite like it."

"I'm intrigued," Eddie said.

"How do restaurants sell duck gumbo if they can't buy the ducks?" Odette asked.

Eddie shook his head and said, "They don't."

"Come to think of it, I've never seen it on the menu anywhere," Odette said.

"Go hunting again tomorrow," Eddie said. "Duck season has just begun."

"I can't," J.P. said. "I have other things to do."

"Me either," Odette said.

"Then we'll all have to wait on Isaac's duck gumbo," Eddie said.

One of Eddie's new employees was Alex Pavlovich. Alex had been a conscripted Russian army officer during the Ukraine invasion. He'd fled with Renata Yatsenko, now the Oyster Bay Canine Training Center's veterinarian.

Separated at the Mexican border, Alex and Renata were reunited on Oyster Island after he and J.P. rescued Renata's mom and daughter from Ukraine. Alex was shorter than Eddie, his receding hair dark and his pate shiny. His shoulders beneath a red floral Hawaiian shirt were broad, his knees exposed by his shorts knobby. Alex grabbed a stool beside Eddie.

"Morning," Eddie said. "You aren't dressed for a chilly January day."

"The weather here is like summer in Russia," Alex said.

Everything okay?"

"Fine," he said. "I forgot something and need to return to my room."

J.P. took the stool Alex had vacated.

"Is he okay?" Eddie asked.

"Confused," J.P. said.

"About what?" Eddie asked.

"Renata."

"He's getting mixed signals?"

"More like no signals at all," J.P. said.

"Renata's daughter and mother are crazy about Alex."

"Sveta and Iryna don't make Renata's decisions," J.P. said. "I advised him to forget her and find someone else."

Eddie chuckled. "With who? Odette or Meika?"

"I was trying to be kind," J.P. said.

"He could move to Chalmette."

"You tell him."

"Hard to worry about Alex when I have problems of my own," Eddie said.

"Don't we all," J.P. said.

You two are close," Eddie said. "Take him to Pauline's."

Pauline's was a truck stop house of prostitution in rural St. Bernard Parish.

"Don't tell Heather about Pauline's. Now that she's pregnant, she thinks Basil's playing around," J.P. said.

"He's the last person I would ever expect to play around," Eddie said.

"Doesn't matter," J.P. said. "It's hard fighting raging hormones."

When Eddie and Odette were alone at the bar, he said, "Can we talk?'

"Sure," Odette said. "What's up?"

"Can we go to your office?" he asked.

"You bet," she said.

When they reached the complex, they entered Odette's office, Eddie shutting the door behind them.

"Basil's leaving me. He said it's partially because you told him I'm running out of money."

"I'm a competent bookkeeper, Eddie. I can read the numbers and know what they mean. I think you do, too."

"Maybe hearing you tell me will help it sink in," Eddie said.

"There's barely enough money to get us through the end of the month. Unless something changes radically, we'll have to shut the doors of the Majestic and let everyone go."

"Is it that bad already?" Eddie asked.

"I think you already know the answer."

"I thought things would turn around. It's like Elvis said, 'You never know how short a month is until you have a Cadillac payment.'"

"Never heard that one," Odette said.

"It's true. It's been three months since the film crew left the island, and the overhead is eating my lunch. Have any suggestions?"

"A convention would be perfect, though there's no easy way to get a large group of people from the airport to the island and back again."

"And not enough nightlife to interest a group of rowdy conventioneers. I know; I've attended a few memorable conventions," Eddie said.

"I'll bet you have," Odette said, "I love my job and don't want to lose it. We'll think of something."

"This place is starting to grow on me," Eddie said. "Will you stay with me until I come up with an answer?"

"I own part of the Oyster Bay Canine Training Facility, and we're about to graduate our first students. Jack, Chief, J.P., and I will have enough money to help you. None of us can afford to lose the island."

"That's a problem," Eddie said. "Basil just quit me. He's packing to leave. The situation was touch and go with him. Without him, I'm toast."

"Damn it!" Odette said.

"Don't panic," Eddie said. "I can keep the wolves at bay until our cash flow increases."

"Then what?" Odette asked.

"Don't ask," he said.

"I'll have a powwow with Jack, chief, and J.P.," Odette said. "Maybe we can staunch the blood until our luck turns. Right now, I have books to keep."

Chapter 4

Eddie had paperwork to do, though his heart wasn't in it. He needed a drink in the worst way and returned to the atmospheric Prohibition-Era bar. Alex and J.P. joined him at the counter. Alex had Meika bring him Russian vodka. J.P. ordered coffee laced with rum.

"I'm sorry I was short with you earlier," Alex said

"I'm a lawyer with thick skin. Sorry to hear about you and Renata."

"Some things aren't meant to be," Alex said. "I have other things on my mind."

"Like what?"

"Business ventures."

"Not much business on Oyster Island," Eddie said.

"There could be," Alex said.

"Like what?"

"A distillery," Alex said. "The island is a perfect location."

"There are thousands of liquor distilleries in the world. Why does the world need another?"

"Russian vodka," Alex said. "I can't buy Russian vodka because of the war in Ukraine. I'm guessing lots of others have the same problem. We could make a fortune if we could supply the market."

"How much does a distillery cost?" Eddie asked.

"A startup would run three to five million U.S. dollars."

"Lots of money," Eddie said.

"J.P. says you're having financial problems. This dream of mine could put us on firm financial ground."

"Don't apologize. I like the idea." Eddie turned his attention to J.P. "I'm guessing you've been talking with Odette, and I'm not happy with that."

"Don't get your pecker bent out of shape," J.P. said. "Everything that happens on Oyster Island is my business and yours. That goes for Odette, Jack, and Chief. If you're in trouble, we're all in trouble. Maybe we can help."

"Sorry," Eddie said. "I keep forgetting you're a client."

J.P. clasped Eddie's hand. "I'm more than a client. We're family on this island. Your problems are everyone's. Tell me how I can help."

"The Majestic needs an infusion of money and needs it quickly," Eddie said. "To make matters worse, Basil just quit me."

"Holy hell!" J.P. said. "That can't be good. What now?"

"Plan B," Eddie said.

"What's that?" J.P. asked.

"A Hail Mary," Eddie said.

"I don't like hearing that," J.P. said.

"I like Alex's business venture. We need someone to fund it for us."

"Have anyone in mind?" Alex asked.

"Frankie Castellano would be perfect for it. Unfortunately, he's our worst nightmare right now," Eddie said.

"Who, then?" J.P. asked.

"Adele Castellano, Frankie's wife," Eddie said as he punched numbers on his cell phone. When someone answered, he said, "Adele, it's Eddie."

J.P. and Alex listened to Eddie's side of the short conversation. Eddie smiled when he returned the phone to his pocket.

"Adele's meeting me in Covington for lunch," he said. "If Frankie finds out, I'll be disbarred."

"Then why are you doing it?" J.P. asked.

"With Basil gone, our other options went down the tube. Can you come with me, Alex?"

"Of course," Alex said.

"I'm coming," J.P. said.

"We don't need you," Eddie said.

"I'd like to share some ideas about the Canine Training Center, not to mention you'll need a bodyguard if Frankie and his men show up."

"Okay, let's go," Eddie said.

They were soon on their way to Covington, a small town on the other side of Lake Pontchartrain from New Orleans in the North Shore area. It wasn't far as the crow flies from Chalmette to Covington, except there was no easy way because of Lake Pontchartrain. You either went through New Orleans to the Causeway, then north across the lake or else took the scenic tour around the lake, which was even longer. Eddie opted for the Causeway.

"Adele's dad, Pancho, has a small café in downtown Covington," Eddie said. "Adele's arguably the finest Italian chef in the south, and Pancho taught her how to cook."

"I love Italian," Alex said.

Still dressed in his Stetson and camouflage fatigues, J.P. sat in the back of the old Ford Sedan.

"Who doesn't?" he said.

33

"No one who likes to eat," Eddie said. "You boys, I promise, are in for a treat."

"I can't believe you sold your Porsche," J.P. said. "How old is this bomb?"

"Not old enough to have fins," Eddie said.

J.P. laughed. I think my granddad owned the last of those. At least the backseat is comfortable."

"It's probably because no one ever sat in it. Quit complaining. The heater and radio work and the tires aren't bald."

J.P. laughed again. "Unlike the last person who owned it."

"Enough about my car," Eddie said. "If I ever get rich, I'll buy another Porsche. Right now, Lizzie is my baby."

"Tell me about this woman we're meeting," Alex said.

"Adele is an attractive fifty-something lady married to the biggest crime boss in the South. Her husband, Frankie, is trying to kick us off the island."

"In Russia, crime lords are greatly feared," Alex said.

"Same here," Eddie said. "Adele and Pancho had an Italian restaurant in Metairie, and I ate there at least once a week. I knew them long before Adele married Frankie."

"You think you can convince her to change Frankie's mind about booting us off the island?" J.P. said.

"Who knows?" Eddie said. "We're running out of options. At best, this is a long shot."

Covington was small, with a population of less than twelve thousand. They quickly found Pancho's Italian restaurant and almost reached the parking lot before they had car problems.

The old car shook when a metallic noise issued from under the hood. J.P. sat straight up in the backseat as gray smoke began pouring out.

"What the hell!" Eddie said.

"Coast into the parking lot," J.P. said. "Lizzy just blew her engine."

Eddie managed to get the vehicle off the street and into Pancho's parking lot. Alex, J.P., and Eddie stood outside the car, watching smoke pour from the hood.

"What now?" Eddie asked.

"Call a wrecker and have them take your car to the nearest junkyard. She's toast."

"The man I bought the car from assured me it was in top condition and had another fifty thousand miles in it."

"Didn't your mama tell you never to believe a used car salesman?" J.P. said.

"Double damn!" Eddie said.

"Call the wrecker," J.P. said. "Alex and I will wait for you in the café."

The little café was empty except for Pancho, an older woman, Adele, and her daughter Toni. Adele was an attractive middle-aged woman whose dark hair had begun to show hints of gray. Her curves were voluptuous, and her dark eyes could serve as both an attraction and a signal of anger.

Adele's daughter, Toni Bergamo, had transformed her once voluptuous figure through exercise, diet, and her dark hair into ash-blond tresses. Both women were gorgeous. Meeting them for the first time, Alex's jaw dropped.

J.P. was acquainted with Adele, though not well.

"We had car problems," he said. "Eddie will be here in a minute."

Eddie was right behind them. When he walked through the door, Adele rushed across the little

35

restaurant, her long black dress rustling, and hugged him. She grabbed his hand and pulled him into an empty chair at her table.

"Eddie, you look great. Is your car okay?"

"Toast," he said. "She's on her way to junker heaven."

"Are you getting enough Italian food?" Adele asked.

"Never going to happen on Oyster Island unless you and Pancho move there and open a reincarnation of your restaurant in Metairie."

"You're always welcome here," Pancho said.

"I'd be here every night," Eddie said. "Unfortunately, there's no easy or fast way to get here from the island."

Pancho was eighty-something with a prominent nose and a twinkle in his eyes, belying his age. His bushy mustache had gone to gray, as had his crewcut hair. The smiling woman beside him was younger than Pancho, though older than Adele. Her hair was gray, and she looked like an aging movie star.

"Eddie," Pancho said. "This beautiful woman sitting beside me is Freya. You can tell by her blue eyes she isn't Italian."

Eddie took Freya's hand and was surprised when she didn't immediately release her grip.

"Pleased to meet you, Freya," Eddie said.

"I'm pleased to meet you as well," Freya said. "Who are these two handsome men with you?"

J.P. didn't wait for Eddie to introduce him. Squeezing Freya's hand, he said, "I'm John Pierre Saucier, and this is Alex Pavlovich. I can attest that Alex is Russian, though not a Putin sympathizer."

Alex wasn't handsome in the truest sense of the word. He had a big head, a shiny pate, and looked more like a barbarian warrior. On the other hand, he exuded masculine sexuality, and women tended to find him irresistible. Alex shook Adele's, Toni's and Freya's hands.

"There are many beautiful women in Russia. My Russian mind is blown by encountering three of the most beautiful women in the world in a wonderful Louisiana restaurant."

"Alex, you are so full of shit!" Toni said. "Doesn't matter because I love it."

"Do all Russians wear shorts in the winter?" Adele asked.

Alex's bald pate reddened. "I love Louisiana. It's so warm and comfortable here."

Toni smiled. "I have a feeling you'll change your tune next July."

"I'll grow accustomed to the warmer weather," Alex said.

Pancho started for the kitchen and said, "I hope everyone likes pepperoni pizza because that's what's cooking in the kitchen."

"Love it," Eddie said.

Everyone smiled when Pancho returned with two steaming pepperoni pizzas and sat them on the table. Adele brought two bottles of Chianti.

"I hope everyone loves Italian wine as much as I do," she said.

The day had grown late, Pancho's little restaurant empty.

"The lunch crowd is gone," he said. "I can enjoy my cooking and a little wine."

"Relax. If any customers come in, I'll serve them," Toni said.

"That's why you're my favorite granddaughter," Pancho said.

"You're only granddaughter," Toni said.

"Not so," Pancho said. "Josie's my granddaughter now."

"But I'm your favorite granddaughter, aren't I?"

"My favorite blond granddaughter," he said.

"Whatever!" Toni said.

When they'd finished eating, Adele motioned for Eddie to join her at a table in the back of the restaurant. She wasn't smiling. When they were seated, she squeezed his hand.

"Eddie, I can't help you with Frankie. Your dispute with him is personal. I love him and can't get in the middle."

"Adele, I'm so sorry," Eddie said. "I shouldn't have put this onus on you."

"You know Frankie as well as I do. He's ruthless when it comes to business. When it's personal, he's Sicilian."

"I understand your meaning," he said. "It was good seeing you, and I always enjoy Pancho's cooking."

Adele squeezed Eddie's hand again and motioned for Toni to follow her to the door. Toni wasn't ready to leave. She touched Eddie's shoulder before following Adele out the door."

"Maybe I can help," she said.

"Don't do anything to get yourself crosswise with Frankie," Eddie said.

"I'm not afraid of Frankie," she said after kissing him.

Eddie rejoined the others at the table, and Pancho refilled their wine glasses.

"Did I do something to offend them?" Alex asked.

"You did nothing," Pancho said. "Did you like the pizza?"

"The best I've ever tasted," Alex said.

A few late diners began entering the restaurant, and Pancho left the table to wait on them. Freya was smiling when Eddie glanced at her.

"So sorry we disturbed your day," he said.

"Pancho loves it. He doesn't care for his son-in-law, and Adele knows it."

"I don't want to get them in trouble with Frankie," Eddie said.

"Toni is like her grandfather: independent. She doesn't mind standing up to Frankie. Adele, well, not so much."

"Adele is why Frankie wants to sell the island," Eddie said.

"He's forgotten the reason why he's angry. I could put a spell on him for you and make him forget," Freya said.

"You're a witch?" Alex asked.

"The head witch of the Covington Coven," Freya said.

"We have a witch on Oyster Island," J.P. said. "A Cajun traiteur."

"Do you, now?" Freya said. "Is the old hotel on the island still there?"

"You kidding?" Eddie said. "That's why we're here. Frankie and I are in a pissing match about who owns the Majestic. I thought Adele could help."

Freya's intense blue eyes flashed when she said, "What is it you need?"

"Business," Eddie said. "The island is near Chalmette, though it might as well be in the middle of the Pacific Ocean."

"I heard the hotel is haunted," Freya said.

"You heard right," Eddie said.

An attractive woman burst through the door before Eddie and Freya could finish their conversation. Eddie and J.P. both recognized Frankie Castellano's daughter, Josie. Josie smiled and joined them at their table.

"Eddie," she said, shaking his hand. "It's been a while."

"Too long," he said.

Josie's dark hair had grown since Eddie had last seen her. She wasn't just attractive; she was drop-dead gorgeous and quickly turned her attention to Alex and J.P.

"Toni called and told me someone has a business proposal. I'm here, and I'm all ears. How you doing, J.P.?"

J.P. hugged her and said, "Like an old hound in a flea dunk. How are Jojo and Velvet?"

"Couldn't be better. Those two love each other," Josie said. "Who is this handsome gentleman with you?"

"Alex Pavlovich. A crazy Russian with an even crazier idea."

"Such as?" Josie asked.

"A distillery," Alex said.

"What's the cost?" Josie said.

"The Whispering Winds Distillery is on the market. We could purchase it for a million American dollars, transport it to Oyster Island, and reconstruct the facilities there."

"Distilleries aren't cheap. You're almost three million dollars shy of what you'll need," Josie said.

"We aren't starting from scratch," Alex said. "We can do this for a million dollars."

"Bullshit!" Josie said.

Alex grinned. "You are American. I am Russian. I'll get us a Russian discount."

"What kind of alcohol does the Whispering Winds Distillery produce?" Josie asked.

Alex pulled a silver flask from the shirt pocket of his Hawaiian shirt, unscrewed the top, and handed it to Josie.

"Please," he said.

Josie took a sip and then another. "Love it," she said.

40

Josie smiled and clutched J.P.'s hand when he said, "Our training facility could use a shot of cash to get up and running. Any interest?"

Josie stood from the table and said, "I'll take these two back to the island. Seems like we have things to discuss."

Chapter 5

Pancho was cooking in the kitchen, and Eddie alone at the table with Freya. From the look in her eyes, Eddie wondered if she was coming on to him.

"How do you know so much about the Majestic?" he asked.

"We witches keep up with certain things."

"Such as?" Eddie asked.

"The Majestic is a nearby place of interest. Most of the witches in the Covington Coven are older, and many are retired. We usually plan a get-together around this time of year. Does the Majestic have meeting rooms?"

"Yes," Eddie said. "While the Majestic is old and quaint, we take pride in our service."

"Are there restaurants?"

"Of course. Isaac, my chef, is versed in Louisiana cuisine. No one goes hungry at the Majestic.

"How many rooms are available at the Majestic?" Freya asked.

"While the Majestic is a boutique hotel, it has around fifty rooms."

"If my group wanted to rent the hotel for a three-day weekend, how much would you charge us?" Freya asked.

"Twenty-five grand," Eddie said. "This doesn't include meals or drinks. Those are extra. I'll provide everything else I can for free."

"Are the rooms worth one hundred fifty dollars a night?"

Eddie nodded. "There's no better deal in the Metro, and the Majestic is one of a kind and haunted to boot."

"We'd like to arrive this coming Friday," Freya said.

"No problem," Eddie said.

Freya pulled a checkbook out of her purse and wrote Eddie a twenty-five-thousand-dollar check.

"One more thing," she said as she handed him the check. "You need a ride to Oyster Island. I'll take you."

Alex sat in the front seat of Josie's shiny black BMW as they left the parking space in front of Pancho's café.

"How's Eddie plan to get back to Oyster Island?" Josie asked.

J.P. laughed. "Don't worry about Eddie. He'll find a way."

Josie glanced at Alex and said, "I like your idea about the distillery. I'd rather put it someplace closer where I could more easily monitor my investment."

"You can't put a distillery someplace because it's close by," Alex said. "Other intrinsic things are needed."

Alex shook his head when Josie said, "Have you ever visited Abita Springs? They brew world-class beer there because the water is crystal clear and wonderful."

"Eddie serves Abita at the Majestic. I agree it's good beer, but. . ."

"But what?" Josie asked.

43

"The perfect water for brewing beer isn't the same as for distilling alcohol."

"What's the difference?" Josie asked.

"The pH of the water is important when brewing beer, as it is when distilling alcohol. In the case of beer, the pH of the mash is more important than the pH of the brewing water. A good brewmaster adjusts many things to create an excellent beer. Unlike beer, the chemistry of the water is essential in distilling the perfect bourbon, rum, or vodka."

"Why are you obsessed with Oyster Island? What makes the water there so good?" Josie asked.

"There must be no iron, and the pH must be neither basic nor acidic. This is all accomplished with limestone filtering. These conditions exist in Jamaica, the Dominican Republic, Puerto Rico, and Cuba. The geologic conditions at Oyster Island are more perfect than all of those places. Quite simply, Oyster Island is the best place on earth to distill alcohol."

Josie slowed the BMW at a stoplight and took the opportunity to glance at Alex.

"You know this for a fact, or are you feeding me a line of absolute Russian bullshit?" she asked.

Alex smiled and said, "When it comes to beautiful women, I've told my share of tall tales to achieve my desires. Regarding Oyster Island water, I am being perfectly candid."

"How can I be sure of your claim?" Josie asked.

"I had water tests done by third-party labs. I'll show you the results," Alex said

"Assuming I believe you, what infrastructure does the island have to support constructing a distillery there?" Josie asked.

"Water mains connect the Majestic and the buildings on the island. There's also a sewage plant and sewage system."

"Who put them there?" Josie asked.

"The WPA in the thirties," Alex said.

"The government did this for property owned by gangsters?"

Alex smiled again and said, "Russia isn't the only country where graft and corruption prevail."

"You're right about that," J.P. said from the backseat. "Louisiana has its share of graft, corruption, and everything in between."

"I'm not a virgin," Josie said. "I know all about crooked politicians and businessmen. I've dealt with my share."

"More money is stolen in white-collar crime every year than in the largest bank heist," J.P. said. "Which way are you going?"

"I hate the Causeway," Josie said. "I'm taking a shortcut."

Instead of taking the Causeway, Josie followed Interstate 10 around the east side of Lake Pontchartrain. A flock of seagulls heading toward the lake winged overhead disappeared into a puffy cloud above them.

"Never been this way before," J.P. said.

"I'm a real estate agent," Josie said. "Since I'm always in a hurry, I've learned every shortcut."

"You're driving, pretty lady," J.P. said. "Nothing much I love better than a good shortcut."

"Okay," Josie said. "We're on our way to Oyster Island. I've stayed at the Majestic. As I recall, the water was good, and the plumbing worked. What else? Do you really want to sell part of your canine training facility, J.P.?"

"If your dad takes over the island, he'll boot us off, and there'll be no canine training facility."

"You think that's going to happen?" Josie asked.

"Basil Doles, Eddie's only legal help, quit him today," J.P. said. "Eddie has already blown through his savings and doesn't have enough money to keep the Majestic afloat. Without him, the rest of us on the island have no chance."

"So, the only reason you're talking to me is because I'm Frankie's daughter?"

"Hell no!" J.P. said. "Eddie didn't call you; he called your mother-in-law. Alex and I came along for the ride. We had no idea you would show up and be interested in what we're promoting."

Josie tapped the brakes. "It doesn't matter. I have a conflict of interest, and I should probably bow out before I become more involved."

Alex reached across the console and touched Josie's shoulder."

"I'm begging you not to do that," he said.

"I can't make your problems mine," Josie said.

"What I'm asking you to share is good fortune. A king's ransom is on the island waiting for someone to take it."

"Okay," Josie said.

She took the I-510 exit, soon crossing the Chef Menteur Highway on her way to Chalmette via Paris Road. Waterfowl abounded in the swampy lowlands they crossed, and a snowy egret glided down to a pristine pool of calm water.

"Thanks for trusting me," Alex said.

"Does it matter who owns the island?" Josie said.

Alex didn't care for Josie's insinuation, frowning when he said, "The knowledge I shared with you is confidential. I'm entrusting you to tell no one. If your father gains control of the island, I swear I'll take the distillery deal with me to the grave."

"The insider information you shared is safe with me," Josie said.

"I believe you," Alex said. "Help me build the best distillery in the world. It can't be bad for anybody."

"My dad would likely disagree if he isn't included in the riches," Josie said.

"At least allow me to detail my plans," Alex said. "You aren't committed in any way. If you decide to become involved, we'll figure a way to include your father."

"What if I don't want to include him?" Josie asked.

Josie grinned when Alex said, "We'll toss him under the bus."

"I'll listen to your proposal," she said. "Tell me about yourself until we reach Oyster Island."

J.P. was asleep in the backseat, Josie laughing as she listened to Alex's lighthearted banter about his childhood in Russia.

"I feel I've known you," Josie said. "I trust you, and I already know what that means."

"What does it mean?" he asked.

"Trouble," she said.

Josie's hand rested on the console. She cast Alex a wistful smile when he clutched her hand and said, "Trust me when I say I'd never do anything to hurt you."

"The last man to feed me that line left me alone at the altar in front of a thousand wedding guests."

Josie nodded when Alex said, "Eddie?"

"He did more than break my heart; he humiliated me in front of everyone I know."

"I'm not asking you to marry me," Alex said. "If I ever do, I won't leave you alone at the altar."

"I don't know if I'm prepared to participate in your business venture," Josie said. "I promised to take you and J.P. back to the island. I won't leave you on the side of the road."

Alex smiled and said, "If you know where you're going, I'm happy to be along for the ride."

J.P. opened his eyes when Josie's BMW crossed the bridge from the Louisiana mainland to Oyster Island.

"Love the backseat of your car," he said. "I haven't slept so well in weeks."

"Show me the well," Josie said. "I want to taste the water straight from the source."

"On the beach," Alex said. "Near the structure where the colorful Volkswagen van is parked."

A young woman in a colorful dress was exiting the bathhouse as Josie parked the BMW beside the Volkswagen van. The attractive, dark-skinned woman smiled when she saw J.P.

"Remember me?" she asked.

"How could anyone ever forget you?" he asked. "Josie and Alex, this is Amani LeClair. She's visiting the island from Jamaica."

"Love your accent," Josie said.

Amani smiled and said, "Thank you. Taking a toilet break?"

J.P. pointed to the water pump. "Miss Josie wants to taste the water at the source."

Amani glanced at Josie and said, "The water is wonderful. Maybe the best I've ever tasted."

"Better than what you have in Jamaica?" J.P. said.

"Why are you worried about the water?" Amani asked.

"Alex thinks it's perfect for distilling alcohol," J.P. said.

"Alex is an intelligent man," Amani said. "My father is the chief distiller at the largest rum distillery in Jamaica."

"Is he now?" J.P. said. "Then you know what I'm talking about."

"Perfect water is necessary for a distillery. Without it, you have inferior swill."

"Do you think the water on Oyster Island is good enough to support a world-class distillery?" J.P. asked.

"Maybe," Amani said. "Are you looking for investors?"

"That's the reason I'm here," Josie said.

Amani nodded and started for her van. "Nice meeting everyone," she said before driving away.

J.P.'s smile disappeared when he saw Josie and Alex's frowns.

"What?" he said. Neither Alex nor Josie answered J.P.'s question. "Amani isn't after your distillery on this island."

"Sure about that?" Josie said.

"Trust no one," Alex said.

"An old Russian proverb?" J.P. asked.

"We keep secrets for a reason," Alex said. "You never know who will try to steal them from you."

Josie frowned when J.P. said, "Didn't sound like Amani wanted to steal your idea."

Alex glanced at Josie and said, "Not to worry. You have the first right of refusal. I guarantee it."

It was getting late, and the sky grew darker as Josie followed Alex to the water pump. A metal ladle hung on the pump. Alex filled it and handed it to Josie.

"Wonderful," she said.

Alex nodded. "The most perfect water on the planet."

"Where do we go from here?" Josie asked.

"Your call," Alex said.

Josie glanced at the darkening sky. "What's your proposition?"

"It's late," he said. "You need to be on your way home."

"I'm a big girl," Josie said. "I can drive after dark."

Josie smiled when Alex said, "But not after a bottle of Dominican rum."

"Do Russians always negotiate over drinks?"

Alex stared intently into Josie's eyes when he said, "Alcohol lubricates the machinery of commerce."

"Is that an old Russian proverb?"

"A universal truth," Alex said.

Josie grinned and said, "Does Eddie have an empty room at the Majestic?"

Josie nodded when he asked, "Are you staying the night."

"Yes, if we plan on drinking a bottle of rum."

"I'll see to it you get the best suite in the hotel," Alex said.

"Good," Josie said. "I'll call Adele and have her take care of Jojo and Velvet. I love the little bar in the Majestic. Maybe we can hash out a deal."

"I look forward to it," Alex said with a smile.

Chapter 6

Freya's baby blue Miata convertible had its top down as they drove out of Pancho's parking lot in Covington. When fat raindrops began falling, Freya raised it.

"I could take an Uber back to the island," Eddie said.

"I'd like to see what I paid for. Don't worry. I won't demand the money back."

"You won't have to," Eddie said. "I think you'll like what you see."

Freya reached across the console and patted Eddie's knee.

"I already do," she said. "You're having financial problems, and I'm sorry. I was eavesdropping and couldn't help but get the gist of your conversation with Adele."

"I hope that isn't the only reason you booked the Majestic for three days," Eddie said.

"Not at all," Freya said. "My coven has a need; Oyster Island and the Majestic Hotel fill that need. It's a match made in heaven."

"I hope Pancho won't become angry with me," Eddie said.

"For what?" Freya asked.

"It's a long way to Oyster Island, and it will be well after dark before you return to Covington."

"Pancho and I maintain our own homes. We have sex when urges occur. We are neither married, engaged, or going steady if people still do that."

"Sorry," Eddie said. "I didn't mean to pry."

"No offense taken," Freya said.

Freya was twenty, maybe thirty years older than Eddie. It didn't matter. He could see the toned muscles rippling in her legs when she shifted gears. Her eyes were vivid and as blue as a summer sky. Even her wrinkles were attractive. Freya smiled as if sensing the pheromones Eddie was exuding.

"Pancho doesn't like Frankie," Freya said. "He doesn't voice his dislike because he sees how happy Adele is in her marriage. Like Frankie, Pancho is Sicilian."

Freya smiled when Eddie said, "Birds of a feather."

Exactly," Freya said. "It takes one to know one."

"My grandfather was Sicilian," Eddie said.

"I sensed as much. Unfortunate."

"Why do you say that?" Eddie asked.

"Sicilians don't like to lose. In the case of Oyster Island, there must be a loser."

"And a winner," Eddie said. "Why can't it be me? I'm a good lawyer. Frankie's no smarter than I am."

"He possesses one thing you don't."

"And what's that?" Eddie asked.

"Infinite wealth," Freya said.

"What about Josie?" Eddie asked. "Does she know Pancho dislikes her father?"

"Josie adores Pancho and thinks of him as her grandfather."

"Few people know it, but I was present when Josie's real grandfather died," Eddie said.

Freya shared a glance with Eddie and said, "I've never heard that. Please explain."

"Frankie is an accomplished musician. His father stole his cornet because he wanted Frankie to focus his attention on the company business rather than music. Frankie hired a friend of mine to find the cornet. Tony Nicosia and I found it for him."

"Please, tell me the story," Freya said.

"It's complicated," Eddie said.

"Condense it for me."

"Frankie's father Paco, Josie's real grandfather was a despicable person, his grandfather Vincento even worse."

"How so?" Freya asked.

"Frankie's father helped Frankie's grandfather murder a victim when he was only twelve."

"Get out of here!" Freya said.

"Paco told me the story on his deathbed. They kidnapped a local banker, trussed him, and put him in the back of a wagon. They drove the man to a bayou where they gutted him, diced him up, and tossed him to the gators."

"Horrible!" Freya said.

"Paco was so bloody, Vincento had to wash him down with a water hose when they returned home."

"My God!" Freya said.

"Frankie's dad and granddad were Black Hand, the original Sicilian Mafia. Frankie has never personally gutted and filleted a victim. Doesn't matter because he's as ruthless as his father and grandfather were, and Pancho knows it."

"He's never shared why he doesn't like Frankie with me," Freya said.

"And he never will," Eddie said. "How do I combat a person indoctrinated by pure evil?"

"Magic," Freya said.

"What?" Eddie said.

"I didn't stutter," Freya said.

"You're asking me to believe in something I can't see, taste, or feel?"

"No one knows everything," Freya said.

"I don't believe in magic."

"Arthur C. Clark said, 'Any sufficiently advanced technology is indistinguishable from magic.'"

"Clark wrote science fiction."

"Jules Verne wrote about ocean-traveling submarines decades before such technology existed. Da Vinci drew a picture of a helicopter centuries before one flew."

"So magic is a technology waiting to be discovered?" Eddie asked.

"Not to me, it isn't," Freya said. "Magic is real."

"If you say so," Eddie said.

"I do say so, and I believe I can help with your situation."

"I'm in no position to turn down help, and you've already helped me with your booking."

"I've practiced witchcraft for decades," Freya said. "I don't know about your concept of witches. I know black magic and have used it occasionally, though my coven attempts to use its powers to help people."

Freya had taken the Causeway to Oyster Island. It was dark when she drove across the bridge from the mainland and parked beside Josie's BMW.

"Josie's still here," Eddie said. "She must be spending the night. Will there be a problem?"

"If there is, I'll handle it," Freya said. "You can show me around tomorrow."

"Great," Eddie said. "Hungry?"

"I could eat something. Pancho's pepperoni pizza is in the rearview mirror, so to speak."

"Wonderful," Eddie said. "Isaac, my chef, never fails to surprise me. Everything's on me, by the way."

Freya turned in the bucket seat and gave Eddie a come-hither smile.

"No, baby," she said. "Put everything on my tab. I like it when people are beholding to me and not vice versa."

The rain had increased as Freya and Eddie hurried down the boardwalk to the hotel's entrance. They were both laughing when they stepped out of the rain.

More laughter echoed from the bar. The people sitting at a large circular table halted their conversation and stared when Eddie and Freya appeared from the darkened hallway.

J.P. was still dressed in his camos. When he saw Freya and Eddie, he said, "What the hell! We thought you were lost."

"Freya was kind enough to give me a ride," Eddie said. "Mind if we join your party?"

J.P. and Alex were sitting on either side of Josie. Odette and Meika were behind the bar, dressed in cowboy boots and buckskin miniskirts. They also wore identical purple and gold LSU tee shirts.

"What are you drinking?" Odette asked.

"Glass of chardonnay," Freya said.

"Dry Martini," Eddie said.

Hearing the commotion, Isaac appeared from the kitchen.

"Who's hungry?" he asked.

"All of us," Eddie said. "Bring us each a plate of your chef special."

"You got it, boss," Isaac said.

"Glad you made it," J.P. said. "It was lucky we got to Covington in that old bomb of yours."

"Enough, already," Eddie said. "I'll take you with me when I buy my next car. Odette, have you got a minute?"

Odette stopped wiping the counter with a bar rag and approached the table. "You bet," she said.

"Freya Becht, this is Odette Mouton, the hotel's general manager. Freya's booking the hotel for a three-day weekend starting Friday."

"Wonderful," Odette said. "How many rooms?"

"Don't know yet," Freya said.

Eddie handed Odette Freya's check. "Freya's the head witch of the Covington Coven. Come Friday, this old hotel will be teeming with witches."

"How fun," Odette said.

"Freya's staying the night," Eddie said. "Book her a room. Tomorrow, you can get all the details and help me give her a hotel tour."

"You got it, Eddie," Odette said. "I'll put the check in the safe and deposit it tomorrow."

Odette returned with Meika, serving dinner to the group at the table. Conversation halted as they feasted on Isaac's blackened redfish with garlic mashed potatoes, coleslaw, grilled asparagus, and hush puppies. Isaac helped Meika and Odette clear the table after everyone had finished eating.

"Hope everyone enjoyed the redfish," he said.

"The best I've ever eaten," Freya said. "You're a culinary genius, Isaac. My coven will love you."

"You've truly made my day," Isaac said.

The little bar/dining area was already dim. When the group finished eating, Odette dimmed them even further and lit several candles.

"I love the ambiance," Josie said. "There's no other place like the Majestic in Louisiana."

"Did Alex and J.P. convince you about the distillery?" Eddie said.

"They haven't stopped twisting my arm since we left Pancho's."

"What's your decision?" Eddie asked.

"I love the idea, though you know as well as anyone there's a question of ownership," Josie said.

"I was hoping you could convince Frankie to call off his dogs," Eddie said. "There's opportunity enough for all of us."

"Dad is like a bulldog. When he sinks his teeth into an opponent's neck, he never lets go. You must think he has a strong chance of prevailing in the lawsuit, or you wouldn't discuss compromise."

"My arguments are stronger than Frankie's," Eddie said. "Problem is, he's spending me into submission. I'm unsure how much longer I can afford to stay in the fight."

"How will my investment in the distillery change that dynamic?" Josie asked.

"You and Jojo are the apples of Frankie's eye," Eddie said. "If you are part owner of the distillery and Canine Training Facility, he won't pull the rug out from under you."

"What about the Majestic?" Is fifty-one percent of the hotel for sale?"

"That would make me a minority owner and you my boss," Eddie said.

"Well?" Josie said.

Eddie grinned. "Sounds like I'm exchanging one problem for a bigger one."

The bar had suddenly gone deathly quiet. Thunder, rattling the rafters, broke the silence.

When the old structure grew quiet again, Josie said, "What's your answer?"

"It's not a deal I have a good feeling about," Eddie said. "That doesn't prevent you from making a deal with Alex and J.P."

Alex and J.P. stared at Eddie when Josie said, "It's all or nothing. Odette, I'm ready to go to my room."

"I have your key," Odette said. "Come with me."

Josie kissed J.P. and Alex on their foreheads and then followed Odette up the stairs to her room.

"Guess that explains how she feels about me," Eddie said.

"What did you expect?" J.P. asked. "You left her standing at the altar."

"I had my reasons," Eddie said.

"Josie's offering us a good deal," J.P. said. "It'll end our problems and guarantee our success."

"For you, maybe," Eddie said. "It would be the beginning of mine."

"We need you, Eddie," J.P. said. "Without you, we'll all be kicked off the island."

"The judge hasn't decided on the lawsuit," Eddie said.

"Basil's gone. I can't help you, nor can any of us," J.P. said.

"Freya's coven gathering is buying us some time," Eddie said. "Things aren't that dire."

J.P. killed his mug of rum and said, "Hell, Eddie, you don't even have a car anymore. How are you going to get back and forth to Chalmette?"

"A damn vehicle is the last of our problems. I'll get a car tomorrow," Eddie said.

Odette returned from upstairs. Meika handed her a bottle of Dominican rum, and she joined the party at the table.

"Someone made a reservation today. He's arriving tomorrow and staying for a while," she said.

"Oh yeah?" Eddie said. "Who?"

"Someone named Carlos."

"What's his last name?" Eddie asked.

Odette looked up the name on her cell phone. "Palacio," she said.

"From where?"

"Miami," Odette said.

"Crap!" Eddie said.

"What?" J.P. asked.

"Carlos Palacio's father, Fernando, is the biggest mob boss in the southeastern United States. He's bigger than Frankie."

"There must be more than one Carlos Palacio in Miami," Odette said.

"When is he arriving?" Eddie asked.

"Tomorrow," Odette said. "He guaranteed his room with his credit card."

"Shit!" Eddie said.

"You could be wrong, Eddie," Odette said.

"I was Assistant Federal District Attorney for New Orleans. Trust me when I tell you I know every mob boss in the South."

Freya drank her wine and then clutched Eddie's wrist.

"You have more problems in the Majestic than lawsuits and mob bosses," she said.

"Like what?" Eddie asked.

"Spirits of the night. The Majestic is seriously haunted," Freya said.

"Impossible," Odette said. "All the spirits are gone from the Majestic. My traiteur friend, Paula, and I performed a cleansing ceremony."

Thunder struck again, followed by an unearthly wail riveting everyone's attention.

"They're back," Freya said.

Chapter 7

Outside of the Majestic Hotel, the storm was intensifying. Inside, the group gathered around the circular table as the candles flickered.

"Why do you think ghosts have returned to the Majestic?" Odette asked.

"I sense them," Freya said. "They are in the room with us as we speak."

"Bullshit!" Odette said. "The ghosts and spirits are gone."

"There are ghosts on the island. We saw them this morning," J.P. said. "Remember?"

"On the far side of the island, not here in the Majestic," Odette said.

"They are here," Freya said. "I can summon them if you don't believe me."

"How can you do that?" Odette asked.

"Séance," Freya said.

Odette snickered. "Did you bring your Ouija board?"

Jack and Chief entered the dark little bar before Freya could answer. Both were drenched. Jack wrung the water out of his dark hair and then went to the bar.

Meika grinned when he pounded the counter and said, "Grog, bar wench."

"I love it when you pretend to be a pirate. I think you need the whole bottle of rum," she said.

Meika threw Jack and Chief bar towels when Jack said, "What I need is a warm fire."

"You're in luck," Meika said. "Odette and I stoked the fireplace earlier today."

Flames licked from the rustic fireplace constructed of limestone blocks quarried from some place in north Louisiana. Jack smiled as he took the bottle of rum and sat at the hearth in front of the roaring fire. Chief joined him.

"What's happening?" he said.

"Staying out of the weather," Eddie said. "What's your story?"

"A little birdie told us Isaac was cooking redfish," Chief said.

"Jack didn't cook anything?" Eddie asked.

"Sometimes, I like eating food I didn't cook," Jack said.

"Jack was a cook in the Merchant Marines," J.P. said. "It's a tossup who is the best chef on the island. Isaac and Jack are each other's biggest fans."

"Aren't you going to introduce us to the pretty lady you're sitting beside?" Chief asked.

"Freya Becht," Eddie said. "These two fine gentlemen are Jack Wiesinski, the lighthouse keeper, and Chief La Tortue, the arguable owner of Oyster Island."

Freya smiled and said, "Please join us."

"Nothing either of us would like better, but we're wringing wet," Jack said.

"Follow me, and you can use one of the rooms," Odette said. "We have bathrobes to fit everyone. I'll throw your clothes in a dryer."

"You're a doll," Jack said as they followed her down the hall.

Alex looked apprehensive and Freya said, "Don't like ghosts, Alex?"

"One of the few things that frighten me," he said.

"Why is that?"

"The orphanage in Russia where I grew up was dank and cold. When the winter winds blew through the cracks in the walls, the older boys would scare us with tales of ghosts and bloody bones."

Freya reached across the table and squeezed his hand. "You have no mother?"

Alex shook his head and said, "Nyet."

He smiled when Freya said, "I'm your mother now. I'll protect you from the ghosts."

"If you were my mother, I would have to be spanked because I would have thoughts of incest."

Freya smiled and said, "Then you do need a spanking."

Everyone turned when a woman with a Jamaican accent said, "I want to watch."

It was Amani LeClair, the colorful shawl wrapped around her shoulders doing nothing to warm her legs, mostly exposed by her thigh-length red culottes and low-cut white blouse.

"Join us, Amani," Eddie said.

"I'm freezing," she said. "Allow me to warm up in front of your wonderful fireplace first."

"What are you drinking?" Eddie asked.

"Something warm," she said.

Amani smiled and nodded when Eddie said, "A mug of Blue Mountain mixed with a shot of rum?"

"You have Jamaican Blue Mountain coffee?" she asked.

"No, but what we do have is hot and tasty, and we have lots of Dominican rum," Eddie said.

"Works for me," Amani said.

Isaac appeared from the kitchen with redfish for Jack and Chief. He smiled when he saw Amani warming her hands in front of the fire.

"Hungry, baby?" he asked.

"Yes, thank you. I've fantasized about your cooking all day," she said.

Everyone chuckled when Isaac said, "I'm glad there's still something about me the ladies fantasize about."

Jack and Chief returned to the bar clad in white terrycloth robes, the group soon conversing like old friends. Chief grabbed the empty chair beside Freya before Jack had a chance. Jack grumbled and sat next to Chief.

Freya smiled and said, "I could see you were a large man. Now that you're sitting beside me, I realize you're even larger than I first thought. Are you Native American?"

Chief grinned and said, "Indian, yes. Wild, not so much."

"Eddie touted your cooking prowess, Jack. What's your story?" Freya asked.

"I joined the Navy when I was fifteen," he said.

"Get out of here," Freya said.

"I served for a year before the Navy learned I'd lied about my age and discharged me."

"What possessed you to join the Navy when you were only fifteen?" Freya asked.

"Long story," Jack said. "The bottom line is that after the Navy, I joined the Merchant Marines. When I retired, the job of lighthouse keeper was available. I took it and have been on the island ever since."

"You're an interesting man, and I'll bet you have many stories."

"Don't get him started," Chief said.

"We'll let Amani, Jack, and Chief finish eating, and then you can perform the séance. Is there anything you need?" Eddie asked.

"A candle, preferably black, if you have one that color; a mirror, preferably a vintage mirror; and lastly, an imaginary circle," Freya said.

Odette got up and said, "I can get you the candle and a mirror. I have no clue what you mean by an imaginary circle."

"When everyone finishes Isaac's wonderful repast, I will show you," Freya said.

Odette set a black candle on the table and dragged an antique cheval mirror—a long mirror mounted on a swivel in a frame, allowing it to be tilted—from one of the rooms. After Amani, Jack, and Chief finished eating, Meika and Isaac cleared the table and joined them. With all attention focused on Freya, she instructed Odette to light the black candle.

Like all good lawyers, Eddie had a pen in his shirt pocket.

Freya glanced at it and said, "May I borrow it?"

Taking the expensive writing instrument Eddie had handed her, she used it to make a black dot on the white tablecloth.

"We need a summoning circle to request the presence of the ghosts," she said.

"That's not a circle," Eddie said.

"It's only a dot on the tablecloth," Odette said.

"Mathematics describes everything in the universe. Every molecule has a mathematical equivalent, no matter how large or small. This dot represents a circle," Freya said.

Eddie snickered and said, "If you say so."

"A circle consists of all the points in the plane which are of constant distance from some fixed point. If the distance from the circle's center is zero, then the result is this dot on the table," Freya said.

"What makes it imaginary?" Odette asked.

Freya scrawled a mathematical equation on the tablecloth.

"If the radius of the circle is less than zero, then this equation will be complex and not real. In other words, this is an 'imaginary circle'. Like our own DNA, everything is a sequence of numbers. Even magic. This imaginary circle will help summon the spirits."

"If you say so," Odette said.

"Extinguish the lights, and you will soon see for yourself," Freya said.

Only the billowing glow of the black candle lighted the room after Odette had turned off the lights. They didn't have to wait for long for the action to begin as a droning sound coming from somewhere deep in Freya's chest began filling the room.

Eddie glanced at Freya, her jaw tilted upward and her blue eyes swallowed by the back of her head. Something white, looking like ticker tape, began issuing from her closed lips. She began to chant, the voice issuing from her mouth seemingly coming from someone other than her.

"By moonlit veil and shadows deep,
Where spirits stir from timeless sleep.
In halls of Majestic, Oyster's embrace
I beckon now, the spectral grace."

A penetrating wail coming from the floor mirror echoed through the old hotel. When the wail dissolved into a tortured moan, Freya continued her chant.

"Whispers lost in ancient lore.

Come forth, phantoms, I implore.
From realms unknown, both near and far,
Reveal the secrets that spirits mar."

The black candle flickered and almost died. It didn't, sparking anew as Freya's words continued.

"Gather 'round, ethereal kin,
In this sacred séance, let the dance begin.
Open the veil twixt worlds unseen.
Speak through me, let truths convene."

Outside, the storm had reached full force, the wind hammering at the windows and lightning striking so close to the old structure that it rattled the walls. White ectoplasm continued pouring from Freya's locked lips, as did the words of her chant.

"By mystic force and magic's might.
Unveil the mysteries of this haunted night.
Let echoes of the past now speak.
In this hallowed space, our destinies peak.

Eddie's and everyone's heads lay on the table. He was trying to speak, though he hadn't the power to open his mouth. The ectoplasm issuing from Freya's mouth was spreading across the table. Some of it got into Eddie's eyes. It didn't matter. He couldn't move. Freya continued to chant.

"Specters old, with stories untold.
In the Majestic's chambers, unfold.
Spirit guides, both kind and wise.
Speak through me, unveil the ties.

Chief's moans overrode the thunder. Eddie was trying to scream. Odette and Amani were screaming, and Jack rolling around on the floor as if possessed by a demon. Ectoplasm spewed from Freya's lips as she continued to chant.

"Through time and space, this sacred plea.
Awaken now and speak to me.
Majestic ghosts, heed my call.
Reveal your tales. . ."

Freya's words died away as she began choking on the spewing ectoplasm. The black candle popped and then went dark. Eddie struggled to move as thunder shook the Majestic. When it ceased, an ethereal glow filled the room as ghostly spirits began exiting the mirror. Eddie rubbed his neck and glanced around. What he saw shook his concept of reality to the core.

A spectral mist had materialized above a weathered table at the center of the room. The atmosphere shifted, and the temperature dropped, sending shivers down everyone's spines. The ghosts of a band of pirates exited the mirror, their eerie forms reflecting the hardships of their seafaring lives.

At the forefront stood the formidable figure of Jean Lafitte, the notorious pirate of history. His eyes glowed with an otherworldly intensity as he began to speak, his voice carrying the weight of centuries.

"In the heart of this island, beneath the sand that has swallowed our legacy, lies a curse more potent than any tempest at sea."

Lafitte's voice echoed through the bar, resonating with a spectral authority. Jack had pulled himself off the floor, and Amani and Odette were no longer screaming.

Everyone's mouths were open as they stared at the spectral entity. Lightning danced outside, casting fleeting glimpses of the pirates' haunted expressions. After a dramatic pause, Lafitte continued his explanation:

"Our treasure wasn't just gold and jewels but a force of ancient magic. A curse that hungers for the greedy and the unworthy."

"What curse?" Freya asked.

Lafitte's spectral appearance shifted, and his hollow eyes seemed to pierce through time itself.

"Beware, for those who dare to unearth the island's bounty will unleash a darkness long kept at bay. The curse is intertwined with the soul of this land, and only the true owners may profit."

"Explain yourself," Freya said.

Without answering, the spirits began disappearing back into the mirror as the wind outside howled in response. Odette hurried to the wall switch as the room dissolved into darkness, flooding the little area with muted light. As she did, a man entered the room carrying a suitcase. He was young, dark-complected, with brown curly hair.

"I had a reservation for tomorrow. I'm here a day early."

Chapter 8

Odette hurried to where the man waited, took his suitcase, sat it on the floor, and shook his hand.

"Welcome to the Majestic. I'm Odette, and I'll get you checked in."

"While she's at it, I'll go with them and have Odette assign me a room," Freya said.

Eddie grabbed her hand and pulled her back to the table. "What about the ghosts?" he asked.

"What about them?" Freya asked.

"Explain the meaning of what Lafitte said."

"I'm a witch, not a psychiatrist," Freya said. "What do you want me to tell you?"

"What we saw," Eddie said.

"I sensed ghosts here in the Majestic," Freya said. "It's the reason I performed the séance. What we witnessed is a matter of interpretation."

"Is that it?" Eddie said.

"Sounds to me like you need to find out about the Curse."

Meika approached the table as Freya walked away. Everyone raised their hands when she asked, "Who needs a drink?"

Isaac went behind the bar to help her, and they were soon dispensing alcoholic drinks to the table.

Eddie turned to Chief, saying, "Know anything about this curse?"

"It was the French that first infected my people with the plague."

"Which plague?" Eddie asked.

"Does it matter?" Chief said. "The Atakapans perished as a result of diseases brought by the French, Spanish, and Americans."

"Then you've heard of this curse Lafitte's ghost spoke about?" Eddie said.

"Yes," Chief said.

"You've never mentioned it to me," Jack said.

"I'd all but forgotten about it," Chief said. "Tell you the truth, I never thought it was real."

"What is the curse?" J.P. asked.

"I don't know. I was young when I heard of it. It went in one ear and out the other."

"You've lived on this island all your life and don't know about the curse?" J.P. said.

"I never thought about it," Chief said. "Everyone who knew anything about the curse is dead. Who would I ask?"

"No idea," Eddie said. "What about the Fountain of Youth? Is there such a thing on the island?"

"The Magic Fountain. It's just up the hill from my teepee," Chief said. "I was a kid when Grandfather took Grandmother to it. She was very sick. Grandfather was desperate. He bathed her in the healing water, and she survived—at least for another decade."

All eyes turned to J.P. when he said, "Before everyone gets all hepped up about the curse, there were likely no ghosts."

"You didn't see them?" Jack said.

"I saw the same thing everyone else saw," J.P. said.

"Then what the hell are you talking about?" Jack said.

"What we thought we saw was an illusion. Freya didn't summon a band of spirits, but she hypnotized us, so we thought she did. We're the victims of her group hypnosis," J.P. said.

"Bullshit!" Jack said. "I saw what I saw."

"What about the white stuff pouring from Freya's mouth?" J.P. said.

"You, me, and everyone else in the room saw it," Jack said. "What's your point?"

J.P. smiled and said, "Then where is it? Maybe what we thought we saw was no more than an induced fantasy."

"Maybe the white stuff was water vapor, and it dissolved back into the air," Jack said.

"That's the point," J.P. said. "Everything has a logical explanation. Every implausible event can be explained. Maybe what we saw was an induced vision. The brain is a complex organ. Do you know for sure if what I'm suggesting isn't true?"

Everyone turned their attention to Amani when she said, "Then what happened to the mirror?"

The old mirror's surface had turned a dull yellow and was no longer reflective. The group at the table stared at it in disbelief.

"Maybe it was like that when Odette brought it," J.P. said.

"Odette wouldn't have brought out a defective mirror," Chief said.

J.P. looked perplexed when he said, "You know that for a fact?"

"You haven't weighed in on this, Alex," Eddie said. "What do you think?"

"I think I'm going back to Russia. It isn't half as frightening as what I just witnessed."

"Could this have been group hypnosis?" Eddie asked.

"J.P. is a professional," Alex said. "During his career, he saw things none of us will ever see. If he says what we experienced was induced by hypnotic persuasion, then perhaps it is."

"Meika," Eddie said. "We're going to need another round."

"You got it, boss," she said.

Odette returned from the front desk with a big smile on her face.

"Why are you so happy?" Eddie asked.

"You kidding?" she said. "Our new guest looks like a Harlequin romance cover model. I did everything I could to keep from ripping open his shirt to see his chest."

"Did he come on to you?" Amani asked.

"If he had, I'd be in his bedroom now," Odette said.

Isaac brought Freya a fresh drink after she had followed Odette to the table.

"Why is everyone staring at me?" she asked.

"J.P. seems to think there were no ghosts, and what we saw was the result of group hypnosis," Eddie said.

"Did he, now?" Freya said.

"Of course, there are ghosts," Odette said. "We saw them this morning in your duck blind. I was skeptical, but I saw what I saw."

"Did you?" Maybe Freya is playing on a description of the group she heard us describe," J.P. said.

"Is all we saw was an induced illusion?" Eddie asked.

"Is that what you think?" Freya said. "What about you, Chief? You think I'm a charlatan?"

"J.P. has never led me astray," Chief said. "Still."

"Still what?" Eddie asked.

"His explanation doesn't explain how Lafitte knew about the island's curse," he said.

Chief nodded when Freya said, "Then the curse is real?"

"How are we going to find out about the curse?" Eddie said.

"I don't know about Lafitte's ghost," Chief said. "I do know there are ghosts on this island, my grandfather. He can tell us what we need to know."

"You can summon your grandfather's ghost?" Freya asked.

"He always appears when I bathe in the Magic Fountain," Chief said.

"Magic Fountain?" Freya said.

"Up the hill from my teepee," Chief said. "I'll dip in the pool and talk with Grandpa."

"When?" Freya asked.

"Soon as my clothes are dry."

"There's a storm outside," Jack said.

"The Magic Fountain is safe in a storm. No harm can come to you when you're in it," Chief said.

"I'm going with you," Freya said.

"Me too," Jack said.

'Lightning will strike you dead," Eddie said.

"No, it won't. Except for light rain, the storm has passed. Grandfather would never let me be harmed," Chief said."

"You don't have to wait any longer," Odette said. "Your clothes are dry. I put them in the room where you changed. You're welcome to stay the night if you like."

"You're a princess, Odette. Any other night, I'd take you up on your offer. Tonight, I'll take a dip in the Magic Fountain."

Jack followed Chief to the room down the hall.

"You're going with them?" Eddie said.

"I want to learn more about what we experienced in the séance," Freya said.

She smiled and patted Eddie's cheek when he asked, "Did you hypnotize us?"

"You saw what you saw. Believe what you want to believe. It isn't up to me to provide pat explanations," she said.

When Chief and Jack returned, Freya followed them out the door. When they were gone, Eddie glanced at Odette.

"I'm relieved about one thing," he said.

"What?" she asked.

"The person you checked in is too young to be Fernando Palacio."

A man stepped from the darkness and said, "Did someone call my father's name?"

As Odette had said, the young man was as handsome as an Italian movie star. He sat beside Amani and slipped something into her hand. Eddie noticed.

"You two know each other?" he asked.

"Though my home is in Miami, I maintain a villa in Jamaica. Amani and I have crossed paths more than once. She's the island's most beautiful woman," Carlos said.

Despite the compliment, Amani wasn't smiling.

Carlos grinned when Eddie said, "Is Amani the reason for your visit to the island?"

"Very perceptive," he said. "My family is into the distilling of rum. Amani thinks Oyster Island is a perfect place to establish a distillery. I'm here to find out."

"Does she now?" J.P. said. "Then you're aware someone is already vying for the rights to the proposed distillery?"

Alex shook his head when Carlos said, "Has a deal already been struck?"

"Not yet," he said.

"Then perhaps you'll tell me more about your proposal," he said.

When Alex smiled and reached across the table, someone descending the stairs said, "Don't you dare shake that man's hand, Alex Pavlovich."

It was Josie Castellano. Carlos Palacio stood from his chair and stared at her.

"Josie, is that you?"

"Carlos," Josie said. "What are you doing on Oyster Island?"

Amani frowned, her arms locked tightly around her chest, when Carlos motioned for Josie to take the empty chair beside him.

"Please join us," he said.

Josie sat between Carlos and Eddie.

They nodded when Eddie said, "You two know each other?"

"We grew up together," Josie said.

"Then your dads know each other," Eddie said.

Carlos turned away from Eddie without answering his question. Josie answered for him.

"Best friends," Josie said. "At least they once were."

Amani didn't like Carlos's reaction to seeing Josie. She got out of her chair and started for the door. As if forgetting something, she turned and said, "You are a wonderful chef, Isaac. Thank you. Eddie, I will settle up with you tomorrow."

Carlos hurriedly left the table and followed her out of the bar. Their ensuing argument was loud though indecipherable. Five minutes passed before Carlos returned to the table alone. Meika and Isaac were polishing glasses behind the bar.

"It's late," Odette said. "You two go home. I'll take care of things the rest of the night."

"You sure?" Isaac asked. "I don't mind staying."

He grinned when Odette said, "You two need your beauty sleep."

"Thanks, baby," Isaac said.

"See you at the house," Meika said.

"Don't wait up," Odette said.

Meika and Isaac stopped what they were doing and disappeared into the kitchen as Odette worked on another round for the people remaining at the table. Alex and J.P. scooted around the table and sat on either side of Josie.

"You do not need to worry," Alex said. "I wasn't going to make a deal behind your back."

"Thanks, Alex. I don't know why I'm so insecure. We haven't even reached the negotiating stage yet on the distillery project."

Josie smiled when Alex said, "When we do, I look forward to constructing the world's best distillery."

"How well do you know Carlos?" J.P. asked.

Josie smiled again. "When our parents visited, Carlos and I would share the same crib."

"Cozy," J.P. said.

"Carlos's father moved to Miami when we were in our teens. Right after the rift."

"Rift?" Eddie said.

"A misunderstanding," Josie said.

Josie gave Eddie a dirty look when he said, "Please explain."

"I've already spoken out of turn," she said.

Feeling the sudden chill, J.P. attempted to change the subject.

"Looks like Carlos and Amani are an item," he said. "I think she thought he was paying too much attention to you."

"She has nothing to worry about from me," Josie said. "Whatever Carlos and I once had is gone."

"Everyone's eyes were suddenly on Josie. "What?" she said.

"You and Carlos were in a relationship?" J.P. asked.

"More than that," Josie said. "Carlos is Jojo's father."

Eddie's mouth dropped open. Before he could comment, an explosion rocked the old hotel. Bolting out of his chair, he started for the front door.

"That wasn't thunder," he said. "Something just blew up."

Chapter 9

The rain continued as Freya, Chief, and Jack reached the Majestic's front entrance. Chief stopped in the hallway without opening the door.

"Looks like rain for the rest of the night," he said. "I'm going to my teepee. There are warm and dry rooms for you here at the Majestic."

"Have you changed your mind about bathing in the Magic Fountain?" Freya asked.

"Not me. I don't mind getting wet."

Freya grinned and said, "Me either. I won't melt."

"Count me in," Jack said.

"You're both crazy as hell," Chief said. "I love it. Follow me and be careful. The wood walkway can get pretty damn slippery in the rain."

Lightning blazed across the sky as the three hurried down the boardwalk. The rain had increased as they reached the foot of the walkway where Chief's Model T Ford awaited them. Jack held the door for Freya and then cranked the engine before sliding into the front seat beside her. They all were wet, and Freya was shivering.

"What a beautiful car," she said.

"Model T Ford," Chief said. "It was my grandfather's."

"I never knew they had windows and windshield wipers," Freya said.

"Henry Ford was an innovator," Chief said. "Thank God, on a night like this."

When Chief pressed the gas, the wheels slipped in the sand, and the car didn't move.

"We're stuck," Jack said.

"Impossible," Chief said. "Old Nellie's never been stuck."

"Seems she is now," Jack said. "I'll get out and push."

It wasn't the first rodeo for either Jack or Chief. When Jack pushed, Chief would accelerate, rocking the vehicle in hopes of dislodging it from the sand. Try as they might, Jack was having difficulty keeping his footing in the slippery sand, and it became quickly apparent he wouldn't be able to unstick the old Ford without help.

Freya nodded when Chief asked, "Can you drive a stick shift?"

"It's been a while. I learned to drive in a car with a standard transmission, and I'm sure I remember how."

"Jack needs help."

Freya squeezed Chief's hand and said, "You can count on me."

When Chief climbed out of the car, Freya slid behind the wheel.

"Jack and I will rock the car. Keep your foot on the gas, but don't spin the wheels. Keep moving once you are out of the rut, and don't stop until you're beyond the deep sand."

"Aye, Captain," Freya said.

Chief was much larger and stronger than Jack, and the car moved forward when he began to push. Wet sand sprayed up from the wheels as the rain increased. They soon had the old Model T out of the rut.

"Don't stop," Chief yelled above the storm's din. "Jack and I will catch up."

Freya hadn't gone far when the car exploded in a fireball of flame, the resultant burst of energy blowing Jack and Chief off their feet. They lay unconscious in the sand as Eddie and the others came running out of the Majestic.

When he saw the fireball, Eddie said, "Good God, all mighty!"

Odette, J.P., Alex, and Eddie began running toward the burning vehicle.

Alex and Eddie grabbed J.P.'s arms, preventing him from trying to wrench open one of the burning vehicle's doors.

"Stop it," Eddie said. "There's no one still alive in the car."

J.P. slammed his fist against his palm and said, "God damn it! No one deserves to die like that."

When an ATV slid to a stop in the sand, Renata, the veterinarian at the dog training facility, jumped out of the vehicle. She gawked at the burning vehicle and began to weep.

Renata's daughter Sveta, mother Iryna, and Meika followed Isaac out of the ATV. Iryna squeezed Renata's hand to console her.

"I knew something terrible had happened," Renata said. "Jack and Chief are dead."

"No, they aren't, Mama," Sveta said. "They're back there."

Jack and Chief lay prone in the sand, on their backs with their arms outstretched and their eyes closed. Renata ran to them. Opening Chief's mouth, she probed it for obstructions and then began administering CPR.

When J.P. and Alex reached her, she said, "Take my place. I need to help Jack."

J.P. didn't miss a beat, taking over where Renata had left off as she rushed to where Jack lay in the sand. After clearing his mouth, she started CPR.

When Alex squatted beside her, she said, "I'll get oxygen from the operating room. Keep Jack alive until I return."

"I'll go with you," Odette said.

Renata didn't hear her because she was sprinting up the slight rise to the Canine Training Facility.

"Can I help?" Isaac said.

"Take the ATV up the hill," Eddie said. "Help Renata and Odette bring down whatever they need. I called 911. An ambulance is on its way from Chalmette."

"Where's Freya?" Isaac asked.

Eddie cocked his chin toward Chief's burning Model T and then shook his head.

"If she was in the car, she's a goner," he said.

Isaac waited outside the canine operating room when Odette and Renata exited with portable oxygen and a surgical kit.

"Hurry, please," Renata said.

When Isaac slid to a stop, Renata jumped out of the ATV and began ministering to Jack and Chief. She soon had them breathing, albeit with difficulty. Jack and Chief's eyes were open when the ambulance arrived.

J.P. shook his head when Chief said, "Freya?"

Chief nodded when J.P. asked, "Was she in the Model T?"

"Jack and I should have been there with her," he said.

"Thank God you weren't. I'm so sorry," J.P. said. "No one could have survived that explosion. Why weren't you and Jack in the car?"

Chief's voice was raspy and barely discernable when he said, "We were stuck in the sand. Jack and I pushed it out of the rut. I told Freya to keep driving until she was out of the loose sand."

J.P. squeezed Chief's hand and said, "Keep your oxygen mask on. None of this is your fault."

The EMTs loaded Jack and Chief on gurneys and transported them to the awaiting ambulance.

"I'm going with them to the hospital," Renata said.

"Me too," J.P. said.

"It's not happening," the lead EMT said. "The pretty lady who saved their lives can come. That's all I have room for. Sorry, regulations."

Renata climbed into the back of the ambulance. Everyone else heard the sirens wailing as the emergency vehicle headed across the bridge to Chalmette. It was still raining, and the State Police and a fire truck were soon to arrive. The Model T was still smoldering, though the rain had doused the flames.

"I'll talk to them," J.P. said. "The rest of you go home or back into the Majestic."

Alex picked up Sveta and carried her to the ATV. Sveta and Iryna were crying.

"The madness has followed us to this island," Iryna said.

Alex took her hand. "None of this has anything to do with Ukraine," he said.

"How can you be so sure?" Iryna asked.

"The old car was probably struck by lightning," Alex said.

Iryna shook her head. "A bomb destroyed it. You know it, and so do I," she said.

"Jack and Chief will be okay," Alex said. "I promise. Take Sveta home, dry her off, and put her to bed."

"I'll stay with them," Isaac said.

Alex nodded and said, "Thank you."

He watched the ATV drive away before returning to the Majestic. Already drenched, he didn't bother running. He found Odette and Meika dispensing drinks. Odette handed him a glass of vodka without bothering to ask if he wanted one. Eddie appeared wearing a dry purple and gold L.S.U. sweatshirt, jeans, and sandals with no socks.

"Odette and Meika, get out of those wet clothes. You too, Alex."

Eddie sat alone at the circular table in the dim bar. J.P. soon appeared, and Eddie handed him a mug of rum.

"I left my door open and some dry clothes on the bed for you. Change out of those wet clothes, and then tell me what the police said."

Eddie waited patiently for everyone to return to the bar. Alex and J.P. were dressed much like Eddie. Wearing hotel robes, Odette and Meika began dispensing drinks.

"What did the police say?" Eddie asked.

"It's too dark to tell much," J.P. said. "They'll have a better idea tomorrow when they can see what's happening."

Eddie and J.P. looked at Alex when he said, "Someone booby-trapped Chief's old car."

Alex nodded when J.P. said, "You know that for a fact?"

"And so do you," Alex said.

"Is he right?" Eddie said.

"That's my first inclination," J.P. said. "I'd like to see what the L.S.B.I. think after they investigate the remains of the Model T."

"The Louisiana State Bureau of Investigation wouldn't get involved unless. . ."

"What else could it be?" J.P. asked. "Cars don't just blow up."

"Who has a motive to get rid of Chief?" Eddie asked.

"You know who," J.P. said. "Frankie Castellano."

"What about Carlos Palacio?" Eddie asked.

J.P. shook his head. "Unlikely. He didn't even know about the island before yesterday."

"Maybe, maybe not. Amani has been on the island for multiple days now," Eddie said. "What's she doing here? Maybe Carlos knows what Frankie knows."

"And Freya?" J.P. said. "What do you intend to do with the money she gave you?"

"Give it back, I guess," Eddie said.

"I didn't get the impression she has a family," J.P. said.

"No clue," Eddie said. "I only met her less than twelve hours ago. Pancho's going to be heartbroken."

"And pissed," J.P. said. "Especially if he thinks Frankie had anything to do with it."

Alex hadn't spoken as he sat in his chair with his eyes closed, rubbing his forehead.

"Are you okay?" Eddie asked.

"I can't see how this will help get the distillery built. Josie will almost certainly drop out of the deal."

Meika and Odette brought fresh drinks and joined them. Odette placed a cell phone on the table. Everyone stopped talking when it rang, and she answered it.

"Majestic Hotel. May I help you?" she said. She handed the phone to Eddie and said, "I think you better do the talking."

"Eddie Toledo," he said. "How may I help you?"

"I need to speak with my mother. Her cell phone isn't working," the woman said.

"Who are you calling for?" Eddie asked.

"Freya Becht. I spoke with her about an hour ago. She's dead, isn't she?"

"Freya is your mother?"

"Yes. Please connect me or tell me what's happened to her."

"Who am I talking to?" Eddie asked.

"Delta Becht."

"Delta, I'm so sorry to tell you. Your mother was killed in an explosion."

Eddie could hear the woman sobbing. "Why was she in an explosion?" she finally said.

"The police are investigating," Eddie said. "Right now, you know everything I know. I am so sorry."

"I want to see her," Delta said.

"Delta, I'm afraid there's nothing to see. Your mother left her purse in her room and her car parked out front. That's all. I know this is a horrible shock, and I'm so sorry."

"Can you bring the purse and the car to me?" Delta said.

"Where are you?" Eddie asked.

"My mother's house in Covington."

"I'll bring them tomorrow," Eddie said. "I'm so sorry I had to deliver the bad news."

"I sensed something terrible had happened. Thanks for confirming it."

Eddie handed the phone to Odette. "I didn't realize you were fielding all the front desk calls. Please forgive me."

"It isn't as if we've been swamped with bookings," Odette said.

"I have just one more problem to rectify," Eddie said. "Thank you, Odette. My miserable life would be unbearable without you."

Odette smiled and said, "Shut up and have another drink."

Chapter 10

Eddie got little sleep and was up early and drinking coffee alone in the bar the next morning. He was thinking about adding some rum to his cup when Josie came down the stairs and joined him.

"You're up early," she said.

"I couldn't sleep," he said.

"Did you wet the bed?"

"Funny. You didn't hear the explosion last night?"

Josie's hand went to her mouth. "What explosion?"

"Chief's old Model T blew up. Freya was killed. Jack and Chief are in the Chalmette hospital."

"That's horrible! What caused the car to blow up?" Josie asked.

"J.P. and Alex think it was a bomb."

Josie didn't immediately reply and because of her facial expression, Eddie could all but read her mind.

"You don't believe my father has anything to do with it, do you?"

"The thought crossed my mind," Eddie said.

"There must be another explanation," Josie said.

"Carlos, your ex-boyfriend?"

"I don't like the tone of your voice, Eddie Toledo."

"Frankie had a motive," Eddie said. "In my mind, he's the number one suspect."

"What motive?" Josie asked.

"Freya was alone in Chief's car when it exploded. Someone planted the bomb with the intent to kill Chief."

"Is that what the police think?" Josie asked.

"The police are studying the scene and haven't issued their prognosis yet. It's what I think."

"Why would my father want to kill Chief?"

"The legal dispute contesting ownership of Oyster Island comes to mind," Eddie said.

"Frankie is lots of things," Josie said. "Stupid isn't one of them."

"Amen to that," Eddie said. "You think someone was setting Frankie up? Who has a reason to do that?"

"Someone with designs on the island," Josie said.

"You think Freya's murder happened because of the ownership of the Majestic?" Eddie asked.

"I'm not interested in the Majestic, and I doubt Carlos is," Josie said. "Our interests lie in the location of a distillery. Who knows why someone else might covet ownership of Oyster Island?"

"Such as?"

"Lafitte's treasure, for one thing," Josie said. "Maybe the island has other hidden treasures we aren't aware of."

"Something so valuable that they're willing to kill for it?"

"Exactly," Josie said. "Have you called Pancho yet?"

"I thought I'd have a few drinks first," Eddie said.

"Coward," Josie said. "I'll call him. He needs to know so he can begin processing his loss."

When Josie stood from the table, Eddie clutched her hand.

"Josie," he said.

"Yes?"

"Thank you."

Josie nodded. "My plans have changed. Can you tell Odette I'll stay on the island for a while?"

"Of course," he said.

Josie had barely left when Eddie's phone rang.

"Hello."

"I'm Seraphina Nightshade. Are you Eddie?"

"Yes, ma'am. Eddie Toledo. The owner of the Majestic Hotel."

"I spoke with Freya yesterday," Seraphina said. "She told me she'd booked your hotel this coming weekend."

"Yes, she did," Eddie said. "Are you a member of the Covington Coven?"

"I'm Freya's second-in-command."

Then we need to talk."

"I'm at Freya's house with her daughter, Delta. She said Freya was killed in an explosion. I had a suspicion last night that something terrible happened."

"That's correct," Eddie said. "I'm so sorry. We need to discuss the money Freya paid me."

"The coven would want the occasion to go forward, and we'll see to it that Freya's money is given to Delta. We'll begin arriving on the island tomorrow. Sometime during our stay, we'll perform a ritual to honor Freya's cycle of life and death."

"Are you sure?" Eddie said. "What about Freya's family? Won't they expect a funeral?"

"Except for the coven, Delta is Freya's only family. She will join us in guiding her mother's transition into the afterlife."

"The Majestic staff will do everything we can to assist in your endeavors and make your stay memorable," Eddie said.

"Are you planning on coming to Covington?" Seraphina asked.

"Freya arrived on the island with only her car and her purse. I want to deliver them to her daughter in person."

"You mean today?"

"I can leave here within the hour," Eddie said. "That should put me in Covington around noon. Can you give me directions to Freya's house?"

"Let's meet at Pancho's. He and Freya were close and I feel he deserves an explanation, and we can grab lunch while we talk."

"You got it," Eddie said.

⌘

The key to Freya's Miata was in her purse. Eddie took it and headed for Covington. He had no idea what to expect from either Seraphina or Delta Becht. He needed to talk with Pancho, and he dreaded it. He parked in front of Pancho's little café just before noon. Pancho was frowning when he met him at the door. Eddie embraced him.

"Pancho, I'm so sorry," he said.

"What the hell happened?"

"Someone planted a bomb in Grogan La Tortue's car. Freya was alone in the car when it exploded."

Eddie nodded when Pancho said, "Frankie?"

"He has a motive. Josie thinks that's precisely why he isn't responsible."

"She may be right," Pancho said. "Frankie isn't stupid."

"Don't I know it?" Eddie said. "That leaves me with a big problem. Who the hell is responsible, and how will it affect everything I do until I figure it out?"

Pancho smiled and slapped Eddie's arm. "You'll figure it out."

"I know you're grieving. Is there anything I can do to help?"

"I'll feel better after Freya's funeral. It is why people have them," Pancho said.

"Freya isn't having a funeral, at least a normal one. Her coven plans to celebrate her life and death in a pagan ceremony on Oyster Island."

"Call it what you want; that's a funeral."

"I guess," Eddie said.

"When?" Pancho said.

"Don't know yet. The coven is having a convention on the island starting tomorrow. The ceremony will take place while the group is there."

"Then book me a room at the hotel," Pancho said. "I'll close the restaurant until I return."

"Where are all your customers?" Eddie asked.

"There's a closed sign on the door. Didn't you see it?"

"Guess I wasn't paying attention. Freya's daughter and one of her coven members are meeting me here for lunch. They'll be disappointed."

"Freya has a daughter?"

"A woman named Delta," Eddie said.

Eddie shook his head when Pancho said, "Where has she been?"

"You know as much about her as I do." Someone knocking on the door interrupted their conversation. "Must be them now."

Two women stood at the door when Pancho opened it. One of the women was dressed in black and had long silver hair. The younger of the two women had shoulder-length blond hair and piercing blue eyes.

"Are you Pancho?" the blond woman asked.

"Yes," he said.

The young woman put her arms around his neck and began to cry. "I'm Delta. My mother loved you. She told me so and I'm sad I never met you."

Pancho began to weep. When he regained control of his emotions, he beckoned the two women to enter the café, shut the door behind them, and motioned them to the table where Eddie was sitting.

"I'm Eddie," he said. "You must be Delta and Seraphina."

Seraphina Nightshade was an attractive sixty-something woman, her stylishly round glasses accenting her handsome face and elegant neck. The red crystal pendant draped from her gothic-style black velvet choker was her only concession to color.

Delta Becht, bedecked in dangling sapphire earrings and a jeweled necklace matching the intense blue of her eyes was Seraphina's antithesis. She was startlingly beautiful and Eddie caught his breath. Pancho saved him from saying something stupid.

"Anyone hungry for shrimp linguini?" he asked.

Seraphina and Delta both smiled and nodded. Pancho brought a bottle of chilled Chianti to the table and opened it and then poured each glass.

"I can see why my mother loved you," Delta said.

"After the linguini is served, you need to explain why I've never met you before," Pancho said.

When everyone had finished their linguini, Pancho served a crisp and flaky cannoli dessert.

"Decadent," Seraphina said.

"Best Italian meal I've ever eaten," Delta said.

"Don't let my daughter hear you say that. She thinks she's the best Italian cook in Louisiana,"

Pancho said. "Now, tell me where you've been keeping yourself."

"I'm a lawyer," Delta said. "Until a few days ago, I worked for a law firm in Baton Rouge. Eighty-five hours a week with little or no recognition or compensation for what I did. My soul was in a dark spot, and yesterday, I finally had my fill of the abuse and quit my job."

"Delta worked for Carns and Holmes, one of Louisiana's most prestigious law firms," Seraphina said.

"Where did you go to law school?" Eddie asked.

"Loyola," Delta said.

"Delta had one of the highest law school admission test scores ever recorded in Louisiana," Seraphina said. "She passed the bar exam on her first attempt."

"Because I worked my butt off," Delta said. "Not because I'm smart."

"You're smart," Pancho said. "I can tell by looking in your eyes."

"Thanks, Pancho. I wish my employers would have thought that."

"Will you hang a shingle here in Covington and try your hand at private practice?" Eddie asked.

"My only plans were to take it easy for a few weeks and decompress. Now, I have Mother's death to contemplate."

When Delta began to cry, Pancho quickly opened a bottle of ouzo and began dispensing shots.

"Delta is a wonderful lawyer, though the law isn't her ultimate calling. Like her mother, she's a witch with powers she has yet to understand," Seraphina said.

"Is that true, Delta?" Pancho asked.

"Freya said my grandmother was a witch and that my powers are destined to be greater than both my grandmother's and hers."

"Are you skeptical?" Eddie asked.

"I think it's total bullshit!" Delta said.

"You are wrong," Seraphina said. "You will soon see for yourself."

"Why did Freya name you Delta?" Eddie asked.

"Because Louisiana's delta is the culmination of the nation's greatest river, and she wanted to give me a powerful name."

Eddie handed Delta Freya's purse and car keys. "The Miata is parked outside," he said.

Seraphina gave the keys to Pancho and said, "Freya left you her Miata in her will because she knew you loved it. Here is the title, signed and notarized."

Pancho pushed the document out of the way and said, "Eddie says you are planning a ceremony for Freya on Oyster Island. Please include me in your plans."

"Wonderful," Delta said. "I'm looking forward to spending more time with you and hearing your take on my mother."

Pancho squeezed her hand and said, "Baby, I'm not sure you want to hear everything I know about your mom."

Delta smiled and said, "I want to hear all your stories."

Seraphina glanced at Pancho's clock and said, "We have to go now. We'll begin arriving on the island tomorrow."

When they were gone, Pancho broke out the scotch and handed Eddie the keys to the Miata.

"I hate that little car," he said. "You can have it."

He signed the title and shoved it across the table to Eddie.

"I can't take your car," Eddie said. "It's probably worth lots of money."

"Doesn't matter. I have my own car and I don't want Freya's," Pancho said.

"I'll admit I need a car. At least let me pay you for it," Eddie said.

"I have everything I need right here at my little café and don't require more money at this stage of my life."

"What about Adele and Toni?"

Pancho shook his head and laughed. "Adele has more money than I'll ever have because of her marriage to the most successful capo in the south. Frankie treats Toni like his own daughter. They both have everything they'll ever need."

"Are you sure?"

"Tell you what," Pancho said. "I have no idea how long I'll stay at your hotel. Throw in the room, drinks, and meals, and we'll call it even."

"You got it," Eddie said. "When are you coming down?"

"Tomorrow," Pancho said.

"I'll have a room ready for you," Eddie said. "Hope you like ocean views."

"You kidding?" Pancho said. "I'm from Sicily."

Chapter 11

The sky over Covington had darkened when Eddie left Pancho's to return to Oyster Island. He squeezed the padded steering wheel, feeling good to have his own car again. When his cell phone rang, he momentarily took his eyes off the road.

"Eddie, it's Basil."

"Everything okay?" Eddie asked.

"I'm good. I heard about the explosion and called to see how you're doing."

"Traumatized," Eddie said. "I was wondering if I should hoist a white flag."

"Because you think Frankie caused the explosion?"

"If not Frankie, then someone willing to resort to violence and even murder to achieve their goals."

"Whoever's responsible, the explosion damn sure raised the intensity bar a notch or two. I'm sorry I left you in a lurch," Basil said. "I know it can be overwhelming when you think no one has your back."

"It's okay," Eddie said. "You had to do what's best for you, Heather, and your unborn son or daughter. You and I are a match for anyone in a court of law. Whoever we're dealing with has upped the ante."

"Someone has done that, for sure," Basil said.

"It's like Sean Connery's character in the movie The Untouchables said, 'You don't take a knife to a gunfight.'"

"Do you remember what happened to Connery's character right after he said that?" Basil asked.

"Not really," Eddie said.

"He was killed by a man with a machine gun who was backing up the guy with the knife."

"Who's backing me up?" Eddie said.

"I am," Basil said.

Eddie laughed and said, "You have a machine gun?"

"Metaphorically speaking."

"Thanks, Basil. Your support is appreciated, and I needed to hear it."

"What did the police say?"

"Haven't heard yet," Eddie said. "They were on the island today. I had business in Covington, and I'm on my way home. I'll know more after I talk to J.P."

"I didn't call just to chat about the explosion," Basil said. "I have something of interest to tell you."

"Like what?"

"I'm working for my dad in Baton Rouge," Basil said. "Lobbyists are rampant around the capitol building. Yesterday, a strange little man visited Dad's office. Maybe the visit is somehow connected to the explosion."

Basil's father was an influential Louisiana state senator, and Eddie was instantly interested in what he had to say.

"And?"

"He asked about Oyster Island."

"What information was he looking for?" Eddie asked.

"Dad said he picked his brain on whether you or Frankie had the strongest case and who the state thought was the island's rightful owner."

"What did your dad tell him?"

"Nothing of importance."

"Who was he representing?" Eddie asked.

"He said he was a journalist doing a story on the island. I checked him out on the Internet though could find nothing about him. My inclination is he was using the cover of being a journalist for an excuse to interview my dad."

"Could it have been someone sent by Frankie?" Eddie asked.

"It seems a stretch that he would approach my dad for information."

"Maybe he was simply trying to gauge your dad's loyalties."

"A possibility," Basil said.

"The explosion doesn't sound like Frankie to me," Eddie said. "He's too wily to show his cards before he's ready to play them."

"If not Frankie, then who?" Basil asked.

"You met Amani LeClair before leaving the island. Her boyfriend is Carlos Palacio."

"I'm not familiar with the name," Basil said.

"His dad is a mob boss in Miami. I dealt with him more than once when I worked for the Department of Justice in New Orleans. Junior is on the island now."

"What for?" Basil asked.

"Ostensibly, to check out the island as a possible location for a distillery."

"Who's pushing that idea?"

"Alex thinks Oyster Island is a perfect place for locating a distillery. Josie Castellano is intrigued and is also on the island pursuing it."

"A perfect place because of what?"

"Alex says the water on Oyster Island checks all the requisite boxes. He should know because he was a liquor distributor in Russia before being conscripted in their army."

"Interesting," Basil said. "How did Josie get involved?"

Basil laughed when Eddie said, "You're a nosy bastard."

"You're the master lawyer I apprenticed under. If I practice bad traits, it's because of your lessons."

"Touché. I called Adele Castellano to see if she could help me work a deal with Frankie."

"You didn't," Basil said.

"I know it wasn't copasetic," Eddie said. "After you left, I was grasping at straws."

"What did she tell you?"

"That blood is thicker than water. I pissed her off, and she walked out on me. Her daughter Toni was with her and called Josie to step in."

"Josie would never cross her dad. I know that much about her," Basil said.

"You're right about that. Alex piqued her interest when he began his sales spiel. J.P. got in on the promotion by offering her a piece of the Canine Training Facility."

"How did that make you feel?"

"Like the captain of the Titanic watching the rats start jumping ship."

"Don't take it personally," Basil said. "Everyone on the island has a stake in what you're trying to accomplish. They're all counting on you."

"Hope they're not betting on the wrong horse," Eddie said.

Basil laughed. "You're neither the captain of the Titanic nor a horse, Eddie. You're the smartest lawyer I know. You'll find an answer and ultimately prevail."

"That makes me feel better," Eddie said. "At least business is looking up."

"How so?"

"Freya, the woman killed in the explosion, was Pancho Bergamo's girlfriend. She was the head witch of the Covington Coven."

"You're shitting me," Basil said. "A real witch?"

"A wealthy witch. Before she died, she paid good money for a witch's convention coming in tomorrow. The hotel is suddenly turning a profit."

"Is that what you were doing in Covington?" Basil asked.

"Part of it. I was returning Freya's purse and car. I had lunch with Seraphina Nightshade, Freya Becht's second-in-command and the new leader of the coven. She confirmed the convention is still a go."

"Wonderful," Basil said.

"The coven intends to commemorate Freya's life and death with some secret pagan ceremony."

"Sweet," Basil said. "What else?"

"Freya has a daughter, a drop-dead gorgeous blond with unreal blue eyes. It took every ounce of my willpower to keep my tongue in my mouth."

"What's her name?" Basil asked.

"Delta Becht."

"I know her," Basil said. "We debated Loyola when I was studying law at L.S.U. I heard she went to work for Carns and Holmes in Baton Rouge."

"You've heard of them?"

"You kidding me? They're the top personal injury lawyers in the state, maybe the world."

"Delta quit her job and was on her way to Covington the day her mom died," Eddie said. "Seraphina Nightshade says she's a witch, though Delta denies it. She'll be on the island tomorrow."

"Maybe she can help you with the lawsuit," Basil said.

"An ambulance chaser?"

"She's the real deal, Eddie. I have no idea how or why she went to work for Carns and Holmes. I do know she graduated tops in her class at Loyola."

"With my sudden change in fortune, I could pay you a salary if you decided to return to the island."

Eddie waited through a long pause on the phone before Basil responded.

"If it were my choice, I'd work for you for nothing. It isn't. I have my wife, a baby on the way, and my dad to answer to now. Doesn't matter because you know I'll continue to help every way I can."

"I know you will," Eddie said.

"I have to go. If I hear anything of interest, I'll call again."

"Thanks, buddy," Eddie said.

After exiting Paris Road, Eddie entered the St. Bernard Parish Hospital parking lot and went inside. The young man at the reception desk informed him Jack and Chief had been released. Relieved, he headed for the island.

Storm clouds had moved north, leaving thousands of stars sparkling in the sky over the Gulf. Eddie pulled up to the front door of Jack's house and entered without knocking. Chief and Jack were sitting at the kitchen's plank table playing gin.

"Damn! Am I glad to see you two," Eddie said. "About this time yesterday, I was worried neither of you would make it."

"Poor Freya can't say as much," Chief said.

"Freya's death isn't your fault," Eddie said.

"Wish I could believe that," Chief said.

"Guilt isn't conducive to recovery," Eddie said. "Freya wouldn't have wanted you blaming yourself. What's that wonderful aroma?"

"Renata and Iryna have been here since we got home, cooking and cleaning," Jack said. "I love Sveta, but I got tired of babysitting and all Renata and Iryna's attention and sent them home."

"Whatever they cooked smells like heaven," Eddie said.

"A one-pot Ukrainian casserole," Jack said. "Kielbasa sausage, cabbage, and pierogies. It's tasty and filling. I'll get you a bowl."

"Save one for me," someone in the doorway said.

J.P. smiled as he wiped his boots before entering Jack's little house. Lucky, his chocolate lab was with him, and he hurried to the fireplace to rub noses with Jack and Chief's dogs.

"I'm happy to see you two," he said. "What did the doctors say?"

"We're lucky we were as far away from Grandpa's car as we were," Chief said. "The explosion knocked us silly, and Jack and I both had concussions."

"The State Police just now finished their investigation," J.P. said. "Someone booby-trapped your vehicle with a sophisticated explosive device."

"I'm amazed they found anything," Eddie said. "There wasn't much left of the car to investigate."

"You'd be surprised," J.P. said. "They found enough to identify a device programmed to explode after the car moved forward about fifty feet. You boys are lucky."

"Grandpa's ghost," Chief said. "He saved Jack and me by sticking the car in the sand and having us get out and push. I hate it he couldn't have saved Freya."

"Any other clues?" Eddie asked. "Tire tracks? Footprints? How did the person who set the bomb get to the car."

"Nothing," J.P. said. "No tire tracks or footprints. It's as if one of Freya's ghosts set the bomb."

"Impossible," Chief said. "It wasn't a ghost who rigged Grandpa's car. Humans leave trails."

"The State Police couldn't find one," J.P. said.

"Let's break out the rum," Chief said.

"The doctors gave us strict orders," Jack said. "No alcohol."

"Screw the doctors," Chief said. "I need a drink."

"You're right," Jack said. "I feel perfectly okay."

Eddie was still working on the last bite of Ukrainian stew.

"I don't know if Renata or her mother cooked this, but I'm ready to marry whichever one did."

"Damn good!" Jack said. "You're lucky we left a bowl for you."

"Don't think I'm not grateful," Eddie said. "Thank you."

Eddie was unprepared for Jack's next question.

"Is this the end of Oyster Island for us?"

"What the hell are you talking about? We're nowhere close to the end. Where did you come up with that crazy idea?"

"You called Adele to ask her help with Frankie," Chief said.

"I had my reasons," Eddie said.

"Is one of those reasons because you're out of money?" Jack asked.

"I'm doing the best I can," Eddie said. "We all just took a blow to the head. I'm reeling, though a long way from down and out. If you two want to throw in the towel, tell me now, and I'll stop worrying about your sorry asses."

"We're not throwing in the towel," Chief said. "Jack and I were worried that you were."

"Hell no!" Eddie said. "I have a witch's convention coming in tomorrow. The Majestic is my life's dream, and things are starting to turn around. The only way I'm leaving the island is by losing our court case, and even then, after an appeal to a higher court. Our fight is far from over."

"What about you, J.P.?" Jack asked.

"I don't know. The State Police knew what they were doing, though something bothers me."

"Like what?" Eddie asked.

"Chief is right. No one could have set that bomb without leaving a trail."

Chief grabbed a flashlight off of Jack's kitchen shelf. "Old Joe and I can find it, and we're doing it now."

"Why not wait until tomorrow?" J.P. said. "Even the world's best tracker can't do it in the dark."

Chief ignored J.P.'s comment and started for the door. "Sometimes, a faint trail is more apparent by the full moon's light than in broad daylight. There was no better tracker on earth than Grandpa, who taught me everything I know."

"Okay," J.P. said. "Me and Lucky can track with the best of them. I'm going with you,"

"Count me in," Jack said.

"You, Eddie, and the other dogs will get in the way. We won't be long," Chief said.

J.P. laughed when Eddie said. "Sure you don't need someone to carry the rum?"

"Leave some for J.P. and me," Chief said. "We'll drink our share when we return."

"We'll do our damnedest to save you some," Eddie said.

Chapter 12

Last night's storm had moved north, leaving a clear sky populated with twinkling stars and a glorious full moon. Waves crashed against the shoreline as J.P. and Chief moved down the slight rise from Jack's house. Walking silently, they followed their dogs until they reached a blackened spot in the sand. Lights were on in the Majestic. It didn't matter. The two men were intent on something else.

After letting the dogs get the scent, Chief and J.P. began tracing a slow circle around the explosion sight, widening their path after completing a rotation of the blackened ground. They continued, their dog's noses to the sand as they followed an ever-expanding circle. They both stopped when Lucky halted. With his tail pointed straight in the air, he glanced first up the hill toward the bridge and then at J.P.

"Go get 'em, Lucky boy," J.P. said.

Chief and J.P. let go of their dog's collars and followed them to the bridge.

"Good thing we brought the dogs," J.P. said. "Whoever planted that bomb may as well have been a ghost. I can't see a damn thing."

"Fucker must be an Indian," Chief said. "He was sweeping his tracks."

"And last night's rain masked what he didn't," J.P. said.

"Didn't fool Mr. Lucky," Chief said.

"Lucky can out-track a bloodhound," J.P. said.

"And a damn good thing," Chief said.

J.P. and Chief hurried across the bridge into the pine forest on the other side. On the scent, Lucky was howling, letting everyone know where he was going. His howls sounded eerie and almost supernatural as they echoed through the pine forest. When his howls ceased, Chief and J.P. stopped and listened.

"They found something," Chief said.

"I brought a light," J.P. said, switching on the flashlight.

"Grandpa never used a flashlight."

"Call him," J.P. said. "If he shows up to help, I'll put the light away."

Chief shook his head and said, "The white man's ways are going to be the death of me."

"Quit your belly aching," J.P. said. "We got work to do.

They followed the beam's light another hundred feet when J.P. raised his hand, motioning Chief to halt.

"Come on, Lucky. Talk to me."

"I hear them," Chief said. "They're off in the bushes."

"Your ears are better than mine. I don't hear anything," J.P. said.

"This way," Chief said, heading off the road into the underbrush.

"Take the flashlight," J.P. said. "I can't see a damn thing."

"You can smell it, can't you?"

"I smell something dead," J.P. said.

"Right about that, Chief said. "Big time dead."

The bushes were so thick that the flashlight was of little use. Chief pushed through the limbs, following his nose. The dogs had already found something and were signaling their location with their barks. They waited when Chief and J.P. broke into a little clearing lit by the full moon.

"Good God, all mighty!" J.P. said when he saw what the dogs had found.

The crumpled body of a large man lay sprawled on the bank of a pond, his dead eyes staring at the moon, and his face contorted into a look of horror frozen in death. Something sharp and deadly had shredded his camouflage fatigues. Worse, a leg and an arm were missing, as if some creature had gnawed them off and eaten them.

"What now?" Chief asked.

J.P. didn't answer as he was already calling the police. Someone he knew answered on the first ring.

"Bureau of Investigations. Trooper Johnson speaking. How may I help you?"

"Claude, it's J.P."

"How the hell you been, Cuz? Need me to get you out of jail?"

"I got bigger problems than that," J.P. said.

"Like what?" Claude said.

"Another body here on Oyster Island."

"Connected to the explosion?" Claude asked.

"Maybe the man who set the device," J.P. said.

"A shooting victim?"

"Don't know," J.P. said. "It's dark, though from what I can tell, some animal has already damaged the body."

"Coyotes?"

"More like a bear, a pack of wolves, or a big cat."

"Give me your location. I'll have someone head your way."

106

"About a half mile north of the bridge to Oyster Island and another hundred feet off the road in the underbrush. I'll text you the coordinates when we hang up."

"It'll be an hour or so."

"Thanks, Claude. We'll be waiting."

When J.P. put away his cell phone, Chief asked, "What now?"

"Go back to the road and wait.

"What about the body?" Chief asked.

"It's going nowhere. I need rum, and I'd just as soon drink it someplace that doesn't stink to high heavens," J.P. said.

"I hear that," Chief said.

"They started away through the underbrush but stopped when growling in the distance riveted their attention. The dogs heard it too, stopped, and wheeled around, the sounds they began making neither barks nor howls.

"What the hell was that?" J.P. asked.

"Grandpa used to say you hear many strange sounds in the swamp at night. Some you recognize, some you don't, and others you don't even want to know."

"Sounds like the latter to me," J.P. said.

"And neither of us has a weapon. Whatever it is, it might be looking for another victim."

"Then let's get the hell out of here."

"If you're waiting on me, you're backing up," Chief said.

J.P. patted Lucky's head and said, "Come on, boys. This body doesn't need guarding."

"What killed him?" Chief asked when they were back on the road.

"You tell me. Something worked him over pretty well."

"Looks like a gator got hold of him, but they're all hibernating. Maybe it's a panther.

107

"There are no panthers in south Louisiana," J.P. said.

"There once was," Chief said.

"There used to be mammoths and saber-tooth tigers," J.P. said. "Is that what you think killed our suspect?"

"The growling we heard sounded real," Chief said.

"So, you think a bear or panther is on the island?"

"Something did a number on that poor fucker," Chief said. "Could have been a bear or a panther."

"Or a gator. We'll know lots more after someone performs an autopsy."

"A dirty job I'm glad someone else has," Chief said.

J.P. took a drink from his flask and then tossed it to Chief.

"Ain't that the truth? Have a pull."

It was almost two hours before the L.S.B.I. arrived. J.P. and Chief were sitting in the dirt beside the road, their flask of rum empty.

Three vehicles, an ambulance, a Ford Bronco, and a State Police cruiser, their red lights lighting the dark road, pulled up to where Chief and J.P. waited.

The officer's crisp uniform marked him as someone who rarely did fieldwork. He wasn't smiling and reminded J.P. of an always angry drill sergeant he'd had in boot camp.

The two troopers with the man snickered when J.P. said, "Damn, Captain Guidry! Since when did the L.S.P. start sending their big dogs to investigate a crime?"

"Filling in," Captain Guidry said. "Even state troopers get sick now and then."

"You're a good man, Captain. It's no wonder that all your men love you."

Captain Guidry ignored J.P.'s blatant compliment and said, "We found a car around the bend. I left some troopers with it, and they're running the tags."

"Wonder why the dead man didn't stay on the road," J.P. said.

"Don't know," Captain Guidry said. "I brought Terry, so we'll know something soon."

Another man, dressed in combat boots and camouflaged fatigues, got out of the Bronco and smiled when he saw J.P.

"Damn, brother," he said. "It's been a while since we worked a case together. How the hell are you?"

"Good seeing you, Terry," J.P. said. "The L.S.P. must believe this is an important case to send the best death investigator in south Louisiana."

"Hell, brother, this is my first field assignment in a year. I was blown away when Hec called and said he needed me."

Terry Felts carried a few extra pounds on his six-foot frame, his white mustache and kung fu beard contrasting with his dark hair and eyes. His use of Captain Guidry's first name marked him as a man of importance.

"Where's the mangled body we need to investigate?" Captain Guidry asked.

"About a hundred yards through the brush, Captain," J.P. said. "That strike uniform of yours won't look as crisp as it is now when we get there."

"Hell, brother," Terry said. "We'll take my Bronco. I haven't found a murder location yet that I couldn't get to."

"How do you know this is a murder?" J.P. asked.

"Hell, brother," Terry said. "It had better be. The captain and I don't go out on accident investigations."

109

"You're the best, Terry. You'll have to tell me," J.P. said.

"Then this must be a doozy because you've covered as many murders as I have," Terry said. "You and the big Indian hop in the Bronco with me. I have loaded the coordinates, and you don't need to tell me how to reach the murder scene."

"Aren't you afraid of scratching your fenders?"

Terry patted a fender and said, "This baby was built for the off-road."

The Bronco powered through the thick brush with no problems, and Terry left the headlights on when they exited the truck. The body wasn't where Chief and J.P. had left it. It was floating face down in the middle of the swampy pond.

"Is that where you found it?" Terry asked.

J.P. shook his head and pointed. "Something must have pulled it out into the pond. We found the body on the bank."

Terry stared at the indention in the muddy bank where J.P. was pointing.

Captain Guidry and the two troopers joined them.

"Jess has a rope," he said. "He can lasso the body and drag it to shore."

"Not yet," Terry said. "I don't see any footprints or signs of a struggle. He must have gone into the water from another location. Let's fan out around the pond and see what we find."

An hour passed as the group methodically checked the perimeter of the pond. J.P. and Chief were the first to find something and called to Terry from the far side of the pond.

"Over here," he said. "This is where he entered the water."

"No blood; no sign of a struggle," Terry said. "Looks like something or someone pulled his body into the pond. Let's follow the drag path back into the brush."

They followed the furrow left in the damp earth to the road.

"Whatever attacked him did it on the road somewhere between here and the bridge," J.P. said.

"And then pulled him to the pond," Terry said. "Let's retrieve the body and see what the marks tell us."

The two troopers lassoed the body and pulled it to shore. Terry put on latex gloves and then flipped the body.

"Whatever got him was big, and it doesn't look like he put up much of a fight," Trooper Jess said.

Terry opened the dead man's mouth with an Archimedes screw. After probing the inside of his mouth, he checked the body's temperature.

"Time of death was about this time last night. He must have parked his car not far from here and walked to the island to set the explosive device. He was on his way back to his car when something or someone killed him and then dragged his body into the brush to the pond," Terry said.

"Maybe an alligator," Al, the other trooper, said.

"It's January," Chief said. "Alligators are hibernating."

"Reptiles don't hibernate," Terry said. "They brumate."

"What the hell does that mean?" J.P. asked.

"Brumation is specific to reptiles and amphibians. When temperatures are cold, they enter a state of inactivity. Their body temperature, heart rate, metabolic rate, and respiratory rate drops. Unlike a hibernating bear, they can become active if the temperature increases."

"It was raining last night and well above freezing," Chief said.

"That wouldn't have abruptly changed the water temperature in the pond," J.P. said.

J.P. and the others looked at Chief when he said, "Stick your hand in it."

Chapter 13

Death investigator Terry Felts followed Chief's advice and stuck his hand in the water. The next thing he did was to use his thermometer to take the temperature.

"Hell, it's almost eighty degrees. How can that be?" he said.

J.P. looked at Chief and said, "Do you know the answer?"

"There's a thermal pool on La Tortue Mountain," he said. "Maybe the thermal properties extend to the area across the bridge from the island."

"You never told me that," J.P. said.

"I'm not aware of a thermal pool in Louisiana," Captain Guidry said.

"What else could it be?" J.P. said.

"Maybe a factory illegally dumping wastewater into a nearby river," Captain Guidry said.

"There are no factories or electrical generation plants anywhere near here," Chief said.

"It's geothermal," Terry said. "Something's going on underground."

"Like what?" J.P. said.

"A geologist told Grandpa that the island sits atop a salt dome," Chief said.

"Salt domes don't cause geothermal activity," Terry said.

"You sound like an expert," J.P. said.

"There are hundreds of salt domes off the coast of Louisiana," Terry said. "I've never heard of one being geothermal."

"Me either," J.P. said.

"Whatever's causing the hot water is affecting the creatures living near here. My guess is it was an alligator that chewed off the victim's arm and leg," Terry said.

"What was the gator doing on the road," Trooper Al asked.

"Good question," Terry said. "Let's get the body bagged. We'll learn more after an autopsy is performed."

"We heard something growling when we found the body," J.P. said.

"You mean like a dog?" Terry said.

"Sounded more like a bear or maybe a wendigo," Chief said.

"What the hell is a wendigo?" Captain Guidry asked.

"A horrible beast that stalks and eats humans or as an evil spirit that possesses humans, turning them into cannibals," Chief said.

Terry laughed and said, "Are there any bears around here?"

"Used to be, though I haven't seen one in a while," Chief said.

"Whatever the hell it is, let's get out of here before it shows back up," Terry said.

They piled into Terry's Bronco. He stopped when they reached the road.

"Want me to take you back to the house?"

"We can hoof it from here," J.P. said.

Chief and J.P. watched the police entourage disappear around the bend before returning to the island. The full moon and open sky made it feel almost like daylight after the darkness of the pine forest. When they reached Jack's house and opened the door, the dogs rushed inside to the roaring fire to join Oscar and Coco. Jack and Eddie were drinking rum and playing gin at the plank table.

"Where you been," Jack asked. "We were starting to worry."

"We're good," J.P. said.

"Find anything?" Eddie asked,

"A dead man," Chief said.

J.P. nodded when Eddie asked, "The bomber?"

"Most likely. We tracked him from the bomb site to a thermal pool in the brush about a hundred yards across the bridge."

"You mean there's another pool like the one on La Tortue Mountain?" Eddie asked.

"This one's bigger and deeper," Chief said.

"Am I the only person on this island who hasn't heard about your thermal pool?" J.P. asked.

"You're welcome to take a dip anytime," Chief said. "Good for what ails you."

"What killed the victim?" Eddie asked.

"Don't know," J.P. said. "He had a missing arm and leg."

"A recent amputation?" Eddie asked.

"The man was dead before the limbs were amputated," J.P. said.

"How do you know that?" Jack asked.

"No blood. The heart had stopped beating some time before the limbs were lopped off," J.P. said.

J.P. nodded when Jack said, "Wild animal?"

"Seems likely," he said.

Eddie glanced at Chief and said, "What do you think?"

"What killed the bomber was wild," Chief said. "It wasn't a bear or any other animal. An evil spirit killed him. A wendigo."

"What's a wendigo?" Eddie asked.

"An evil spirit that takes the form of a hairy beast and eats people," J.P. said.

Eddie shook his head when Chief said," Wendigos exist."

"What's that in your hand?" Eddie asked.

Chief dropped a yellow flower on the table.

"Where'd you find it?" J.P. asked.

"By the body?" Chief said. "I've never seen a flower like this."

"You shouldn't have picked it up," J.P. said. "It might be evidence."

"A flower?" Chief said. "Seems unlikely to me."

"Where did it come from? It doesn't look like any flower I've ever seen. Does it grow on the island?" J.P. asked.

"Beats me, boss," Chief said. "I picked it up because it's pretty, and Terry and his men didn't bother with it."

Everyone turned their attention to Eddie when he said, "It's a cerasee flower that grows in Jamaica."

"How do you know that?" J.P. asked.

"Amani has a cerasee plant in her van. She showed it to me. My guess is that flower probably came from her plant."

"That makes her a suspect," J.P. said. "I better call Terry."

Eddie grabbed J.P.'s wrist when he reached for his cell phone.

"Amani didn't kill that man and eat his arm and leg. There must be another explanation as to why the flower was beside the body," Eddie said.

"Like what?" J.P. asked.

"I don't know," Eddie said. "Whatever it is, we need to keep this to ourselves."

"We can't withhold evidence in a murder investigation," J.P. said.

"You think a flower implicates Amani as a murder suspect?" Eddie asked.

"What's your point?" J.P. said.

"Few people have as much investigative experience as you and I do. My gut tells me it isn't in our best interest to involve Amani in the murder investigation."

"I don't know," J.P. said. "A clue is a clue."

Eddie threw up his hands. "You can't believe in bureaucracy any more than I do. We keep this information to ourselves until we see how it plays out."

J.P. glanced at Jack and then at Chief. "Well?" he said.

"I'm on Eddie's side," Chief said.

"Forget about the flower," Jack said. "It could have gotten where it was a thousand different ways that don't implicate Amani."

"Maybe so," J.P. said. "What now?"

Jack poured rum into mugs and said, "We get a little drunk."

"I'm not sure I'm ready for this," J.P. said.

"The flower isn't all I found," Chief said.

J.P. was shaking his head when he said, "What else?"

"This," Chief said, dropping a beautiful blue stone on the table.

"Looks like turquoise," Eddie asked.

"That's what I thought," Chief said. "When I looked closer, I could see it wasn't."

Someone stuck their head in the door. It was Alex.

"Having a party without calling me?" he asked.

"Chief and J.P. found a man's body on the other side of the bridge," Jack said. "Chief found a flower blossom and a blue stone. Now, J.P. thinks Amani killed the man."

"I never said that," J.P. said.

"Enough already," Eddie said. "Lay off of J.P. He's on our side."

Alex picked up the yellow flower from the plank table. "It is Amani's," he said.

Jack poured Alex a mug of rum. "Sit," he said. "Explain yourself."

"I awoke from a dream last night," Alex said. "Amani was standing at the foot of my bed."

"You're shitting us!" J.P. said.

"It was Amani. Except. . ."

"Except what?" Eddie said.

"She wasn't quite real. Her naked body was all aglow, wisps of vapor swirling around her. She had a flower like this behind her ear."

Alex nodded when Jack said, "She was naked?"

"It was a dream," Alex said.

No one noticed the person standing in the doorway, listening to Alex's story. It was Odette, and everyone turned when she spoke.

"It wasn't a dream," she said.

"Odette, what are you doing here?" Eddie asked.

Odette's dogs, Bruiser and Mudbug were with her and quickly joined the other dogs by the fireplace.

"I was feeling lonely and had a hunch something was going on," she said.

"How do you know Alex's experience wasn't a dream?" Eddie said.

"Because Amani also visited me. It was the ghost woman J.P., and I saw in his duck blind."

Odette smiled when Jack said, "Was she naked?"

"I can tell you're loving every minute of this story," she said.

"Better than a table dance," he said. "Tell us what happened."

"Amani was like Alex described. She wasn't quite real. She pulled back the sheets and crawled into bed with me. I couldn't touch her, and she couldn't touch me because she was a ghost. A visitor from the spirit world."

"What did she want?" Eddie asked.

"To tell me something," Odette said.

"What?" Eddie said.

"I'm not sure. I had the feeling we had some unexplained cosmic connection. One thing I'm sure of."

"Quit stalling and tell us," Eddie said.

"Her live persona is here on the island for a purpose," Odette said.

"She couldn't have been a ghost. I was either dreaming, or else she was real," Alex said.

"If she were real, how did she get into your room?" J.P. asked.

"She couldn't have," Alex said. "My door was locked. "Her visit was a dream. A vivid dream. It was as if she were real."

"Damn!" Jack said. "I'd like to have dreams like that. Mine are always about recipes."

"Speaking of food, I'm starving," Chief said. "Have any leftovers in this place?"

"You're always hungry," Jack said. "I'll see what I have."

"I'll help," Odette said. "What's in the refrigerator?"

"A little bit of everything," Jack said. "What sounds good?"

"Duck gumbo," J.P. said.

"Get over it until we bag some ducks," Odette said.

"Gumbo takes too long," Jack said. "How about some bacon, eggs, and grits?"

"I can go for breakfast," Chief said.

"You could go for the rear end of a horse," Jack said.

"Count me out," Eddie said. "The Covington Coven is arriving tomorrow, and I need to be firing on all cylinders."

"We're never going to make it unless you hire some cleaning people," Odette said. "The convention is going to expect clean sheets every day."

"What the hell are we going to do?" Eddie asked.

"Kind of late to put an ad in the paper," Odette said. "Meika and I will have to make do until you get somebody."

"Iryna can help," Alex said. "She told me she feels worthless and wants a job."

"I'll talk to her tomorrow," Odette said. "Isaac may know someone in Chalmette who can help us."

"Something else is bothering me," Eddie said.

Chief's attention had turned to the wonderful aroma coming from Jack's little galley as he and Odette began dishing up bacon, eggs, and grits.

"What's bothering you?" Jack asked.

"Something Freya said during her séance," Eddie said.

"Like what?" Jack asked. "She said lots of things."

"Maybe it wasn't Freya," Eddie said.

"It was Lafitte's ghost," Chief said. "He said, 'Beware, for those who dare to unearth the island's bounty will unleash a darkness long kept at bay. The curse is intertwined with the soul of this land, and only the true owners may profit."'

Eddie finished Chief's thought. "When Freya asked him what he meant, he said, '"Eternal life.""

"The Fountain of Youth," Chief said.

"Of course," Eddie said. "No other place in Louisiana has thermal water."

"I know someone who might be able to tell us what's going on underground and why we have thermal water on Oyster Island," J.P. said.

Eddie said, "Who?"

"There is an old geologist named Professor Enos Quinn. He lives on Goose Island, not far from here," J.P. said. "I met him a few years back. He knows as much about the geology of south Louisiana as anyone."

"You think he'll help us?" Eddie asked.

"I'll call and ask him," J.P. said.

"And?" Eddie said.

"He's a crusty old bastard with a heart of gold. I think we can count on him."

Chapter 14

The witches from the Covington Coven began arriving at the Majestic before Eddie could drink his first cup of morning coffee. Odette had things under control and invited him to join her, Iryna, and Isaac at a table in the bar. Before speaking, Odette poured him a cup of coffee from a carafe.

She grinned when Eddie said, "Remind me to give you a raise once the hotel begins turning a profit."

"That would be today," she said. "Have you seen all the new guests?"

"That's what worries me," Eddie said. "We're so shorthanded; how the hell will we ever handle them?"

"We aren't as shorthanded as you think," Odette said. "I hired Iryna earlier."

Eddie thrust his hand across the table and said, "Wonderful news. Welcome aboard, Iryna."

"Thank you," she said. "Oyster Island is a dream come true, and the house you assigned us is more than wonderful. The only thing I lacked was a cure for my boredom. This job will do the trick."

"Trust me when I tell you I'm eternally grateful," Eddie said.

"Isaac has more good news," Odette said. "His nephew and wife, Ron and Marian, recently relocated to Chalmette from Houma, where they worked in the hotel business."

"Their daughter Mariah lives in Chalmette and just had twins," Isaac said. "They wanted to move closer to her."

"And?" Eddie said.

"They needed jobs and a place to live," Odette said. "I've hired them to run the front desk and help Iryna. They'll live in the quarters behind the counter."

"Great news," Eddie said.

"Ron is a handyman," Isaac said. "You name it; he can fix it. They are arriving on the island today and will start work as soon as they're situated."

"Thanks, Isaac," Eddie said.

"They're hard-working Cajuns," Isaac said. "You can count on them to give you more than a day's work."

Before Eddie had finished his second cup of coffee, J.P. showed up at the table with a short little man of indeterminate age. A buckskin sportscoat covered a Western shirt complete with a bolo tie. His tan corduroy pants didn't quite cover his well-worn cowboy boots.

"This fine gentleman is Professor Enos Quinn. He runs the L.S.U. ornithology lab on nearby Goose Island."

Professor Quinn shook everyone's hand, lingering too long before releasing Iryna's.

"Is something the matter?" Iryna asked.

"Your accent. Are you from Ukraine?"

"How did you know?" she asked.

"I met my deceased wife during a trip to Ukraine. You remind me so much of her, I may ask you to marry me."

123

Iryna's face flushed crimson red. "Your wife was Ukrainian?"

"Yes," Professor Quinn said.

"What were you doing in Ukraine?"

"Before retiring, I was a vertebrate paleontologist."

"Big words," Iryna said. "Please explain."

"I studied dinosaurs and traveled to Ukraine to research the Riabininohadros, the only known dinosaur found in modern Ukraine."

Iryna smiled and said, "My granddaughter, Sveta, would love it. You no longer study dinosaurs?"

"Alas, I discovered I loved bird watching more than dinosaurs and retired to Goose Island. L.S.U. learned of my skills and hired me. I've been there ever since. It's where I met J.P."

"Where is Goose Island?" Isaac asked.

"Practically next door in Plaquemines Parish," Professor Quinn said. "I live in a rustic house built on stilts that juts into the bay."

"You're here on Oyster Island to study the birdlife?" Iryna asked.

"J.P. called me. It seems Mr. Toledo has questions about the island's geology. I'm here to hope to supply him with answers.

Eddie dropped the blue mineral on the table and said, "Then maybe you can tell me what this is."

Professor Quinn rolled the mineral and said, "I know exactly what it is. It's a semi-precious stone known as Larimar."

"I'm impressed you recognized it so quickly," Eddie said.

"It comes from only one place on earth," Professor Quinn said.

"Where?" Eddie asked.

124

Eddie, Odette, and J.P. exchanged glances when Professor Quinn said, "The Dominican Republic."

"It was found here on Oyster Island. Is it possible there's a second source?" Eddie asked.

"Heaven's no," Professor Quinn said. "Larimar's origin is associated with volcanic activity. There are no volcanos in south Louisiana."

"Sure about that?" Eddie asked.

"This stone is polished and likely disconnected from its jewelry setting."

"Are you sure it didn't come from Oyster Island?" Eddie said.

"Quite sure, Mr. Toledo. I've never heard of anything more cockamamie in my entire life," Professor Quinn said.

"Is it possible you're wrong?" J.P. asked.

Professor Quinn frowned and said, "I'm old, and I've been called a fool more than once. I'm not an old fool. If you can supply the evidence, I'm prepared to do a one-eighty in my thinking."

"Thanks, Professor," Eddie said. "That's all I ask."

"You've raised a high bar, Mr. Toledo. I'll keep an open mind."

"Please, just call me Eddie."

"Why don't you stay with me, Enos?" Isaac said. "I have a beautiful house with several empty bedrooms in a little enclave on the island. Iryna, her daughter and granddaughter, and Odette are my neighbors. I'd love to have company."

Professor Quinn shook Isaac's hand. "I'm not alone. I brought my rottweiler, Chuckie, and cat King Tut. They're waiting outside in my Jeep."

"Do they bite?" Isaac asked.

"Only if you attack me," Professor Quinn said. "Otherwise, they're as gentle as lambs."

"You are all welcome," Isaac said. "I think I'm the only person on the island without a dog."

"None of them as big as Chuckie," Professor Quinn said.

Odette smiled and said, "Bruiser's twice as big as your dog, and he isn't fully grown."

"Then Chuckie, King Tut, and I look forward to meeting him," Professor Quinn said.

"Come with me," Isaac said. "I'll get you and your pets situated. You can rest and then return to the Majestic for dinner."

"Isaac is the chef," Eddie said. "You won't be disappointed."

"That sounds like heaven," Professor Quinn said. "I've been cooking for myself for twenty years."

Professor Quinn's dark eyes lit up when Iryna said, "Do you like Ukrainian cuisine?"

"Adore it," Professor Quinn said. "I can't remember the last time I had Ukrainian cabbage rolls."

"My daughter Renata and I can cook you a traditional Ukrainian dinner you won't soon forget," Iryna said. "Are you interested?"

"You had me at pryvit," Professor Quinn said.

Iryna blushed, hearing Professor Quinn use the Ukrainian word for hello.

"What about me? Am I invited?" Isaac asked.

"Everyone's invited," Iryna said. "It'll be a party."

J.P. and Eddie were left alone at the table when Isaac took Professor Quinn to see his accommodations, and Odette accompanied Iryna on a tour of the hotel.

"What do you think about Professor Quinn?" J.P. asked.

J.P. grinned when Eddie said, "I'm going to be surprised if he finds any dinosaur bones on Oyster Island."

Eddie nodded when J.P. said, "Your expectations are low?"

"Hell, J.P.! It seems like we're grasping at straws. He did put a name on the mineral Chief found."

"And it comes from the Dominican Republic. How strange is that?"

"What do you mean?" Eddie asked.

"Alex compared the water we drink here on the island to the water in the Dominican Republic. Maybe Professor Quinn can tell us its connection to Oyster Island."

"Could be a coincidence," Eddie asked.

"Maybe."

"You don't think so?" Eddie said.

Before J.P. could answer, Delta Becht and Seraphina Nightshade appeared at the table. Both men stood.

"May we join you?" Delta said.

"Please do," Eddie said. "J.P., this is Delta Becht, Freya's daughter, and Seraphina Nightshade, the new head of the Covington Coven."

J.P. smiled ear-to-ear when he said, "Pleased to meet both of you."

"My room is lovely," Seraphina said. "I can't believe the view of the bay."

Delta was staring at the object in Eddie's hand. He handed it to her when she said, "May I look?"

"It's larimar," Eddie said.

"I know," Delta said. "My mother had a larimar necklace that my dad bought for her on their honeymoon in the Dominican Republic."

J.P. glanced at Eddie and said, "I remember seeing it around your mom's neck."

Everyone grew quiet as Eddie clutched Delta's hand and said, "I'm so sorry."

"It's okay," she said.

"I just met your mom," J.P. said. "She was a wonderful person."

"I want the person responsible brought to justice," Delta said.

"Something or someone already took care of it," J.P. said.

"How do you mean?" Delta asked.

"He's dead," J.P. said.

J.P. nodded when Delta asked, "You know who killed my mom?"

"We found a man's body on the other side of the bridge. A friend and I tracked him from the bomb site. Something killed him shortly after he perpetrated the attack."

"Something and not somebody?" Delta asked.

"The body produced more questions than answers. The Louisiana State Police is investigating. We'll have answers soon."

Delta fingered the polished gemstone. "Where did you find this?"

"Near the body of the bombing suspect," J.P. said. "It probably landed near the bomber following the explosion."

Delta began to weep and said, "May I keep it? It's the most personal thing remaining to remember my mom by."

"Evidence," J.P. said. "When the investigation is complete, I'll get it to you. I promise."

Delta nodded and said, "Thank you."

"Freya told me she intended to help you with your lawsuit concerning the island," Seraphina said.

Eddie said, "Did she? How did she intend to do that?"

Seraphina winked and said, "Magic. Freya's specialty. Mine too."

Eddie grinned and said, "You have a magic wand?"

"Maybe," Seraphina said. She took Delta's hand and pulled her up from the table. "The coven is arriving, and I need to get busy. Delta is helping me," she said. "We'll talk later."

Eddie and J.P. watched them disappear into the growing crowd.

"What do you think?" Eddie asked.

"That I'm in love," J.P. said. "They are both fine-looking women."

"Lust is more like it. When was the last time you had a date?"

"Been a while," J.P. said.

"I can see," Eddie said.

Someone Eddie recognized pushed through the crowd and joined them at the table.

"Pancho," Eddie said. "You made it."

Pancho shook J.P.'s and Eddie's hands and said, "I feel out of place. I think I'm the hotel's only male guest."

"Lucky you," J.P. said.

"Are you okay?" Eddie asked.

"I'll be lots better when we lay Freya properly to rest."

"Is your room acceptable?" Eddie asked.

"Beautiful," Pancho said. "I just feel out of place."

"How so?" Eddie asked.

"Freya and I never took a trip together. I feel as though I'm betraying her."

"Nonsense," Eddie said. "She'd have wanted for you to enjoy yourself."

Isaac interrupted them when he returned to the table.

"Forgot my keys," he said.

"Isaac, this is Pancho Bergamo. He was Freya's close friend, and he's here to mourn her death."

"I'm so sorry for your loss. I ate at your restaurant in Covington a few months back. It was the best Italian food I've ever tasted," Isaac said.

Pancho's demeanor instantly changed. "Thank you, Isaac," he said.

"You two have something in common," Eddie said. "Isaac is the chef of the Majestic,"

Pancho beamed when Isaac said, "Is there a chance I could get you to teach me a few of your recipes while you're on the island?"

"Love it," Pancho said. "Kitchens are my business and my hobby?"

"Staying at the hotel?" Isaac asked.

"I have a lovely room upstairs, though I would rather stay with people I know to commemorate Freya's passing."

"Bunk with me and Professor Quinn," Isaac said. "I have a big house at an enclave on the island and an unused bedroom."

Pancho glanced at Eddie and then back again at Isaac.

"You mean it?"

"You kidding me? It would be an honor. I've known about your cooking for years, and learning from you will be an honor."

"Eddie?" Pancho said.

"Knock yourself out," Eddie said. "I'll have Odette reassign the room to someone else."

"Professor Quinn is waiting at the door. I'll introduce you, and then we'll go upstairs and get your bags."

Pancho beamed as he disappeared through the crowd with Isaac. Again, alone at the table, J.P. and Eddie smiled.

"That takes care of some of your problems," J.P. said.

"Some, but not all," Eddie said.

"At least it sounds as if we're in for a few days of really good eating," J.P. said.

"Thank God for small favors," Eddie said.

Chapter 15

Eddie sat alone at the table after J.P. left him to begin work at the Canine Training Center. He gazed around the crowded room at the eclectic women chatting and getting situated in the hotel. Every one of them, he thought, had secrets to hide. Finally deciding to do some work, he left the bar and walked down the hall to his office. He found Delta Becht waiting for him.

"Everything okay?" he asked.

"I was wondering," she said.

"About what?"

Eddie nodded when she said, "You know I'm a lawyer."

"What about it?" he said.

He glanced at the carpet when she said, "I can help with your lawsuit." When Eddie didn't immediately respond, she said, "I know you think I'm nothing more than an ambulance chaser."

"No way," he said. "It's just that. . ."

"I don't have enough experience to help you?"

"The case is complicated and involves American Indian Law."

"I graduated first in my class at Loyola and took several courses in American Indian Law. It wouldn't take me long to get up to speed."

"I won't mince words," Eddie said. "Frankie Castellano has every lawyer in Chalmette on retainer. I had help until a few days ago when Basil Doles took a job with his dad in Baton Rouge."

"Then you need help," Delta said.

"Yes, but. . ."

"But what?"

"You're here for your mother's memorial service. You don't even live in this parish. I'm looking for someone more permanent."

"I don't want to return to Covington just yet," Delta said. "Too many memories there. I need to come to grips with them first."

"I don't have enough money to pay your salary," Eddie said.

"Then make me your partner. I'll work for a split."

"I have nothing to split. I have no clients, and my suit with Frankie Castellano is the only legal work I have on my plate."

"You're a famous lawyer. Companies will pay good money to have you on retainer," Delta said.

"I don't have time," Eddie said.

"I do," Delta said. "My undergrad degree is in marketing with a minor in public relations. I'll get us the customers and do all the work."

"I don't know," Eddie said.

"How does Becht and Toledo sound? We'll make a fortune, and you can run the Majestic as a hobby."

"You mean Toledo and Becht, don't you?"

Delta glanced away and said, "I was pulling your chain. You must admit, the name has a ring to it."

What else do you want?" Eddie asked.

"Name recognition. Partnership with you will elevate my status from ambulance chaser to respected legal mind."

"Sounds like you need to pay me," Eddie said, smirking.

"Right now, you need me as much as I need you," she said.

"All right," Eddie said. "You got a deal."

"Just like that?"

"Yes."

"When do I start?"

"Now. I'll show you your office."

Delta followed Eddie down a short hallway to a suite of a half-dozen fully equipped offices. The place was empty, and no one sitting behind the reception area desk.

The offices were plush with polished wood floors, hand-installed molding, and expensive original art on the walls. She followed Eddie to his office.

"You're probably familiar with the movie recently filmed on location at the Majestic. The construction crew built out this suite of offices. We have computers, internet, and a state-of-the-art phone system. Want to see your office?"

"If it's half as plush as yours, I can't wait," Delta said.

"Plusher," Eddie said as he led her down the hall. "This was the director's office, complete with a leather couch, side chairs, and a giant TV on one of the walls."

Delta was shaking her head when she said, "Oh, my God! At Carns and Holmes, I had a folding table for a desk."

"Get used to it," Eddie said. "Toledo and Becht is a blueblood law firm, the finest Oyster Island has to offer."

Delta ignored Eddie's levity and pulled a chair behind the ornately carved desk.

"Won't take me long to get used to this office," she said.

"Basil Doles's former office is down the hall. He has reams of information concerning the Castellano lawsuit. I'll show you."

"Thanks, Eddie," Delta said.

"For what?" Eddie said.

"Giving me a chance."

"I'm not keeping score," he said. "If you're thirsty around five, I'll be in the bar."

"You got it," Delta said.

Eddie had left his cell phone on his desk, and it rang when he returned to his office alone.

"Hello."

"It's Frankie," the voice said.

"I recognized your number. What can I do for you, Frankie?"

"Two things. One- I had nothing to do with the bombing. Two- This lawsuit is between you and me. Leave my family out of it."

"Understood," Eddie said. "I'm not responsible for Josie's actions."

Eddie patiently paused before Frankie said, "What about Josie?"

"She's here on the island."

Eddie grinned when Frankie said, "I'm going to kill you, Toledo."

"She isn't here to see me," Eddie said.

"Then what's she doing there?"

"It's her business, not mine. Maybe you should ask her. Someone else is on the island who might interest you."

Another long pause, and then Frankie said, "Who?"

"Carlos Palacio."

Eddie heard a crash as if Frankie had just thrown something against the wall.

"Holy crap!" he said. "Does Josie know he's there?"

"They had drinks together like old friends or old lovers."

"Hold a room for me. Adele and I are on our way," Frankie said.

"You can't do that," Eddie said. "We're in the middle of a lawsuit."

"I'm calling a truce. We can resume the suit after I get Josie off the island."

"The judge isn't going to like this," Eddie said.

"Then don't tell him," Frankie said.

"I won't have to," Eddie said. "It'll be all over the news by tomorrow. Your lawyers will mutiny."

"Wouldn't that be nice for you?" Frankie said.

"I have no illusions," Eddie said. "You would have another lawsuit filed before the end of the week."

"Smart man," Frankie said.

"That's not all. It was Pancho's girlfriend who was killed in the bombing, and he's here on the island, along with a pagan coven of witches, to celebrate her life and death."

"It was Freya who was killed in the bombing? Holy hell!"

"You knew her?"

"Course I did," Frankie said. "Jojo was starting to call her grandma."

"So sorry," Eddie said. "I didn't know."

"Are they burying Freya on Oyster Island?"

"There's nothing left to bury," Eddie said. "Her coven is staging a memorial ceremony sometime in the next few days."

"Holy hell!" Frankie said. "Freya was a witch?"

"You didn't know?"

"You think I'd have let Jojo meet her if I did?"

"I'm not responsible for this situation; we have a bigger problem."

"What could be bigger than this?" Frankie asked.

"If you aren't responsible for the bombing, then someone else is. Someone interested in the Majestic and Oyster Island and who will stop at nothing to achieve their goal."

"Palacio?" Frankie said.

"I don't think so. He and Josie were talking with Freya shortly before she was murdered. He seemed just as surprised about her death as anyone."

"And you should know, Mr. former prosecutor. Any ideas?"

"We're embroiled in a lawsuit, Frankie. We shouldn't even be talking."

"I'm dismissing the suit," Frankie said. "As soon as I hang up, I'll call my lawyers. Get me that room."

"Does this mean everything is copasetic between us?"

Frankie paused and said, "We need to work together on this. When we're done, I'm going to kick your ass."

Eddie's mind was reeling when he knocked on Delta's office door.

"Let's get a drink," he said.

File folders and legal filings littered Delta's desk.

"Don't have time," she said. "I have a case to get up to speed on."

"Forget it," Eddie said. "I just settled the case."

"How did you do that?" she asked.

"Frankie Castellano knew your mother. Jojo, his grandson, was starting to call her grandma. He's mad and hell-bent to find out who murdered her. He and his wife Adele are on their way to the island to attend her ceremony."

"Holy shit!" Delta said. "Is this a cover-up?"

"I don't think so," Eddie said. "He sounded genuinely surprised to me."

137

"Chief was the target of the bombing and not my mom. You said so yourself. Even if Castellano didn't intend to kill her, he might still be responsible."

Eddie popped his forehead with the flat of his hand. "Of course. You're thinking like a prosecutor, and Frankie's playing me for a chump. At least he's dropping the lawsuit."

"Maybe he intends to refile once the smoke settles," Delta said. "Did he agree to a settlement in writing?"

Eddie shook his head. "I need a drink," he said. "I've been out of the courtroom too long and not thinking straight."

"First, we need to draft a settlement," Delta said. "If he refuses to sign it, then he's likely complicit in my mom's murder."

"I can't do it now," Eddie said. "It'll have to wait.

"No, it doesn't. I'll do the first draft, and then we can work on it."

"You sure?"

"Sit," Delta said. "I have just the right contract template to use. Still, this will take a while, and I'll need your help."

Delta began keyboarding and exchanging suggestions with Eddie. More than an hour had passed when the printer began to hum, and the first draft of the contract emerged. She handed a copy to Eddie and began studying one of her own. After a dozen changes, Eddie grinned.

"This is brilliant," he said. "Who taught you how to write contracts?"

"Sister Louisa was one of my professors at Loyola. She's a Catholic nun."

"Remind me never to sue anyone Sister Louisa is representing," Eddie said.

"You think it suits our purpose?"

"You kidding? This settlement agreement is perfect."

"Thanks," Delta said. "Coming from you, that's high praise."

"Now, if we can only get Frankie to sign it," Eddie said.

Someone opened the office door and stuck their head in without knocking. It was Odette.

"Thought I heard something," she said. "What's going on?"

"World-rocking developments," Eddie said.

Odette made a face and said, "Like what?"

"I just spoke with Frankie. He's agreed to call off the lawsuit, at least temporarily."

"What brought that about?" Odette asked.

"Frankie and Adele were familiar with Freya because of her relationship with Pancho. He wants to attend her celebration of life ceremony. He can't do that without compromising the lawsuit, so he's dismissing it."

"What's to stop him from refiling after the ceremony?" Odette asked.

"Not so easy," Frankie said. "He'll have to start over again with a new judge." Eddie showed her the agreement. "And we have this."

"What is it?" Odette asked.

"An ironclad settlement agreement my new law partner and I hashed out."

"Delta is your law partner now?" Eddie nodded without explaining, and Odette let the subject drop. "How will you get Frankie to sign the agreement?"

"Haven't figured that one out yet," Eddie said. "Are there any rooms left?"

"About half a dozen. Many of the guests are doubling up."

"Save one for Frankie and Adele," Eddie said.

"Isaac's nephew and wife have arrived and are already working the front desk. They're pros and everything is going smoothly for once."

"Good to hear," Eddie said.

Odette started to back out of the room. "I'll alert Ron and Marian now."

"Thanks, Odette. Delta and I are headed for the bar. Please join us when you get a minute."

"Will do," Odette said. "One more thing."

"What?" Eddie asked.

"Professor Quinn was anxious to see the island. J.P. arranged for Chief and Jack to take him out beyond the breakers in the boat so he could get a shoreline view," Odette said. "They won't return until after dark."

"That's good, I guess," Eddie said. "The professor is wasting no time."

"That's not all," Odette said. "Josie, Amani, Alex, and Carlos are going with them."

"Cozy," Eddie said. "Thanks for the info."

"See you in the bar," Odette said, shutting the door behind her."

"I'm parched," Eddie said. "Let's get that drink."

Delta followed Eddie out the door, stopping him before they reached the end of the hall.

"Is this the end of our legal partnership?"

"You kidding me? I'm ordering champagne to celebrate it. You're the best thing that's come down the pike for me since I can't remember when."

"You mean it?"

Eddie shook her hand. "From this day forward, we're partners. I'm lots of things. Liar isn't one of them."

Chapter 16

Once a haven for dozens of yachts, beautiful Oyster Bay was now mostly devoid of boats. It remained a home for pelicans, gulls, and other seabirds. One of the big birds swooped over the group, heading up the wooden dock to one of the two remaining boats.

Jack and Chief led the group down the wooden walkway to an old trawler. A cloudy sky blocked the sunlight, and everyone was dressed warmly to repel a chill wind blowing off the Gulf of Mexico.

J.P. had arranged the outing to allow Professor Enos Quinn to look at Oyster Island from the shoreline. The rest of the group included Alex, Josie, Amani, and Carlos Palacio. Jack went to the wheelhouse of the trawler and started its diesel engine. Chief untied the rope, mooring it to the dock, and followed the others aboard.

The old diesel engine, silent for so long, sputtered and popped before leveling into a powerful purr. As they motored out of the channel leading to the Gulf of Mexico, Chief glanced at the gray sky and wondered how far they'd get before the rain began falling. Professor Quinn's question interrupted his thoughts.

"Your boat is beautiful," he said.

"It was a rumrunner during the Prohibition Era," Chief said.

Sensing a story, the rest of the little group gathered around.

"I can guess what the role of a rumrunner was," Professor Quinn said.

"This beautiful old lady's name is Argo," Chief said. "During Prohibition, people who smuggled rum into this country illegally were called rumrunners, and so were their boats."

"We're all ears," Josie said. "Please tell us the story of this boat."

"A rumrunner who lived part-time on Oyster Island owned her. Its original name was the Island Mistress because though the rumrunner had a wife and family in New York, he had a mistress who lived with him while he was on the island."

"Interesting," Professor Quinn said.

"The Argo was built in 1928. The decks are teak, the hull constructed of the finest Douglas fir. A 180-horsepower diesel engine propels it, and its dual 200-gallon fuel tanks are big enough to get you all the way to the Bahamas."

"So, the Argo was used to smuggle illegal alcohol?"

"This boat was registered as a fishing vessel. Her crew would pick up the hooch, store it in the hold, and top it with fish. She's so slow the Coast Guard never suspected she carried illegal booze in her hold."

"Sounds like the rumrunners were taking quite a chance," Professor Quinn said.

"Pretty much so. The Coast Guard had a fleet of fast boats armed with cannons. Most rumrunners, much faster than the Argo, were shot out of the water."

"Sounds like a dangerous profession," Josie said.

"But lucrative. The man who owned the Argo lived like a king on Oyster Island."

"The Feds never caught him?"

"No, but his jealous wife finally did," Chief said. "Shot off his kneecap and crippled him. Stopped his running around forever. She's also responsible for making him change the name of the Island Mistress to Argo."

They were soon beyond the breakers in the crashing waves of the Gulf of Mexico. The little group watched with interest as Professor Quinn studied the shoreline with a pair of binoculars. Gulls followed the boat, jutting in and out of the dark clouds, looking for fish brought to the surface by the wake. The Argo coasted to a stop when Professor Quinn signaled Jack to cut the engines.

"What are you staring at so intently?" Josie asked.

"The anomalous topography," Professor Quinn said.

"Please explain," Josie said.

"The hill behind the lighthouse seems to have an elevation above sea level of at least forty feet."

"So?" Josie said.

"There are no hills in south Louisiana," Professor Quinn said.

"Seems there are," Josie said. "We can see the one you're talking about even without your binoculars."

Chief motioned to Jack when Professor Quinn said, "I've seen enough. Return us to shore."

Professor Quinn didn't immediately answer when Josie said, "What do you think?"

He finally said, "I'm unprepared to conclude anything, young lady. I want to see more of the island before I do."

Everyone except Professor Quinn got out of the wind and joined Jack in the wheelhouse as he navigated the old trawler through the choppy water of the Gulf. The Professor remained on deck, braving the elements as he gazed at Oyster Island with his binoculars. The boat stabilized when Jack entered the pass into Oyster Bay.

"The Professor seems out of sorts," Amani said.

"I told him there was a hill on Oyster Island," Chief said.

"I don't think he believed you," Josie said. "What's the explanation?"

"A geologist for an oil company told me it's because the island overlies a salt dome."

"There are underground salt domes all over the Gulf of Mexico," Jack said. "It's how the oil companies know where to drill their wells."

Jack and Chief took offense when Amani said, "If you already know what causes the hill, why did you invite Professor Quinn to study the island?"

"J.P.'s idea," Jack said. "The Professor is a friend of his."

Amani persisted. "You're just humoring him?"

"You might say that," Jack said.

"Grandma always said Oyster Island is magical," Chief said. "I've lived here all my life and never ceased to be amazed."

"None of us are scientists," Alex said. "I know the island is perfect for the location of a distillery. I have no explanation for Chief's hill or thermal water."

Josie, Carlos, and Amani stopped staring out the window and turned their attention to Alex.

"No one ever mentioned thermal water to me," Josie said.

Chief shrugged and said, "Magic."

"It's something more than magic," Alex said. "I agree with J.P. that Professor Quinn will give us the necessary answers."

Jack pulled the trawler into the dock. After Chief had secured the ropes, the group exited the boat. Carlos held Josie's hand, ensuring she didn't slip when she stepped on the damp plank leading to the dock. Jack smiled and winked at Alex when he saw him frowning.

"Jealous?" he said.

"Worried," Alex said.

"Don't worry," Jack said. "Josie won't go around you on the distillery deal."

Eddie had bought a stretch ATV for transporting hotel guests, and they needed every inch of the extended-frame vehicle to carry the group to the water well on the beach. Alex filled an aluminum ladle with water from the pump and handed it to Professor Quinn. The group waited as the professor tasted it. The smile on his face told them everything they wanted to know.

He pointed his thumb upward and said, "Worldclass. Easily the best tasting water in Louisiana."

Professor Quinn passed the ladle to Josie and she smiled after sipping the water from it. Everyone was soon smiling, though Alex seemed especially happy.

"One more stop before we go to La Tortue Mountain."

Chief directed Jack to a spot on the far side of the Oyster Island bridge and then pointed into the trees.

"About a hundred yards that way," Chief said.

Jack pulled to a halt on the side of the road. "The ATV can't make it through there," he said.

"Terry, the death investigator, blazed a trail through the brush in his Bronco. The ATV can't use the trail, but it'll make it easier for us to walk to the site," Chief said.

The group unloaded from the ATV and followed Chief. They were soon staring at the deep blue surface of the pond where they had found the body of the bomber.

"What am I supposed to make of this pond?" Professor Quinn asked.

"Dip your hand in it?" Chief said.

Quinn squatted and stuck his hand into the water. "Impossible," he said.

Everyone soon tested the temperature of the water.

"The death investigator said the water is geothermal. He had a thermometer and measured the temperature at eighty degrees," Chief said. "What do you think?"

Professor Quinn didn't answer. Instead, he began walking around the pond. The little group waited until he'd circled the body of water.

"What were you looking for?" Josie asked.

"The pipe transporting hot water into the pond," Professor Quinn said.

Chief opened the bag he'd carried from the ATV and handed a metal detector to Professor Quinn.

"J.P. had the same question. There's no pipe. At least no metal pipe. You're welcome to check it for yourself."

Professor Quinn waved away the metal detector. "I'll take your word for it. Doesn't matter because I'll require more proof before I even begin to consider that the pond is geothermal."

"What else could it be?" Josie asked.

"Factory waste water dumping for one thing," Professor Quinn said. "Artificial heating for another."

"There are no factories for miles from here, and why would anyone heat the pond?" Josie said.

"Ever heard the phrase 'salting the mine,' young lady?"

146

Josie gave Alex a dirty look and said, "Is that what this is?"

"This is the first time I've ever seen this pond. Why would I heat it? There's no logical reason."

"You're Russian," Professor Quinn said.

Alex opened his mouth to reply but thought better of it and remained silent. Jack spoke for him.

"You have something against Russians?"

"Very much so," Professor Quinn said. "It starts with Ukraine."

Alex started to speak, but Chief cut him off with a wave of his arm.

"Wait just a minute, Professor. You met Iryna Kalinichenko earlier. She and her granddaughter Sveta are alive because Alex and J.P. rescued them from Ukraine. Alex is honorable, and I won't allow you to malign him."

"Me either," Jack said. "You may be a great scientist, but you're ignorant of basic humanity if you judge people by nationality. Let's go, Chief."

They stopped when Professor Quinn said, "Wait, I apologize. I let one of my many prejudices get in the way of my good senses. Please forgive me."

"It's Alex you need to make amends to. Not us," Jack said.

"Alex, I sincerely apologize."

"Accepted, Professor. An old Russian proverb says, 'Best is enemy of the good.'"

"What the hell is that supposed to mean?" Jack said.

"The professor knows," Chief said.

"Do you now believe the pond is geothermal?" Josie asked.

"No, but I don't rule out the possibility, and I promise not to jump to any more absolutely inane conclusions," he said.

"Next stop is La Tortue Mountain," Chief said. "It's going to ring your bell."

"Can't wait," Professor Quinn said. "Lead the way."

They were quickly on their way to La Tortue Mountain, and it was raining lightly when Jack parked the ATV at the base of Chief's hill.

"We'll get wet in the rain," Jack said. "Want to postpone until later?"

"The others can return to the Majestic if they desire," Professor Quinn said. "I'm not sugar and won't melt. I'm ready to investigate Mr. La Tortue's mountain."

"Count me in," Alex said.

"We're all going," Amani said.

The group followed Chief up the sandy path to the top of the hill and the clearing where his teepee sat. In the distance, through the trees, they could see the Majestic Hotel, and the Gulf of Mexico beyond it.

"I love your teepee and the view of the Gulf is truly grand," Amani said.

Chief's chickens, because of the rain, were in their coop, his cat Buttercup asleep in the teepee as he led them to a rustic water well. He lowered the wooden bucket into the well and drew water from it.

With an aluminum ladle identical to the one they had used on the beach he offered the group a taste of the water. Their smiles and responses to the water was the same as it was on the beach.

"Though I have no explanation for this hill, I can't deny the water on this island is perfect," Professor Quinn said.

"There's a rock-bottomed pool of water further up the hill," Chief said. "An artesian flow feeds it. I'll show it to you."

They followed Chief to a clear pool fed by water pouring from the solid rock wall. Professor Quinn stuck his finger beneath the flow and tasted the water.

"Wonderful," he said.

"My grandmother called it the 'Magic Fountain,'" Chief said.

"I can feel the spirits of the people who have bathed in the pool," Amani said. "It is truly magical."

Surprised by Amani's reflection, no one commented. Chief finally said, "One more thing to show you."

The path up the hill grew ever steeper. Soon, they reached a triangular-shaped obelisk at least twenty feet from the ground.

"What is it?" Josie asked.

"Lick your finger. Rub it over the white rock and taste it," Chief said.

Josie followed Chief's directions and said, "It's salty."

"It's rock salt," Chief said.

"How long has this been here?" Professor Quinn asked.

"Not long," Chief said. "I was bathing in the Magic Fountain when an earthquake shook the hill so violently, I thought I would roll down the hill. After the tremor, I walked up the hill and found this rock feature penetrating the earth's surface."

"I've never seen anything like it," Alex said.

"There's more," Chief said. "A cave inside of the rock formation."

Chief pointed to a dark opening in the otherwise solid rock."

"Can we enter?" Professor Quinn asked.

"I've installed a ladder," Chief said. "I'll go first and light a torch."

Chief disappeared into the darkness. When he reached the bottom of the ladder, he lit a torch that illuminated the cave.

"I'm coming down," Professor Quinn said.

"Watch your step. It's slick down here," Chief said.

The rest of the group followed Professor Quinn down the ladder. Quinn was staring at a steaming pool of water. He stuck his finger into it, quickly pulling it out.

"It's hotter than eighty degrees," he said.

"More like a hundred," Chief said. "It feels great once you get used to it."

Alex had a small test kit and began using an eyedropper to add chemicals to the sample he collected. Josie, Carlos, Jack and Amani looked on with interest. Professor Quinn was interested in something else: black rock piercing the salt. He had a geologist's pick hammer on his belt and used it to collect a sample.

The professor didn't answer when Chief said, "What do you think now?"

Chapter 17

The dark bar was crowded in the late afternoon when Eddie and Delta took seats at the large table Meika reserved for Eddie and his guests.

"Bring us a chilled bottle of Dom Perignon," Eddie said.

"We don't have any Dom. Will Cook's do?"

Remembering he'd nixed Odette's order of Dom Perignon because it was too expensive, Eddie said, "Bring us what you got." When Odette joined them, he asked, "Have a glass?"

She smiled and said, "No thanks. I'm drinking rum."

J.P. arrived at the table. When he saw the label on the champagne bottle, he said, "Big night?"

"Celebrating," Eddie said.

"What are you celebrating?" J.P. asked.

"Delta's a lawyer and was going to help me kick Frankie's ass."

"Was?"

"Frankie dropped the lawsuit," Eddie said.

"You kidding me? Wonderful news. How did you talk him into dropping the suit?"

"His grandson Jojo was calling Freya grandma. He wants to attend her ceremony but can't in good faith while the suit goes on."

"Is he going to refile after the ceremony?" J.P. asked.

"Delta and I hacked out an ironclad settlement agreement. Now, all we have to do is convince him to sign it."

"How do you do that?" J.P. asked.

"I don't know yet," Eddie said. "That isn't the only reason for our celebration."

"What could be better than having Frankie drop the lawsuit?"

"Delta and I formed a partnership. The Toledo and Becht law firm is now official," Eddie said.

J.P. glanced at Delta and said, "Congratulations. At least, I think."

Delta had finished the champagne, draining the last of it straight from the bottle. The silly grin on her face informed them that she was intoxicated. She exited her chair, sat in J.P.'s lap, and draped her arms around his neck.

"Whoa, girlfriend," Odette said. "J.P.'s the last person whose lap you should sit on."

"He's cute," Delta said.

"So are baby alligators," Odette said. "It won't stop them from biting you."

"Leave the girl alone," J.P. said. "She's just having fun."

Odette got out of her chair, unraveled Delta's arms from around J.P.'s neck, and pulled her to her feet."

"You're done," she said. "I'm taking you to your room."

Eddie was frowning and shaking his head after watching Odette and Delta disappear through the crowd.

"What the hell were you thinking?" he said. "She's my law partner."

"She sat in my lap," J.P. said. "I didn't grab her hand and pull her into it."

"Then don't," Eddie said. "We need her to help with Frankie."

"You're worried, aren't you?"

"Good attorneys never stop worrying," Eddie said. "I'm taking no chances."

J.P. showed Eddie his palms. "I'm hip. Lucky and I don't want to lose our happy home."

"Then show a little restraint," Eddie said.

"I didn't do anything," J.P. said.

Odette interrupted the conversation when she returned to the table alone. "That girl can't hold her liquor," she said. "It might have been different if you'd have let me order good champagne."

"I stand corrected," Eddie said. "Nothing but the best from this point on."

Odette turned the empty champagne bottle upside down into the silver ice bucket and pushed it aside.

"Delta liked it," she said.

"Something to remember if I ever have a date with her," J.P. said.

"Don't even think about it," Eddie said.

It was dark outside when Frankie and Adele Castellano appeared through the crowded bar. Frankie pulled up a chair without asking. Adele wore a white blouse, a short black leather skirt, and stylish calf-length boots. Her dark hair may have come from a bottle, though you couldn't tell if it had. Eddie got to his feet and hugged her.

Frankie was wearing a ridiculously expensive light brown Brioni suit complete with a thousand-dollar tie, five-thousand-dollar brogans, and a Rolex that cost more than most people make in a year. Like Adele, his hair and eyes were dark. His slicked-back hair was thinning, leaving him with a shiny forehead. His bulldog expression made him look angry even when he was smiling.

"Adele," Eddie said. "You're more gorgeous every time I see you."

"You're a liar, Eddie Toledo, but I love it," she said.

Meika was already at the table with a scotch for Frankie and a glass of chardonnay for Adele.

"Good memory," Frankie said.

He smiled when she said, "I never forget a good tipper."

"Thanks for saving us the best suite of rooms in the hotel," Adele said.

"When I heard Jojo and Toni were coming, I made sure you'd have plenty of room," Odette said.

Adele took her hand and took pains so that Frankie saw her do it: a not-so-subtle demonstration that she'd forgiven Odette for whatever transgression Frankie thought she may have committed. Frankie noticed.

"Toni's in the room watching TV with Jojo."

"Toni's a wonderful daughter," Odette said. "You and Frankie are blessed."

Frankie was frowning, his arms clasped tightly around his chest. "She's on my shit list right now," he said.

"Why is that?" Eddie asked.

"I heard through the grapevine that she called Josie after Adele had given you your walking papers."

"Josie's a grown woman with a career of her own," Eddie said. "Alex Pavlovich presented her with a business deal. She was here on the island doing due diligence."

"What business deal?"

"That's for Josie to tell you," Eddie said. "I don't betray confidences."

Adele frowned and shook her head when Frankie said, "Maybe the only thing I like about you."

Frankie smirked when Adele said, "You promised me you'd be civil."

"Eddie's a lawyer," he said. "He doesn't expect people to be civil to him."

"So sorry, Eddie," Adele said.

"Frankie's correct. No need to apologize," he said.

"Josie's not in her room. Where in the hell is she?" Frankie asked.

"On a field trip to study the island's geology," J.P. said."

"What's to study?" Frankie asked.

"No comment," J.P. said. "Like Eddie said, you need to ask Josie."

J.P. didn't answer when Frankie said, "Carlos Palacio isn't in his room. Is he still on the island?"

Though Eddie, Odette, and J.P. exchanged glances, no one at the table answered. Frankie noticed. Odette motioned for Meika to bring the table more drinks.

Adele wasn't happy with the direction the conversation had taken.

"Please, Frankie. Josie is a friend of everyone at the table. You've never given away a personal secret, and you shouldn't expect others to."

Frankie's arms unfolded, and he sipped his fresh scotch.

"Sorry," he said. "Josie's my daughter and mother of my only grandchild. I'm upset about her well-being."

"You're a smart man, Frankie, and your beautiful daughter is just as smart and savvy as you are," Eddie said. "Smart enough to run your business if she wanted to."

"You're right, Toledo. I don't know why hearing it from you pisses me off, but it does."

"Life takes unusual turns sometimes," Eddie said.

Frankie glared and asked, "What's that supposed to mean?"

"Just that Josie's destiny isn't marriage to a chump whose only claim to fame was his stint with the Justice Department."

Adele clutched Eddie's hand and said, "You're no chump, Eddie."

Frankie threw his hands into the air and said, "Hell, I'm not worried about Eddie. Carlos Palacio and that snake of a father of his are the ones cramping my style."

Adele grabbed one of Frankie's wildly gesticulating hands and placed his scotch glass into the other.

"You're going to have a heart attack if you don't calm down," she said.

Odette exited her chair and put her arms around Adele's shoulders.

"Why don't you take Frankie to your room," she said. "There's plenty of booze in the mini-fridge, and I'll get a menu and come with you and take your dinner order. Nothing will happen here tonight, and you'll get a fresh start tomorrow."

"Frankie?" Adele said.

"You got it, doll. Let's go."

Odette grabbed a menu from the bar and followed Adele and Frankie.

"Save a place for me," she said. "I'll be back."

Once Frankie had left the table, J.P. said, "Ever hear of Conexco?"

"Seems I've heard the name, though I can't remember where or when," Eddie said.

"The dead person we found on the other side of the bridge was a man named Wayne King. If you aren't squeamish, I have a picture of the body on my cell phone," J.P. said.

Eddie took a minute to study the picture before handing it back to J.P.

"He's very dead, all right," Eddie said.

"The police haven't found squat about the bomber. They did find a business card with a handwritten phone number on the floorboard of his rental car. The name on the card said Conexco," J.P. said.

"What else?" Eddie asked.

"Nothing except the phone number," J.P. said.

"What's the story on Conexco?" Eddie asked.

"There are dozens of companies using that name. The police have no idea which one it is," J.P. said.

"Now I remember," Eddie said. "A lobbyist in Basil's father's office asked about Oyster Island. I'll call and see if Basil's learned anything else."

J.P. waited as Eddie dialed his cell phone. Basil answered on the first ring.

"What's up, boss?" Basil asked.

"Just checking to see if you'd learned more about the man who visited your office?"

"Nothing," Basil said.

"What was his name?"

"Wayne King," Basil said.

"Bingo!" Eddie said. "Thanks, Basil. I'll call you back when I know more."

"What did he say?"

"The man posing as a journalist to interview Basil's father was none other than Wayne King, the dead bomber you and Chief found on the other side of the bridge."

J.P. had no time for questions as Odette returned with Toni Bergamo, Adele's daughter, in tow. She looked like a younger version of Adele except for her ash-blond hair. J.P. and Eddie got out of their chairs and hugged her, J.P. whistling as he ogled her toned body, highlighted by her red-flowered miniskirt.

"Look at those legs. You been working out?"

"Training horses for Frankie and riding my bike on weekends." She pirouetted and said, "You like?"

J.P. whistled again. "You're as pretty as your mom," he said. "You could be a movie star or a runway model."

"J.P. Saucier," she said. "Are you trying to get into my panties?"

"I've never seen a woman yet that J.P. hasn't tried to get into her panties," Odette said.

Laughter filled the dark bar as Meika arrived at the table and asked, "What are you drinking?"

"Abita," Toni said.

"With a chilled mug?" Meika asked.

"Just the can," Toni said. "Has anyone seen Pancho? I'm worried about him."

"In the kitchen cooking with our chef Isaac," Eddie said. "He couldn't be happier."

"Good," Toni said. "What sort of ceremony is Freya's coven having for her?"

"Who knows," Eddie said. "They're pagan witches; your guess is as good as mine."

"Freya was the most uninhibited person I ever met," Toni said. "She had more lovers than Casanova."

"Pancho didn't seem to mind," Eddie said. "He wasn't jealous when she offered to drive me to the island."

Meika returned to the table and said, "Isaac and Pancho cooked shrimp scampi. Anybody hungry?"

Everyone raised their hand. When Meika returned to serve their dinner, Pancho was with her.

"Hey, baby," he said, touching Toni's shoulder. "I was hoping you'd make it."

Toni patted his hand. "I wanted to be here for you. The couple at the front desk said you don't have a room in the hotel. Where are you staying?"

"Not far from here at Isaac's house. He's an old man like me, and we have lots in common. I'm teaching him a few Italian recipes."

"Good," Toni said. "I was worried about you being alone."

"Strangely, I don't think I am alone. I feel as if Freya is with us," he said.

"Considering her magical abilities, I wouldn't doubt it," Toni said.

"I'll catch up with you later," Pancho said. "I need to get back in the kitchen and help Isaac."

When they'd finished eating, Toni said, "I'd love to see the beach from the observation deck."

"I'll go with you," J.P. said.

When they were gone, Odette said, "Maybe we're in luck with Frankie. From how he's acting, it seems he may have forgiven me."

"Let's hope so," Eddie said. "Toni and Adele are doing everything they can to help."

A group of people approached the table, Josie Castellano among them.

"Did I hear someone mention my stepmom and sister?" she said.

Chapter 18

Eddie's jaw dropped as he watched Josie standing behind Odette at the table. What surprised him wasn't her appearance. It was the hand of Carlos Palacio she was holding ever so blatantly. Professor Quinn, Alex, Jack, and Chief were with them.

"Join us and tell us what you learned," Eddie said.

"Thought you'd never ask," Chief said.

Eddie smiled and said, "You never have to ask for a seat at this table. You're always welcome."

They had barely sat when Meika arrived from behind the bar and began delivering drinks.

"What can I get you, Professor Quinn?" she asked."

"Abita, please," he said.

"Chilled glass?"

"Just the can will do," he said.

"You and Toni have similar tastes."

"Who is Toni?" Professor Quinn asked.

"Josie's stepsister," Meika said.

Josie's smile faded when she said, "Toni's on the island?"

"Along with your mom, stepdad, and Jojo," Odette said. "They're here for Freya's ceremony of life and death and their room is around the corner from yours."

"Who's Jojo?" Carlos asked.

"My son."

"You have a son?"

"The love of my life."

"How old is Jojo?"

Josie hesitated a moment before saying, "Eight going on twenty-one."

Josie's pronouncement seemed to disturb Carlos, and he reached for a drink before remembering he didn't have one. Meika noticed.

"What can I get you, Mr. Palacio?"

"Brandy, please," he said.

When Meika returned with drinks, Carlos drained his brandy in a single gulp.

"Another?" Meika asked.

"No, thank you. I'm feeling ill and going to my room. Please excuse me."

Josie looked shocked as Carlos hurried away from the table. Eddie and Odette noticed and exchanged a knowing glance as Professor Quinn drank from his can of Abita.

"Jack and Chief," he said. "I want to thank you both for my tour of Oyster Island. It was quite eventful."

"Then please share your findings with us," Eddie said. "I'm all ears."

"Professor Quinn hasn't told us anything either," Jack said.

When Pancho appeared at their table and rested his palms on Josie's shoulders, conversation about the field trip ceased.

"Eddie said you were here during the explosion," he said.

"Pancho, I'm so sorry. I wish there were something I could have done," Josie said.

"Just your being here means the world to me," he said. "Who's hungry?"

"Pancho, have you met Professor Quinn?" Josie asked.

"The professor and I are old buds," Pancho said. "We're both staying with Isaac."

"And I can't wait to taste one of your culinary masterpieces," Professor Quinn said.

"Count me and the rest of us in," Jack said.

Pancho smiled and said, "Shrimp scampi and bottles of Chianti coming up."

Pancho, Isaac, and Meika soon appeared at the table with plates of food. Polite conversation ceased while everyone enjoyed their shrimp scampi. Everyone except Josie. Her expression was pained as she used a fork to play with the scampi on her plate. Eddie wasn't eating and noticed.

"Carlos didn't know about Jojo, did he?"

Josie shook her head. "I never told him."

"What happened between the two of you?" Eddie asked.

"I don't want to discuss it," she said.

"No problem. I understand."

Josie stood from the table and said, "I enjoyed our outing today immensely, but now I must go. Please excuse me."

"Josie didn't eat her scampi," Pancho said when he and Meika returned to the table to clear the dinnerware."

"She was exhausted from the field trip and decided to go to her room," Eddie said.

"Hope she's okay," Pancho said.

"She's tired and has things on her mind she needs to work out."

Before Pancho could ask what was troubling her, Professor Quinn interrupted their conversation.

"Your scampi was wonderful," he said.

Jack agreed. "Best I've ever eaten."

"Same here," Chief and Alex said.

Pancho was smiling as he and Meika returned to the kitchen. Eddie turned his attention to Professor Quinn.

"Please tell us what you learned. Does the island sit atop a giant salt dome?"

"There's a salt dome involved. That isn't all that's occurred geologically on this island."

"Please explain," Eddie said.

"I was skeptical about Chief's claims when we began our field trip. I even accused Alex of salting the mine. I'm sorry. I was wrong."

"Then the pond is hydrothermal?" Chief said.

Professor Quinn nodded. "It took seeing your cave and thermal pool to convince me."

"The hundred-degree water?" Alex asked.

"That and something else," Professor Quinn said.

The professor had a leather collection bag on a strap around his neck. He removed something from it and sat it on the table. It was a slab of grainy black rock.

"What is it?" Chief asked.

"Basalt. An igneous rock resulting from volcanic activity. This island overlies an active craton likely filled with molten rock."

"You have to be kidding," Eddie said.

"This must be a fairly recent occurrence because there's no evidence of volcanic activity in Louisiana."

"Then what's the answer?" Eddie asked.

"Geology is a complex science that involves many forces such as plate tectonics and seafloor spreading. Believe me when I tell you there's a plausible explanation."

"I believe you," Eddie said.

"So sorry I accused you, Alex. Right now, I'm stupefied, and I stand corrected."

Alex smiled. "Your apology is appreciated, though completely unnecessary. I only wish Josie was still here to hear your prognosis."

"I'll fill her in tomorrow," he said, glancing at the old Bulova on his wrist."

"If you're ready to leave, Chief and I will give you a ride to Isaac's house," Jack said.

"Wonderful," Professor Quinn said. "I like going to sleep with the chickens."

"I'll see if Isaac and Pancho are ready to leave," Odette said.

Odette returned with Isaac and Pancho, and they were soon heading home.

"I'll finish in the kitchen, then go to bed," Odette said.

"Thanks, Odette," Eddie said.

"For what?"

She smiled and nodded when he said, "Everything."

"Where's Amani?" Eddie asked.

"She begged off," Alex said. "Said she had things to do. We dropped her off at her van."

"She isn't staying with Carlos?"

"It was apparent to everyone that Josie and Carlos are a couple. They never got more than a few feet from each other."

"Frankie's going to be pissed," Eddie said.

"Josie's a powerful woman. I doubt she's worried about what anyone thinks."

"Except for Carlos," Eddie said.

"I hate to leave you alone," Alex said. "I have notes to transfer to my laptop."

"Is Carlos's appearance going to flummox your funding arrangement with Josie?"

"Hope not. The distillery has become my dream. I hope circumstances don't dash that dream."

"See you tomorrow," Eddie said. "I'm going to play the part of a good host, circulate the bar, and introduce myself to the guests."

"Have fun," Alex said.

Eddie spent the next hour meeting the coven members in the bar. He learned that they were a diverse group, all interesting and brilliant. He was ready to call it a night when he spotted Seraphina Nightshade sitting with two other women at a table. He stopped to say hello.

"Hope you're enjoying yourself, Seraphina."

"Immensely, she said. "Please join us."

"I don't want to interrupt your conversation."

"Nonsense," she said. "We only have a minute anyway. This is Eddie Toledo, the owner of the Majestic.

The three women looked enough alike to be sisters, maybe even triplets. They were all attractive, of indeterminant age, and had long hair.

"I'm Beth," the woman with dark hair said.

"Arabella," the blond woman said.

"It's nice to meet you," Eddie said. "I hope you're enjoying your stay at my old hotel."

"It's lovely," Arabella said.

"We have a meeting in the conference room in ten minutes," Seraphina said. "Will you be in the bar in a couple of hours?"

"Probably so," Eddie said.

"Then maybe we'll see you then," she said.

Meika was smiling when she brought Eddie a scotch.

"Looks like you're in for a wild ride later on tonight," she said.

"Really?" Eddie said. "You mean with Seraphina?"

"And her two friends," she said.

She nodded when he said, "All three?"

"Why not? This is the kinkiest bunch of females I've seen since I worked at a nurse's convention in New Orleans."

"Nurses are kinky?" he asked.

Meika nodded again. "You'd be surprised what all they can do with a stethoscope."

"Sounds like I should go to my room," he said.

"Suit yourself," Meika said.

Instead of calling it a night, Eddie decided to walk on the beach. It was cold and misting rain as he followed the boardwalk to the sand. Toward the beach, he could see a dim light illuminating the interior of Amani's van. He pulled his shirt up around his neck and headed toward it.

The sand was damp, and the wind blowing off the Gulf chilled him. He wished he had worn his windbreaker. It was no use worrying about it now. If Amani weren't awake, he would hurry back to the hotel and take a warm shower before going to bed.

The thought comforted him as he stood outside the colorful van. He had chickened out of knocking on the door and was preparing to head back to the hotel when the van door opened.

"Eddie, is that you?"

"I was worried and decided to check on you."

"You're wet, and it's cold out there. Come in."

"You sure?"

"I was hoping you'd come," she said.

"Really?" he asked.

She took his hand and said, "I'm glad you're here."

Eddie's eyes opened wide when he saw Amani was scantily dressed in only a light blue nightgown.

She smiled when he blurted out, "You're beautiful."

"And you look miserable in those wet clothes. Take them off. I have a blanket you can wrap yourself in while we talk."

"You sure?"

"I have brothers," she said. "There's nothing I haven't seen. I promise you won't embarrass me."

Eddie stripped to his boxer shorts. Amani was having none of it, smiling as she pulled them off and placed them on a shelf to dry. He lost his self-consciousness when she draped a warm throw over him.

Amani smiled when he said, "I forgot my flask."

When Amani opened a cabinet to retrieve a bottle of rum, Eddie noticed her cat for the first time.

"The big boy's a stray. I found him eating out of a trashcan at a roadside park in the middle of nowhere."

"He's beautiful," Eddie said.

"His name is Blanco because he's white. He's part tabby and Siamese. He's jumpy because his beautiful blue eyes are congenitally crossed."

When the big cat brushed against the blanket, it began purring as Eddie stroked its back.

"I didn't know you like cats," he said.

"Blanco doesn't take to many people. I can see he trusts you. Have some rum. It will warm your soul."

"I'm sorry about you and Carlos," Eddie said.

"Why are you sorry?"

She laughed when he said, "He's your boyfriend."

"Do you believe in karma?"

"Sure. At least I think I do."

"There's a reason for Josie's appearance on the island. Everything happens for a reason," Amani said.

"If you say so."

"I'm on Oyster Island for a reason, and you're here with me tonight to help."

"What reason?" he asked.

"To find something lost here and to return it to its rightful owner."

"Like what?"

Amani didn't answer Eddie's question. "The boat ride on the trawler today was eventful. Do you know how to operate it?"

"Jack taught me," Eddie said. "I've had it out on many occasions."

"Can you take me somewhere in it?"

"Wouldn't you rather go with Jack? He knows the waters around the island better than I do."

"There must be only the two of us," Amani said. "Will you take me?"

"No problem," he said. "When do you want to go?"

"Tomorrow."

"After lunch, maybe? I have a few things to do in the morning."

"That will work."

Amani took a drink from the flask and then offered it to him. Outside, the rain had intensified, drumming a steady beat on the van's metal roof. A thin mattress occupied the floor. After putting away the flask and extinguishing the dim light, she climbed under the blanket with Eddie and then eased him gently into a recumbent position.

Amani whispered in Eddie's ear, "Stay the night with me."

Chapter 19

When Eddie left Amani's van the following morning, the rain had ceased. He sat at the bar, badly needing a cup of coffee. Meika smiled when she saw him.

"Rough night?"

"I had a wonderful night, thank you," he said. "Why do you ask?"

"You're wearing the same clothes you wore last night, and you haven't combed your hair."

She grinned when he said, "And I'm in desperate need of a hot cup of coffee, so please don't ask any more personal questions."

"Yessir, boss. Coffee coming right up."

Eddie drank his coffee and hurried upstairs before anyone saw him. He felt better after a hot shower and changing into clean clothes. His stomach growled, and he headed back to the bar for breakfast. He found the place buzzing with early morning activity. Seraphina saw him sitting at the table and stopped by.

"We missed you last night," she said.

"Something came up," he said.

"Beth and Arabella were disappointed. So was I. Will you be in the bar tonight?"

She smiled when he said, "Unless something comes up again."

Without commenting, she blew him a kiss, turned, and walked away. Delta joined him at the table, interrupting his thoughts.

"Sorry about last night," she said.

"No apologies necessary. No one's perfect. Have you ever heard of a company named Conexco?"

"Of course I have. According to the discovery we did, Conexco is the company Frankie Castellano tentatively sold the Majestic and the island to. You remember, don't you?"

"Yes, now that you jog my memory."

"Why do you ask?"

"The man they found dead on the other side of the bridge was named Wayne King. He had a business card in his rental car for a company named Conexco."

"Maybe you should confront Mr. Castellano with that information," Delta said.

"Maybe so," he said.

"Eddie, do you still need me now that you've settled the lawsuit?"

"We haven't officially settled anything. Even if we had, our partnership is a wonderful idea. I look forward to it lasting for years to come."

"You're not just saying that, are you?" she asked.

"I mean every word of it. There is one little thing you can help me with."

"Name it," she said.

"It's Seraphina. I think she's coming on to me."

Delta's eyes rolled. "With the convention in full swing, women outnumber the men on this island ten to one. Every man is fair game, including Pancho. I can't help you."

Meika appeared at the table and said, "Breakfast?"

"I'm starved," Eddie said. "What's on the menu this morning?"

"Bacon, eggs, and grits," Meika said.

"Sounds wonderful. Delta?"

"I'm stuck attending this convention and will have to pass. Have you seen J.P.?"

"You're wasting your time on him," Meika said. "He's good-looking and knows it. He'll go to his grave a bachelor."

"Sorry to hear that," she said,

Meika was all ears when Eddie asked, "Are you a pagan?"

"I've no idea what I truly am, though I know I'm not a pagan."

"What about your mother?"

"Mom was many things; a good parent wasn't one of them. I'm even unsure who my real father is or if he's dead or alive. Mom always said I was a witch. I don't think so."

"Sorry I brought it up," Eddie said.

She smiled and said, "What issues I haven't resolved, I've managed to hide away in the dark recesses of my brain. Got to go. See you later."

Meika and Eddie watched her meld away into the growing crowd.

"Too bad," Meika said. "She's one hot mama, though I doubt she realizes her sexual effect on people."

Meika smiled when Eddie asked, "Is that good or bad?"

"Depends," she said.

"On what?"

"Whether you're trying to get into her pants, or she's trying to get into yours. I'll bring your breakfast.

Eddie had almost forgotten about promising to take Amani out on the Argo. He was reminded when she showed up at his table dressed for a day on the water.

"I'm ready," she said.

"I thought you were kidding about going out in the boat last night."

"It's important to me. I wasn't kidding."

"Okay. Want something from the bar first?"

Amani smiled and showed him her silver flask. "I have everything I need. Eat your breakfast. It's early yet."

Eddie thought he saw Seraphina staring through the crowd at him as he and Amani left the hotel. He decided not to worry.

The day was gloomy, a hangover from the previous night's rainstorm. The water in the bay was calm as they motored out of the marina, Eddie a bit nervous about captaining the boat for the first time without Jack standing beside him.

Once they'd exited the breakers and entered the Gulf of Mexico, Eddie said, "Where to?"

A point of land in the distance protruded out from the shoreline.

"I don't know," she said. "That headland is a good place to start."

Eddie steered the Argo toward the headland in the foggy distance.

"If you don't know where we're going, how will we get there?"

"No person alive knows the location of what I'm looking for," she said.

"What exactly is it?"

"A Spanish galleon sunk during a hurricane," she said.

"Odette and Chief have found Spanish gold on Oyster Island," Eddie said. "Could it be from your sunken ship?"

"Maybe," Amani said. "Lots of ships sank during storms of the past. The one I'm looking for carried something more valuable than gold."

"Like what?" he asked.

"I can't share that information with you now."

"Why not?"

"You do not need to know. You'll learn the answer in due time," she said.

An hour had elapsed before they motored past the headland.

"What now?" Eddie asked.

"There's a barrier bar just ahead. The water depth drops off quickly on the Gulf side and about fifty feet deep where we'll be diving, the water fairly clear."

Armani ignored him when he said, "You didn't say anything about diving."

He nodded when she said, "You know how, don't you?"

She handed him the binoculars hanging from a peg. He used them to see a barren island paralleling the shoreline.

"Is this the location of your Spanish galleon?" Eddie asked.

"I'm not sure," she said.

The wind had picked up, the height of the waves intensifying as they approached the low-lying island.

"Look at those dark clouds over the Gulf. Last night's storm was tiny compared to the one heading our way," Eddie said.

"Looks dangerous. It shouldn't stop us from our dive." Amani asked.

"You're always in danger in open water," Eddie said. "We must hurry, or the storm will catch us before we return to Oyster Island."

"You think the boat could sink?"

173

"This old ship is seaworthy. According to Jack, the Argo has traveled to Jamaica. She's good to go in anything short of a hurricane."

"The dive site isn't far, just beyond the barrier island," Amani said.

A flock of brown pelicans lifted skyward as the Argo motored past the barrier island. A hundred yards beyond the seaward side, Eddie killed the engine, drifted to a stop, and dropped anchor. The wind whipped up whitecaps as Amani followed him out of the wheelhouse and down the ladder to the main deck.

Eddie had been diving more than once since moving to the island and knew the tanks and wetsuits were stored in a hold on deck.

He handed a wetsuit to Amani and said, "This one should fit you."

Amani stripped off her clothes and pulled on the wetsuit. Eddie did the same. A dull gray sky had only grown dimmer as they readied their equipment.

"We better hurry before the water gets too rough," Eddie asked.

Amani gave him the high sign. "Let's do it."

"Then follow me down," Eddie said.

Eddie dropped backward into the Gulf's blue water, and Amani followed him off the side of the boat. His anxiety disappeared as he sank beneath the surface, the bubbles from his regulator rising upward as he tracked the anchor line to the bottom.

The water was a hazy shade of bluish-green, and ambient light faded as they reached the bottom. Bits of metal and other debris lay on the sandy floor, and red and green organisms grew on top, moving like slow-motion dancers in the current. A school of groupers swam between them. Not far away, Eddie saw something else.

174

A jumble of old cars and boat hulls lay on the sandy surface. Eels and tiny fish swam among the cracks and crevasses, and he realized why the large school of groupers had congregated. The old vehicles formed an artificial reef on the Gulf floor, and all manner of fish and vegetation had taken advantage.

Amani swam past the maze of wrecks after giving the man-made reef a cursory inspection. Enthralled by the plethora of life assembled around the discarded junk, Eddie looked closer. A glint of light reflected off something rocking in the current. Scooping it up, he placed it in the pouch attached to his wetsuit.

Amani was looking for something else and moved around the vehicles in ever-widening circles. A large shark swam past them as she turned back toward the anchor. When they reached the line, she grabbed it and pointed upward. They got a surprise when they reached the surface.

The rapidly moving frontal edge of the storm was already upon them, heavy rain rippling the Gulf's surface. Athletic Amani heaved her fins over the railing and started up the ladder to the deck of the Argo. Lightning streaked across the dark sky, thunder sounding almost immediately as Eddie followed her up the ladder.

"Let's hurry," he said. "This old tub's too slow to outrun the storm, and we're about to catch hell."

Heavy rain began battering the deck as they stripped, stowed their gear, grabbed the clothes they'd left on the deck, and made for the ladder up to the wheelhouse.

Rain pelted them as they climbed the ladder and bounded through the door that Eddie shut with difficulty. After raising anchor, he turned the boat around and pointed the bow toward Oyster

Island before bothering to get dressed.

When Amani joined him at the wheel, he smiled and said, "Nothing better than cruising naked."

Amani didn't share his smile. "The ship wasn't where I first thought. We need to keep looking."

"Forget it. Not today, we're not. The Argo is seaworthy, but so were the ships remains we saw down below. I'm heading back to the island. We can return later and find your Spanish ship when it's not so stormy."

Eddie felt the warmth radiating from Amani's naked body as she clasped her arms around his free arm.

"I can't believe we didn't find the galleon."

"No, but I found something," he said.

"What?" she asked.

"A gold doubloon. Not just a piece of eight; the entire coin."

Eddie handed her the coin. "Gold," she said as she hefted it in her hand.

The Argo rocked and rolled in the storm that didn't wait for them to reach the island. Eddie was relieved when they motored through the narrow breach leading to the bay, the water instantly calmer.

"Sure you won't tell me exactly what we're looking for?" he asked.

"You'll know soon enough."

Amani smiled and hugged him again when he said, "I'm getting attached to your van. Need company again tonight?"

"We've been away from the island for most of the day. I have things I need to do and so do you."

"I'm disappointed," he said.

"There are plenty of nights ahead of us," she said.

"And it would be all right with me if I spent

them all with you." Amani didn't reply and he said, "Do you still have feelings for Carlos?"

"Carlos provided a mechanism for me to reach the island; no more and no less."

"That's not how you think of me, right?" Eddie asked.

"You're a special person," she said. "We were destined to meet."

She smiled when he said, "What else does our destinies hold?"

"Maybe nothing more than a moment in time," she said.

Chapter 20

Eddie was drenched when he entered the Majestic. The old hotel was buzzing, the dim bar filled with happy patrons as he hurried upstairs to change into dry clothes. Adele met him as he descended the stairs.

"Eddie, thank God I found you," she said.

Adele's expression told him she was distressed. He took her hand and said, "What's the matter?"

"Josie and Frankie are in the bar. They're in a terrible argument and probably already said too much. Can you do something?"

"What are they arguing about?"

"Jojo. Frankie's angry that Carlos Palacio is on the island. He doesn't want Carlos to have anything to do with Jojo. He's refusing to let him and Josie be alone."

"Frankie can't do that," Eddie said. "Jojo is Josie's son."

"Tell that to Frankie," Adele said.

"Take me to them," he said.

Adele shook her head. "Can you do this alone? I don't want to appear to take sides."

Eddie nodded and kissed her forehead. "I'll do my best," he said.

Delta spotted him as he entered the bar. "Where have you been?"

"Business," he said. "I need your help. Come with me."

They found Frankie and Josie at a table in the back of the room. As Adele had said, they were in a heated conversation.

"Sorry to interrupt," he said. "I need to talk to you in private."

"I'm in the middle of something. Can't it wait?" Frankie said.

"Afraid not," Eddie said. "This is my law partner, Delta Becht. She'll take you to my office. I need a moment to speak to Josie, and then I'll join you."

Josie looked at Frankie and said, "Go. We can continue this later."

Frankie was grumbling as he followed Delta down the hallway leading to the complex of offices.

Josie nodded when Eddie asked, "May I sit?"

"I'm not in a good mood," she said.

"I see that. Adele told me Frankie's forbidding you from seeing Jojo alone."

"Carlos is refusing to meet his son. Even if I could convince him, Dad's making a meeting impossible."

She nodded when he said, "You need my help?"

"I have no idea why I trust you. I need to do something, but I'm at my wit's end. Can you help me?"

Eddie glanced at the hall leading to his office. "I'll think of something. I need some information. What's the deal with you and Carlos, and why is Frankie so adamant that he never meets Jojo."

Eddie smiled when Josie said, "I don't know why I should trust you."

Josie didn't pull away when Eddie took her hand.

"I've been hearing a lot about destiny lately," he said. "Maybe I simply played a part in causing you to realize who you love."

Josie smiled and said, "Maybe, though I'm not letting you off the hook that easily."

"How did you and Carlos meet?"

"Complicated story," Josie said.

"Give me the short version."

"Carlos is Dad's godson, and I'm Carlos's dad's goddaughter. Fernando and Dad grew up together. They were best friends and inseparable. I've known Carlos for as long as I can remember." She smiled when she said, "When we were babies, our moms used to bathe us in the same tub."

"Cozy," Eddie said.

"Even when we were young, we knew we were destined to marry."

Josie shook her head when Eddie said, "What happened?"

"Dad and Fernando had a falling out."

"About what?"

Josie shook her head again. "Something to do with our families is all I know. Carlos and his family moved to Miami, and I hadn't seen him since then until he showed up on the island. I was pregnant with Jojo when they moved and barely seventeen."

"I can see why Frankie's angry," Eddie said.

"So can I, though it's maddening."

"Is the spark still there between you and Carlos?"

"He's pissed because I never told him about Jojo."

"Understandable," Eddie said.

"Until I met you, I intended never to marry. You can imagine how Frankie and Adele felt when you left me waiting at the altar."

Eddie was still holding Josie's hand, and he squeezed it. "I've told you how sorry I am."

"It's okay. Maybe it's like you said."

"What?"

"Destiny," Josie said. "Right now, it all seems to be falling apart. What can I do?"

"I'll work on Frankie," Eddie said. "You shouldn't be here when he returns. Go back to your room."

Eddie didn't wait to see if Josie took his advice as he headed to his office. He found Delta sitting behind his desk and Frankie smiling, enjoying a scotch as he occupied a comfortable chair across from her. When Delta stood, Eddie motioned for her to stay where she was and sat in the chair beside Frankie. A crystal scotch decanter occupied a side table, and Eddie poured a glass.

"Sorry for the wait," he said.

"No problem," Frankie said. "I enjoyed talking with your attractive and very intelligent law partner. She's a sweetheart. One thing, though."

"What's that?"

"I always took you for a lone wolf. I would never have expected you to take a partner."

"Neither did I," Eddie said.

"Then why did you?"

"If you see a diamond in the sand, you pick it up."

"Your scotch is good. What's so important that you needed to speak to me privately?"

"The man who bombed Chief's car and killed Freya was Wayne King," Eddie said. "The police found a business card in the floorboard of his rental car. The name on the card was Conexco. Are you familiar with the man or a company named Conexco?"

Frankie's smile had disappeared. "Wayne King is a company hitman. You already know the answer to your Conexco question."

"Frankie, I need to know. Are you connected with Conexco in any way?"

Frankie smiled and said, "Is it Eddie asking or Prosecutor Toledo."

"Any way you want it," Eddie said.

"Like I told you, I wasn't responsible, or know anything about the bombing. I do know some things about Conexco that you don't."

"Such as?"

"Conexco has been around since before Prohibition. It was the company that built the Majestic. They ran rum and other alcohol through Oyster Island back in the day. They were, and are, into every illegal activity imaginable."

"And you're not?"

Frankie laughed. "Most of my businesses are legal, tax-paying entities. I don't hold a candle to Conexco."

"What about Fernando Palacio?"

"What about him?"

"His son is on the island. That gives him a motive," Eddie said.

"Palacio and Conexco aren't connected," Frankie said.

"Are you vouching for him?"

"It's common knowledge that I don't like the bastard. Doesn't matter because I won't stoop to telling lies about him."

"What happened between you and Palacio?"

"My business, not yours," Frankie said.

"He's the grandfather of your grandson. Have you ever bothered to tell him?"

"That's about enough, Mr. Prosecutor. Congratulations on landing a world-class law partner. Now, I'm out of here."

Frankie started for the door when Eddie said, "Wait. One more question."

Frankie turned and said, "Ask it."

"You have no right to keep Josie from being alone with her son. Won't you change your mind?"

Frankie pointed his finger at Eddie. "You were almost Jojo's father. You're not, so keep your long Italian nose out of other people's business."

When the door slammed, Delta said, "What did he mean by that?"

"Josie and I were engaged. I jilted her. Now, I'm about as welcome as a bad case of the flu."

"Then how did you wind up with the Majestic?"

"Frankie gave me a second chance in hopes Josie and I would reconcile. He probably also believes in Santa Claus and the Tooth Fairy."

"What now?" Delta asked.

"If what Frankie said is true, Conexco is our problem. I need to speak with J.P. and find out where the investigation is."

"What do you need me to do?" Delta said.

"If Conexco wields as much power as Frankie says they do, we're probably in for more trouble. Find out as much about them as you can."

"What exactly am I looking for?"

"Conexco wants something on this island. We need to know what it is."

Eddie left Delta to contemplate his words as he left the office and returned to the bar. He wanted to talk with J.P. and found him sitting with Alex.

"Just who I needed to see," he said as he sat between them.

"What's up?" J.P. said.

"Problems," Eddie said.

"What problems? The hotel is full, and you're raking in the dough."

"I just spoke with Frankie. He says Conexco is the original company that built the Majestic and smuggled liquor through Oyster Island. He also told me that Wayne King was a company hitman."

"Pretty much what the LSP learned," J.P. said. "Makes me wonder why they want the island back after all these years."

"Me too," Eddie said. "Where are the police going with this case?"

"They've closed it," J.P. said.

"They can't do that."

"Other than the business card, there's no link between the bomber and Conexco. There are no other leads."

"Frankie said Wayne King works for Conexco."

J.P. frowned and said, "Maybe as an independent contractor. He's not on the payroll."

"Makes sense," Eddie said.

"What now?" J.P. said.

"Find out why Conexco has the hots for Oyster Island."

"How do you intend to do that?"

"I haven't the foggiest idea," Eddie said.

Alex was drinking Russian vodka and gazing around the crowded room.

"So many attractive women," he said.

"And all looking for a good time, according to Meika," Eddie said.

"Too bad I have things to do tomorrow," Alex said.

"It's a long time until tomorrow," J.P. said. "Relax, unwind, and have some fun."

"I'm showing Josie and Carlos where I would put the distillery," Alex said. "I want to be sharp, as this may be my only chance."

"Where do you want to put it?" J.P. asked.

"Beside the storage building. It's flat with connections for both water and electricity."

"Perfect," J.P. said.

"I think so," Alex said.

Someone in the room knocked a glass off their table, and Eddie, Alex, and J.P. became aware of the growing activity around them when it shattered on the floor.

"Your guests are enjoying themselves," J.P. said.

"That's what they're supposed to do at a convention. Odette says our liquor sales are through the roof."

"Wonderful! When are they having the ceremony for Freya?"

"Friday night," Eddie said.

"Full moon," J.P. said. "Bet it'll be interesting. Are you going?"

"I was responsible for Freya being on the island. I'll be there. You?"

"Going with Toni."

"The walk you took last night must have gone well. Are you two an item now?"

"We like each other. We're taking it slow and seeing where it goes. She doesn't have much time because she's watching Jojo."

"Oh?"

"Velvet, Jojo's dog, is staying at Jack's house. Tomorrow, Toni, Jojo, and I are taking Velvet for a walk."

"I have another problem," Eddie said. "Maybe the two of you can help me with it."

"What's your problem?" J.P. asked.

"Jojo is Carlos's son. Josie wants them to meet, but Carlos is resisting. Even if he weren't, Frankie won't let Josie be alone with Jojo."

"What do you want us to do?" J.P. asked.

"Tomorrow, while on your walk, drop by the place where Alex is showing Josie and Alex the location for the distillery."

You mean to set up a meeting between Carlos and Jojo?" J.P. said. "Frankie will kill us."

"No one will know it was planned except the three of us," Eddie said. "It's what Josie wants and will ensure she'll invest in the distillery."

"Toni won't go for it."

"Then don't tell her," Eddie said.

Alex wasn't convinced. "It'll kill the distillery deal," he said.

Alex smiled when Eddie said, "Remember that old Russian proverb? The best is the enemy of the good."

"You aren't good with proverbs," he said. "Doesn't matter. I'll help you stage your ambush."

"Me too," J.P. said.

Jack and Chief arrived as the men were shaking hands.

"What's up?" Chief asked.

"Nothing," Eddie said.

"You're hiding something," Chief said.

"We have nothing to hide," Eddie said.

"Chief's right," Jack said. "Everyone quit talking when we arrived. Tell us what's going on."

Pancho and Professor Quinn arrived at the table before Eddie could answer.

"May we join you?" the professor asked.

"Pull up chairs," J.P. said. "The more the merrier."

Meika arrived at the table with drinks and said, "Isaac's cooked up fried catfish, jalapeno hushpuppies, and fresh-cut fries. Who is hungry?"

Everyone was. They had barely finished eating when Seraphina appeared at the table.

"What a handsome group of men," Seraphina said. "May I join you?"

"Please do," Professor Quinn said. "What's your name?"

"Seraphina Nightshade."

"Charmed. I'm Enos Quinn, a history buff who would love to hear all about paganism, its origins, and practices."

Chief drew closer as Seraphina began explaining paganism.

"That sounds a lot like Native American beliefs," he said. "Maybe I'm a pagan."

"Before organized religion, everyone was a pagan," Seraphina said.

Two days before Freya's celebration of life and death, the Majestic was rocking. Eddie was dog-tired. He went to the bathroom and didn't return, going upstairs to his room instead.

Eddie didn't hear the rain on the roof or the storm outside his window. He'd stripped and fallen asleep almost immediately, remaining in the same somnolent state until something at the foot of his bed awoke him. He opened his eyes to see Freya dressed in black from head to toe and standing at the foot of his bed.

Chapter 21

A dark specter dressed in black from head to toe stood at the foot of Eddie's bed. He sat up, not knowing if he was dreaming or seeing a ghost.

"Freya," he said. "Is that you?"

He grinned when she said, "It's me, pretty boy."

"Am I dreaming, or are you a ghost?"

"Very much a ghost," she said.

"Death didn't take away your sense of humor."

"Or my sex drive. Your bare chest turns me on. Too bad I can do nothing about it."

"What are you doing here?" he asked.

"Attempting to keep you from joining me in the spirit world."

"Is that a possibility?"

"Very much so," she said,

"Then you're an angel?"

"Something like that. Let's call my presence here divine intervention."

"Love it," Eddie said. "Tell me what I need to do?"

"You have a mystery on your hands, which means big problems for you, this island, and everybody on it."

"Tell me about it. Are you here to help me solve them?"

"Would if I could. It's not that easy," Freya said. "I can help, though you must solve this mystery alone. I'll do my best to point you in the right direction."

"Then point me," he said.

"The night I died, Chief, Jack, and I were on our way to La Tortue Mountain to bathe in his magic fountain. There was a reason."

"What?"

"Do you remember the séance?"

"Vividly," Eddie said.

"Your friend, J.P., thought I was a charlatan and called my performance an induced illusion. Do you believe him?"

"I'm unsure what I believe. The séance seemed very real to me."

"It was real, just as I am now. Get out of bed and come to me," Freya said.

"I'm naked."

"And I'm a spirit of the night. Your nudity is of no consequence."

Eddie got out of bed and went to where Freya waited.

"Now what?"

"Touch me," she said.

Eddie's hand disappeared into her body. "You could be a ghost, and I might be dreaming. This feels like a dream. How am I supposed to know?"

"You aren't dreaming. Even if you were, dreams sometimes answer questions you can't even ask when you are cognizant. I need some trust here."

"I trust you, and I'm listening," Eddie said.

"Seraphina has a strong attraction for Chief. They are on their way to La Tortue Mountain to bathe in the Magic Fountain and to encounter the ghost of Chief's grandfather."

"To what end?" Eddie asked.

189

"The curse and the treasure Lafitte searched for are inextricably intertwined. I'm dead now because of the curse, and every person on this island is in danger."

"And you think Chief's grandfather has the answers?"

"Sometimes only the dead have the answers we seek," Freya said. "Chief's grandfather was on Oyster Island during Prohibition and possesses a wealth of otherwise forgotten information."

"I'm a former prosecutor," Eddie said. "Knowing the questions to ask is as important as who you ask."

"Seraphina is a witch and understands things that others never contemplate. If Chief's grandfather has relevant information to share, she and will ferret it out."

"Sounds like witches make good lawyers," Eddie said. "Is Delta a witch?"

Freya smiled and said, "Questions about my daughter are for you to answer."

She disappeared into a flickering mist as Eddie stood naked in the muted darkness.

⚜

The ATV's headlights cut a swath through the darkness as Chief steered the electric vehicle across the island. He'd erected a covered carport at the base of the hill where he lived. It came in handy as it was misting rain.

"This is it," he said. "La Tortue Mountain."

Seraphina grinned when she got out of the car. "There aren't many hills in south Louisiana, much less mountains. Yours is impressive. How do you explain it?"

"Oyster Island sits atop a salt dome. The salt is pushing up from the subsurface, causing this prominent hill. I learned earlier there is also a volcano beneath us."

"Are you a geologist?" Freya asked.

"No, though Professor Quinn is. He says the island is connected to the volcanic islands of the Caribbean."

"Don't know about that," Seraphina said. "I do know it's magical. I can feel the magic."

"There's a path up the hill to my teepee. You go first. I know the way like the back of my hand and can catch you if you slip."

"Good to know," she said as Chief pointed her to the base of the trail.

When Seraphina slipped, Chief gently nudged the small of her back. As they continued up the trail, the rain intensified, and lightning illuminated the way. Seraphina saw the little homestead where Chief lived when the narrow path flattened. Opening the flap of his teepee, he pulled her inside.

The crimson glow of a firepit dimly lit the teepee. Chief's cat Buttercup lay asleep on a pallet of warm fur and colorful blankets. Seraphina smiled as she took it all in.

"This is a real teepee," she said. "I can't believe how big it is."

"And warm," Chief said.

"The teepee is warm. It's also cozy and inviting. You have a cat?"

"Miss Buttercup. She's usually out tomcatting, though she doesn't like the rain."

"I took you more as a dog person," she said.

"I have two dogs. Coco, a chihuahua, and Old Joe, a German shepherd. They're safe and dry at Jack's house, asleep by the fire alongside his bulldog Oscar."

"Freya had a black cat named Jinx. He's my cat now. He has special powers."

"How so?" Chief asked.

"Jinx was a wizard in another lifetime. At least according to Freya."

"Sounds like a great cat." Chief took Seraphina's hand and said, "You miss Freya, don't you?"

"More than you will ever know. I spoke with her on the phone the night she died. She said you were a beautiful man."

"I'm surprised she said that. I'm so big and wild-looking; most people are afraid of me," he said.

"I'm not. Freya told me she intended to make love to you. Now, I know why."

"I didn't bring you to my mountain to take advantage of you."

"Why not?" she said. "That's why I'm here."

"Then why bother going to the Magic Fountain? My pallet is warm, and Buttercup will scoot over."

"Freya is with us. She wants to experience the Magic Fountain and meet your grandfather."

"That's a given if we bathe in the pool," Chief said.

"Then let's do it," she said. "We'll have the rest of the night to enjoy your pallet."

"We'll leave our clothes here," Chief said. "If we hang them near the fire, they'll be dry in the morning. I have a large bath towel if you're shy."

Seraphina let her clothes drop to the floor of Chief's teepee. "Pagans aren't ashamed of their bodies," she said.

Though Seraphina was probably older than sixty, she had the toned body of a much younger woman. She didn't mind Chief's admiring gaze.

"Most people would envy your body," Chief said. "What's your secret?"

"Hours of yoga, Pilates, and tai chi," she said. "And yours?"

"Genetics," Chief said. "I chose my parents well."

Seraphina used two hands to measure Chief's biceps.

"You must not be afraid of anything," she said.

"Everyone has something they fear," Chief said.

"What is it that you fear?"

"Same thing as everyone else," he said. "The unknown."

"I don't believe anything frightens you," Seraphina said.

"The moment something triggers my anxiety, I follow the 333 rule," he said.

"You're making this up."

He shook his head and said, "Identify three objects and three sounds you recognize, then move three body parts."

"Does it work?"

"It works. When anxiety seems overwhelming, the 333 rule concentrates your focus and grounds you."

"Do you live your life by rules?"

"Don't we all?" Chief said.

"No, but yours is one I can't wait to try," Seraphina said. "Now, show me your Magic Fountain."

The rain had grown stronger as they climbed the Magic Fountain hill. Lightning streaked across the sky and Seraphina pulled her bath towel tightly around her chest.

"We're going to be struck by lightning," she said.

"We'll be safe in the pool."

"How do you know?" she asked.

"It's sacred. No harm comes to those bathing in it. You'll see."

When the path flattened, the sound of water pouring from a rock wall riveted their attention.

Chief stopped at the edge of a clear pool with a cobblestone bottom.

Chief nodded when Seraphina said, "Is it artesian?"

"Water has poured from that rock wall for as long as I can remember."

Chief dropped his towel, stepped into the water, and took Seraphina's hand.

She hesitated and said, "Is it cold?"

"A long way from freezing. You'll quickly get used to the temperature."

Seraphina stepped into the water and followed Chief to the middle of the clear pool. It wasn't deep, the water only rising to their chests.

"Where does the water go?" she asked.

"Down the hill in a little creek to a ledge where it drops to another pool."

Chief nodded when Seraphina said, "You have a waterfall?"

"A very small waterfall at the base of the hill on the far side of where we parked the ATV. It's tranquil, and I go there when I need to meditate. Something I need to do more of."

"You're Native American and Native American beliefs are similar to mine. Will you help me with Freya's ceremony?"

"How can I help?" Chief asked.

"I need someone to construct a large pile of wood for a bonfire on the beach," Seraphina said.

"How large?"

"Twenty feet tall or more."

"Why so large?" Chief asked.

"It needs to burn or at least smolder from midnight until dawn."

"Jack and I will build it for you," Chief said.

"Thank you," Seraphina said. "One more favor?"

"Name it," Chief said.

"I'd like for you to do the ceremonial lighting of the bonfire."

"I can do that," he said.

A glow lighted the pool with dim phosphorescence, and Seraphina said, "What's causing the light?"

"Bioluminescence created from algae in the cobblestones," Chief said.

"Is it harmful?" Seraphina asked.

"Just the opposite. I noticed the bruise on your thigh. Look at it now."

"It's disappearing before my eyes," she said. "How is it possible?"

"The pool has restorative properties," Chief said.

"I feel my skin tightening," she said. "Is this the Fountain of Youth the Spanish sought?"

"It isn't the Fountain of Youth," Chief said. "It does cure your body of illness."

"You mean like water from the spring in the Grotto of Our Lady of Lourdes, France?"

"The same," Chief said. "Cures only occur for those who believe in the water's power."

"Is this water blessed?" Seraphina asked.

"I'm not a religious person," Chief said. "Grandfather knows. When he bathed my grandmother in this pool, it cured her of the plague. I've always called it magic. You'll have to ask him."

"I'd love to," Seraphina said.

"Then turn around. He's right behind you."

The glowing image of an old Atakapan man floated in the darkness above the sand surrounding the cobblestone pool.

"Who are you?" Seraphina asked.

"Nashoba Nowa," he said.

"That's Atakapan for Walking Wolf," Chief said. "How are you, Grandfather."

195

"Doomed to walk the sands of this island for eternity," he said. "Why did you summon me?"

"I didn't," Chief said.

"Someone acted on your behalf," the spirit said.

"Freya?" Seraphina said.

"The woman killed when my car exploded," Walking Wolf said.

"You got Jack and me out of the car because you knew it would explode, right?" Chief asked.

"I wanted to save everyone. The woman refused to leave the car," Walking Wolf said.

"My fault," Chief said. "I needed someone to steer the car while Jack and I pushed it out of the deep sand that had it trapped."

"I'm sorry I didn't save her," Walking Wolf said. "She's a spirit now and, like me, doomed to walk this island in endless circles."

"Is there anything I can do?" Chief asked.

"Return the island to the Atakapans," Walking Wolf said."

"We're trying," Chief said. "Thanks for saving me and Jack. Do you know who set the bomb?"

"The same white men who bought the island during the Great Turmoil. The men who built the Majestic."

"Do you know why?" Chief asked.

"They left something valuable on the island and want it back."

"What did they leave?" Chief asked.

"Lafitte's treasure."

"They had the map. Why didn't they dig it up before they abandoned the island?"

"They did dig it up. That's when their troubles began."

"The treasure was cursed?" Chief asked.

"Yes. They returned it to the ground. It didn't help. They finally gave up and left the island."

"What else?" Chief asked.

"The cursed treasure brought death and wasn't meant to be here."

As Walking Wolf began to disappear, Chief said, "Wait, I have more questions."

The words, "I have no more answers," echoed through the darkness.

Chapter 22

Eddie and Alex were eating breakfast, waiting for Josie and Carlos to come downstairs. The rain had finally passed over the island, and it was a glorious mid-January day.

"Tell me again what happened last night," Alex said.

Eddie made a face and laced his coffee with rum before answering.

"Freya's ghost appeared to me. She said that not only was I in danger, but everyone on the island. She told me Chief and Seraphina were on their way to La Tortue Mountain to bathe in Chief's Magic Fountain and to encounter the ghost of Chief's grandfather."

"For what purpose?" Alex asked.

"To find out why Conexco would kill to regain control of the island."

"How much did you drink before you went to bed?"

"I saw what I saw," Eddie said.

"Are you sure it wasn't one of J.P.'s induced trances?"

"You witnessed the ghosts of the Lafitte pirates. Were they real enough for you?"

"I am unsure what I saw or what someone programmed me to see. You know that it was we Russians who invented brainwashing."

"Don't be so presumptuous. It was the Chinese who first employed brainwashing, and even now, scientists disagree about its efficacy."

Eddie snickered when Alex said, "What does a lawyer know about mind control?"

"Good lawyers know how to benefit from it. Bad lawyers, . . . well. . ., they're bad for a reason," Eddie said.

"I respect you, Eddie. Let's agree to disagree on this one," Alex said.

Alex's eyes grew wide when Chief and Seraphina entered the room arm-in-arm.

"We're having breakfast. Join us," Eddie said.

Chief and Seraphina pulled up chairs at the table. "Thought you'd never ask," Chief said. "I'm starving."

"You talked with Freya last night, didn't you?" Seraphina said.

Eddie glanced at Alex and said, "What makes you think that?"

"Because I can tell by your expressions you know Chief and I spent the night together," she said.

She touched Chief's arm when Eddie said, "Did you see your grandfather?"

Meika arrived at the table before Chief could answer.

"The breakfast special today is Andouille Sausage Cajun Scramble," she said.

"Sounds wonderful," Seraphina said. "That's what I'll have."

"Me too," Chief said. "With extra grits and biscuits."

"Got it coming," Meika said.

"What about your grandfather's ghost?" Eddie said.

"The people who built the Majestic believe Lafitte's Treasure is theirs," Chief said. "They want the island back so they can retrieve it."

"Then why did they give it up in the first place?" Eddie asked.

"Grandfather said the treasure is cursed, and their troubles began when they dug it up. They reburied it, but when that didn't help, they abandoned everything and left the island."

"What could have happened that would have caused them to leave the island?" Eddie said.

"Walking Wolf didn't say, though he implied it was something horrible," Seraphina said.

"Josie and Carlos are coming down the stairs," Alex said. "Wish me luck."

When Josie waved as she followed Alex out the door, Eddie made a phone call to J.P.

"They're on their way. Is everything still a go?"

"Yes, and not a minute too soon," J.P. said. "Toni and Jojo are getting antsy, and I was running out of excuses."

"Good luck," Eddie said.

"You have something cooking with J.P. you haven't told me about?" Chief asked.

"Frankie's being a dick and not letting Josie see Jojo alone?"

"Why not?"

"He doesn't want her introducing him to Carlos," Eddie said.

"Excuse me?" Seraphina said. "Are Carlos and Josie dating?"

"More than that," Eddie said. "They've known each other since they were very young. Carlos is the father of Jojo. Josie never told him he had a son, and he's pissed about it."

Eddie nodded when Seraphina said, "Let me guess. Josie wants to change all that."

"She asked me to help, so Alex, J.P., and I devised a plan. I just checked with J.P. to see if everything is a go."

Seraphina squeezed Chief's hand and said, "I love a good love story. Right now, I must run upstairs and prepare for the day." Chief nodded when she said, "See you tonight?"

"Looks like you got a hot one there," Eddie said.

"A tiger by the tail is what I have, and I don't know how to let go."

"Good luck on that," Eddie said.

"Thanks," Chief said.

Eddie tapped his fingers on the table. "Wish I knew why Conexco abandoned the island. Any ideas?"

"Have you checked the Internet?" Chief asked.

"Neither Basil nor I could find anything about it on the Net," Eddie said.

"Jack's always spouting random facts about the island. Maybe he knows something," Chief said.

"Remind me to ask him," Eddie said.

The original owners of the Majestic maintained a large storage facility where they kept everything from kitchen supplies to period costumes and old slot machines. They'd spent lots of money installing electricity and water lines. Plenty of land existed near the facility, and Alex envisioned it as the site for his distillery.

"This is the spot," he said.

"Let's take a look," Carlos said. "What's the large building?"

Alex exited the ATV and said, "A storage facility. Since this is the commercial part of the island, I thought it would be a perfect spot for the distillery. There's a well. The tests I've run on the water are remarkable. This is, quite simply, the best place on earth to put a distillery."

"The facility will require lots of electricity," Josie said. "Where will it come from?"

"Buried electrical lines connect the warehouse," Alex said.

"Mind if we look?" Josie asked.

"This way," he said.

Alex had a key to the storage building and led them to a loading dock. They climbed the stairs and waited as Alex raised the large door. When he went inside to turn on the lights, nothing happened.

"Looks as if you need an electrician," Carlos said.

"Sorry," Alex said. "The building has gone unused for decades."

"Nothing that can't be fixed. I'm sure," Josie said.

"Right," Alex said. "I'll show you the well."

The well had a manual pump, and Alex finally smiled as water poured onto the ground. Josie didn't notice. Jojo's dog Venus was running toward her. Dropping to her knees, she grabbed the big dog around its neck.

"Good girl," Josie said. "What are you doing out here all alone?"

Velvet was a beautiful half-breed, mostly German Shepard. Josie had paid the Oyster Island Canine Training Facility sixty-thousand dollars for her. Jojo loved the highly intelligent dog, and Josie had never regretted the purchase.

Velvet couldn't stop wagging her tail as Josie hugged her. Jojo, Toni, and J.P. weren't far behind. When Jojo saw his mother, he ran to her.

"Mama," he said. "What are you doing here?"

"Looking at a property," Josie said.

Toni gave J.P. a dirty look when she saw Jojo and Josie. She took his hand.

"Your mother's doing business here. We need to go."

"Wait," Carlos said.

As the two stared at each other, there was no doubt who Jojo's father was. Both had dark eyes, dark hair, and the same facial bone structure.

"What's your name, young man?" Carlos asked.

"Jojo," the boy said.

"Is that your real name or a nickname?"

"It's what Grandpa calls me."

"What's your real name?" Carlos asked.

"Carlos," Jojo said.

Carlos looked at Josie. "Why didn't you tell me?"

"I couldn't," Josie said.

Carlos put his hands on Jojo's shoulders, dropped to his knees, and said, "I'm your dad. I'm taking you back to Miami with me."

Jojo frowned and slapped his hands away. "You're not my dad," he said.

"I am," Carlos said.

"Then why did you leave my mama?"

"Long story," Carlos said.

Jojo walked back to where Toni and J.P. waited. When he whistled for Venus, she ran to him.

"Can we go somewhere else?" he said.

Toni gave J.P. another dirty look and started back down the way they had come. Jojo and Venus followed. Carlos lowered his head and closed his eyes.

When he opened them, he said. "I'm returning to the hotel."

"Me too," Josie said. "I'm too upset to think about the distillery."

"I understand," Alex said.

No one spoke during the short drive to the Majestic. Carlos exited the ATV, not waiting for Josie as he hurried up the boardwalk to the front door.

"Don't feel bad," Josie said. "Eddie cooked up the meeting with Carlos and Jojo because I asked for his help. It didn't go the way I'd hoped."

"We Russians say, 'Plaster for a dead man.'"

Josie smiled and said, "You'll have to explain that to me."

"A plaster is a death mask. It has insignificant meaning in the scheme of a person's life. Your story is long from over, and I sense things will work out well."

"Thanks, Alex. With or without Carlos, I want to do the distillery deal. Let's talk later and decide where to go from here."

"Thank you," Alex said. "Your words are music to my ears."

Josie went into the Majestic alone and found Eddie at his table.

"May I join you?" she said.

"Please do. You look as if you need a drink."

"Is it that obvious?"

"Carlos stalked through the bar a few minutes ago. I take it the meeting didn't go well."

"Jojo's name is Carlos. I didn't realize their resemblance until I saw them beside each other. Carlos told Jojo he was his father. Jojo didn't react the way I thought he would."

"What did he do?"

"He became angry," Josie said.

"Sounds like the three of you need a few months of family counseling," Eddie said.

"It's never going to get to that point. Carlos is leaving the island and returning to Miami."

Josie nodded when Eddie said, "Do you want him to stay?"

"Until seeing him for the first time in years a few days ago, I didn't realize how much I love him. Now, I'm terrified I'm going to lose him."

"Call Fernando," Eddie said.

"I can't do that. Dad would kill me."

"Jojo is Fernando's grandson. They both have a right to know. Call him now."

"I don't have his number," Josie said.

"I do," Eddie said. "I spoke with him a half-dozen times while at the D.A.'s office. Call him on my phone. He'll answer on the first ring."

"Is that you, Eddie?" Fernando said when he answered the phone.

Josie waited through a long pause when she said, "It's Josie Castellano."

"How are you, Josie," he finally said. "How's your father?"

"Cranky as ever," she said. "My father isn't the reason I called."

"What is the reason?"

"I'm on Oyster Island with Carlos and my son, Jojo. Carlos is Jojo's father, and you are his grandfather."

Josie waited through another long pause. "Does Frankie know Jojo is my grandson?"

"He knows," Josie said.

"What do you want me to do?" Fernando asked.

"Help me," she said.

Josie hung up the phone before Fernando could answer. Ten minutes passed before Carlos stormed down the stairs, looking angry enough to chew nails.

"Sit," Eddie said. "I'll get you a drink."

Carlos's arms were crossed, and he was fuming. His demeanor calmed when he drank the brandy Meika brought him.

"Why did you call Fernando?" he asked.

"I had no other place to turn," Josie said.

"Dad is on his way here and told me not to leave. He and your dad will kill each other," he said.

"They need to resolve their differences and there's no better time than now," Josie said.

Frankie followed Carlos into the bar, glaring at Eddie when he reached the table.

"I've had just about enough out of you, Toledo," he said.

"Calm down and have a scotch," Eddie said.

When Meika handed Frankie a scotch, he slammed the glass against the floor.

The dim bar went deathly quiet as everyone was riveted on the angry man in a coffee-stained undershirt, plaid Bermuda shorts, thousand-dollar dress shoes, and black socks.

"This hotel and island are mine, Toledo. As soon as Freya's ceremony is over, I'll boot you back into the gutter where you belong."

Chapter 23

When Meika arrived at the table with a broom and dustpan, Frankie stalked away amid applause from everyone in the bar. Eddie helped Meika with the mess, killing his drink when he returned to the table.

"I think I'm going back to bed," he said.

"Not everyone's mad at you," Josie said. "I appreciate all you've done."

"How did you know my father's cell phone number?" Carlos asked.

"Your dad and I go way back," Eddie said. "I was the Assistant Federal D.A. in New Orleans and tried to prosecute him more than once. I could never make anything stick."

"And he still talks to you?"

"You're dad's a businessman. He knows I was only doing my job," Eddie said.

"He told me to beware of you," Carlos said.

"Neither of you have anything to worry about. I left the Federal D.A. office a while ago and don't intend to return. You can rob the Pope for all I care as long as you don't harm me or anyone on this island."

"What will you do about Frankie's threats?" Carlos asked.

"Frankie may think he owns this island, but it's the property of the Atakapan Indian Tribe, namely Grogan La Tortue, the last of the Atakapans."

"Frankie and my dad have ways of getting around federal laws."

"Hell, Carlos, the Federal Government has ways of subverting federal laws. It doesn't matter because no one alive knows more about Federal law than I do. You two enjoy yourselves. The tab's on me. I have work to do."

Despite Eddie's bravado, Frankie's threat had shaken him. He wanted to get away from people for a while and fled down the hall to his office. Delta met him at the doorway.

"Your face is so red you could strike a match on it. Are you okay?"

"Come into my office," Eddie said.

Delta sat in the chair in front of Eddie's desk, crossed her long legs, and said, "What's up?"

"Frankie Castellano just threatened to boot me off the island."

"What provoked him?"

"Josie asked me to help her introduce her son to his father, Carlos Palacio. Frankie found out and took offense. Doesn't matter because I have a plan."

"Tell me," Delta said.

"Frankie's never going to sign the agreement we prepared. We need to try another tact."

"Such as?" Delta asked.

"The lawsuit against me and Chief was in state court, which is not the correct place to argue American Indian Law. Now that the state case has been dropped, we can sue Frankie in federal court in New Orleans. It's my old backyard."

"What gave you that idea?" Delta asked.

"It just came to me. I want to file it tomorrow. Can you stay up all night and help me draft the pleadings?"

"Let's do it," she said.

The next morning, Eddie awoke in his overstuffed chair. He walked down the hall to Delta's office where she was finishing the pleadings. When she saw him, she smiled and hit the print button.

"Good morning," she said.

"Is it? There are no windows."

"I went out earlier. Odette is bringing us coffee. Want to read our case?"

Eddie nodded and followed her to the copier. They returned to Delta's office, and Eddie had just finished reading the document when Odette arrived with a carafe of coffee.

"Brilliant," he said. "You set more traps in this pleading than Grizzly Adams. Let's see Mr. Castellano try to wriggle out of this one."

"What's up?" Odette said.

"We're back at war with Frankie. When he awakens tomorrow, he'll realize he's been ambushed. By then, it'll be too late."

Delta loaded the pleadings into her briefcase and started for the door.

"Where are you going?" Odette asked.

"New Orleans to file the suit," she said. She returned in a minute. "I rode to the island with Seraphina. I have no car."

Eddie fished in his pocket for his recently acquired Miata and tossed them to Delta.

"Your mom's Miata. It's parked out front. Pancho traded it to me," Eddie said.

Delta exited the offices for the second time without commenting.

"What now?" Odette said.

209

"Breakfast. I'm starved."

Still very early, the bar was empty. Meika gave him a look when he grabbed a stool at the counter.

"Another wild night?" she asked.

"If you call writing a legal brief wild, then yes."

"Isaac isn't here yet," Meika said. "There's no one to cook breakfast for you.

"I'll fry him some eggs," Odette said.

Meika was too busy cleaning the bar area to chat, so Eddie moved to his table. He was checking the newsfeed on his cell phone when Josie joined him.

"You're up early," he said.

"I could say the same for you."

"I had office work to do and haven't been to bed yet," he said.

"I couldn't sleep, so I dressed and came downstairs."

"What's wrong?"

"I thought Carlos and I had found what we had lost. Turns out I was wrong."

"You didn't misinterpret anything. I've seen how he looks at you," Eddie said.

"That changed when he met Jojo."

"Maybe Carlos isn't your problem," Eddie said.

"Then who is?"

"His dad. Fernando is exactly like Frankie; he is a powerful man. I'm guessing Carlos doesn't handle his fatherly pressure like you."

"I can't change that," Josie said.

"Maybe you can."

"Tell me," Josie said.

"Turn the tables on him," Eddie said. "Make him realize he can't live without you."

"How?"

"Convince him you're head over heels with someone else. Make him so jealous that he can't see straight. Worry him to the point that he has no choice but to give in to his emotions."

"How am I supposed to do that," Josie said.

"Make a convincing play on someone else."

"I'm not a dishonest person. Even if I were, I'm not an actress."

"Bullshit!" Eddie said. "Every woman is an actress, and this ruse has nothing to do with dishonesty; it's about forcing Carlos to realize he can't live without you, even if it means defying his father's wishes.

"I can't."

Eddie laughed and said, "Of course you can."

"How am I supposed to accomplish this feat?"

"Make a play on someone, and don't hold back. I'm talking about an Academy Award-worthy performance. You wrapped me around your little finger like no woman I ever met, and Frankie can't say no to you."

"Will you help me on this?"

"Me? I'm already in so much trouble with Frankie I don't want to risk death with the son of Miami's most powerful person."

"Fernando is like my dad. He talks big but has a heart of gold."

"And I promise his heart will melt when he meets his grandson."

Josie squeezed Eddie's hand and said, "Please help me?"

"When?"

"Tonight."

Josie took Eddie's silence as a yes and blew him a kiss as she exited the bar. She was gone when Odette arrived at the table with eggs, toast, and grits.

"Is the hotel in trouble again?" she asked.

"No more than it was yesterday," Eddie said.

"You're not reassuring."

"It's the best I can do."

"I was just getting comfortable with my job. I love it and everything about it. I don't know what I'll do if I have to return to stripping."

"Then don't," Eddie said. "You have a degree in hotel and restaurant management from L.S.U."

"I'm a semester short. Remember?"

"We're a long way from losing the island," Eddie said.

"You sure?"

"Positive. Now, get back to work."

Odette smiled as she left the table. Eddie finished breakfast and then started up the hill to Jack's house without bothering to go to his room, shower, or change clothes. He found Jack feeding the dogs.

"Where's Chief and J.P.?" he asked.

"Training dogs," Jack said. "Hungry?"

"I ate at the Majestic before heading this way."

"Chief and J.P. won't be here until lunch," he said.

"It's you I'm here to see," Eddie said. "Got any rum in this place? I'll take a shot of that."

"Grab a seat at the plank table. I'll bring the rum and coffee pot."

Jack also brought a cinnamon roll on a napkin when he served the coffee and rum.

"Take a bite," he said. "Tell me if it needs anything."

Eddie bit into the cinnamon roll. "Damn, Jack!" he said. "This is decadent. I'd weigh two hundred pounds if I ate your cooking daily."

"You like it?"

Eddie licked the sugar off his fingers. "You know I'm a sugar freak. I need to save my empty calories for booze."

"They aren't empty if you enjoy them," Jack said. "Now, why are you here?"

"I have some questions about the Majestic, and Chief said you're the person to ask."

"The lighthouse keeper whose place I took told me most everything about the Majestic and this island."

"Can you call him?"

"He moved to Phoenix. Wasn't there a year when he died," Jack said. "What is it about the Majestic that you want to know?"

"Why did the people who built it abandon Oyster Island?"

"Beats the holy hell out of me!" Jack said. "Maybe because it wasn't profitable any longer."

"They had quite an investment in this island. Why didn't they try to sell it?"

"To tell you the truth, I don't have a clue," Jack said.

"Is there anyone still alive I can ask?"

"Jesse had an old housekeeper who cleaned for him. She worked for the Majestic's owners when she was young."

"Super," Eddie said. "You know how to contact her?"

"She was old when I met her, and I have no idea if she's still alive. She lived in a Cajun trapper's village not far from here."

"Can you take me there?"

"Hell no!" Jack said. "J.P. knows where it's at. He can take you."

Eddie and Jack were playing gin when J.P. and Chief arrived from the canine training facility. His breakfast had worked off, and Jack's gumbo smelled wonderful.

"You got me into lots of trouble yesterday," J.P. said.

"You mean with Toni?"

"She thought I planned the rendezvous with Jojo and Carlos."

"Did you convince her you didn't?"

"Don't know for sure yet. We have a date tomorrow night to talk about it."

"Good luck," Eddie said.

"Odette called and said we have a new problem with Frankie."

"News travels fast on Oyster Island," Eddie said.

"Any truth to it?"

"He's after my ass and intends to take down the rest of the island with me."

"Should we be worried?" Chief said.

"Delta, my new law partner, and I stayed up all night working to get the jump on Frankie. He'll be surprised when he wakes up tomorrow."

"You're the best, Eddie; we trust you," Chief said.

"How's it going with Serafina?"

"Good. Jack and I are helping with Freya's ceremony."

Doing what?"

"There's going to be a big bonfire on the beach. Jack and I have been cutting wood and preparing it for the ceremony."

"What else?" Eddie asked.

"I'm going to do the ceremonial lighting of the bonfire."

"Why did she choose you?" Eddie asked.

"Because I'm an Indian, and my spiritual beliefs are similar to those of pagans."

"Aren't you a bit uneasy dating a pagan?" Eddie asked.

"You kidding? She's the most sensual and interesting woman I've ever known."

"Glad you're into her," Eddie said.

Chief added an extra dollop of rum to his coffee and said, "You aren't here to talk about me and Seraphina, are you?"

214

"I had a question for Jack," Eddie said. "He told me an old Cajun woman who used to work for the people who owned the Majestic might know."

"What's the woman's name?" J.P. asked.

"Martha Sonnier," Jack said. "She lives in a little trapping community not far from here. You know where I'm talking about, don't you, J.P.?"

"Mosquito Flats. Visited it more than once when I was a parish cop," J.P. said. "Anytime there was an altercation, I got sent to handle it because I speak Cajun."

"Can you take me there?" Eddie asked.

"They don't like authority and don't trust outsiders. They fish, hunt, trap, make moonshine, and have no electricity or running water. They live off the land, only deal in cash, and Eddie, like I said, they don't trust strangers," J.P. said.

"Do you know if the old lady is still alive?"

"Only one way to find out," J.P. said.

Chapter 24

Eddie sat in the backseat of J.P.'s big truck because the passenger seat was reserved for Lucky, J.P.'s chocolate lab.

"Sorry you have to sit back there," J.P. said.

"No problem," Eddie said. "I worked for the D.A. office long enough to get used to it. How far away is this place."

"It's over on Slithery Bayou," J.P. said. "Not far from here."

"Sounds ominous."

"It's only a nickname," J.P. said. "There are no more reptiles than anywhere else around here. The mosquitos are a different story."

"Hope you have repellent in the truck. Do you know Martha Sonnier?"

"Haven't had the pleasure. She must be old if she worked at the Majestic during the Depression."

"More than a hundred," Eddie said. "I'm not holding out much hope she's still alive."

"Even if she's not, she may have kin who know about the history of the Majestic."

J.P. turned off the blacktop and followed a barely visible road through the trees and brush. After days of rain, the road was muddy and rutted.

Glad you have four-wheel drive," Eddie said.

"Don't need it," J.P. said. "The road has a solid base, and the families who live in Mosquito Flats use it all the time."

"If you say so," Eddie said.

"We're almost there, and I need to give you some instructions."

"I'm listening."

"These people have no electricity or running water. Though some of them understand English, they speak Cajun French. It's changed so much since their ancestors left France that a French person can't understand it, and they don't understand French.

"The people of the village still live much like they did when they were deported from Canada. When you get to know them, they are wonderful people but don't take to outsiders, so watch what you say and do."

"You got it," Eddie said.

The village dogs heard the truck long before they reached the little settlement."

"Don't pet the dogs unless you want to get bit," J.P. said. "They don't like strangers."

A dozen dogs were running with the truck, and everyone in the village awaited them when they rounded the final bend. Eddie was enthralled by what he saw.

Slithery Bayou opened up into a small lake. A dozen pirogues lay tethered to the wooden dock, snaking out into the still water. Fishermen occupied several of these primitive boats carved out of a single tree.

Probably a dozen wooden shacks on five-foot stilts sat among the trees. They all had porches, some with rocking chairs and others with porch swings. A young woman was stirring something in a large black cauldron with a boat paddle over an open fire. A man in overalls was waiting when J.P.

parked the truck. He wasn't smiling, and the shotgun in his arms looked dangerous.

J.P. opened the door and said, "Comme ça va?"

The barking dogs stood at bay, waiting for J.P. to leave the truck."

"Ain't nobody misbehaving here," the man said.

"I'm not a cop anymore, Mr. Robert," J.P. said. "This is a personal visit."

"Who you here to see?"

"Ms. Martha Sonnier," J.P. said.

Mr. Robert shooed away the dogs and cocked his head in the direction of an old woman sitting in a rocking chair on the front porch of the nearest shack.

J.P. tipped his Stetson and said, "Mèsi, monsieur."

Lucky and Eddie followed J.P. to the porch, where a smiling old woman awaited them.

In good English, she said, "I haven't had a visitor in twenty years. Pull up a rocker."

"I'm J.P. Saucier, Ms. Sonnier, and this is my dog Lucky and friend Eddie."

The old woman's false teeth were in a glass of water on a little table beside her chair. She quickly put them into her mouth.

"My name is Martha, J.P. Why are you here to see an old lady?"

"If I'd known how pretty you are, Ms. Martha, I wouldn't have waited so long to visit."

Martha Sonnier smiled when she said, "You're a liar, J.P., but you're so good-looking I could listen to your lies all day long."

"A lie has never crossed my lips," J.P. said. He pulled the flask from his pocket. "Like a nip of rum?"

A smile crossed Ms. Martha's face when she took the flask and had a drink.

"Smooth," she said, wiping her mouth with the sleeve of her blouse. "Eddie's almost as good-looking as you. What's your story, Eddie?"

"I'm the new owner of the Majestic. I understand you once worked there."

"Are you part of the mob?"

"No, ma'am," Eddie said. "I stole five bucks from my sister when I was ten. She never let me forget it, and that's about the extent of my crimes."

"Good to hear," Ms. Martha said. "The people I worked for were evil."

"You couldn't have been very old when you worked there," Eddie said.

"I'm a hundred and two and was only twelve when I helped my mother clean the hotel rooms. Trust me when I say I have stories to tell that would curdle your blood."

"I'll bet you do," Eddie said. "Do you know why they abandoned the island?"

"The people who owned it dug up Lafitte's treasure and exposed the curse," she said.

"What happened?"

"Started with yellow fever," Ms. Martha said. "Killed practically everyone on the island. People stopped coming, and they had no guests. One thing after another. It just kept getting worse."

"And they blamed the bad luck on the curse of Lafitte's treasure? What made them even consider that a curse was the cause of their problems?" Eddie asked.

"The old Indian that sold them the island," Ms. Martha said.

Ms. Martha nodded when J.P. said, "Walking Wolf?"

"He had a map showing the location of Lafitte's treasure. They took it from him. Like I said, their troubles started when they dug up the treasure."

"How did they know Walking Wolf had the treasure map?"

"Don't know," Ms. Martha said. "All I know is it marked the end of me and Mama's jobs. You wouldn't need some help, would you?"

"I'd hire you in a minute," Eddie said.

"Not me," Ms. Martha said. "My granddaughter. She would be perfect at my old job."

"What's your granddaughter's name?" Eddie asked.

"Narcisse Denis. She's pretty as a picture and only twenty."

"Have her come by the island tomorrow. I'll have Odette, my manager, interview her," Eddie said.

"Pull out that silver flask of yours. We'll drink to it," Ms. Martha said.

Mosquito Flats was in the rearview mirror when Eddie said, "That old lady is quite a character."

"Bet she was a wild one back in the day."

"Probably so," Eddie said. "She may be suffering from a touch of dementia."

"She didn't seem that way to me," J.P. said. "What did she say that caused you to think that?"

"I never heard any reports of yellow fever in Louisiana as late as the 1930s."

"It wouldn't have been something the owners of the Majestic would want to publicize," J.P. said.

"I'm sure you're right about that. Chief never told me his grandfather ever had the Lafitte Treasure map," Eddie said.

"Maybe he didn't know."

"If he did have it, how did he get it?" Eddie said.

"More importantly, how did the rumrunners find out he had it?" J.P. said.

"Maybe something we'll never know," Eddie said.

"Unless we take a dip in Chief's Magic Pool and ask Walking Wolf's ghost."

"I thought you didn't believe in ghosts," Eddie said.

"Maybe not, but it would be a perfect opportunity to go skinny dipping with a couple of good-looking pagans."

"What about you and Toni? I thought you were having a date with her tomorrow night."

"She agreed to discuss our disagreement but is still slightly miffed at me."

"Doesn't sound like much of a date," Eddie said.

"I like her enough to try and work things out, J.P. said.

"Then why are you talking about skinny dipping with other women?

"Toni and I aren't married," J.P. said. "Doesn't hurt to fantasize."

"Maybe it's time for you to meet someone else," Eddie said.

"Who?"

"Like you said, the island is teeming right now with attractive pagan women. It's a bachelor's dream come true," Eddie said.

"You're a bachelor. Why don't you introduce yourself to some of your gorgeous guests?"

"Because I have enough problems as it is," Eddie said.

"What problems?"

"Josie Castellano."

"She's no longer your fiancée. How is she your problem?" J.P. said.

"We're still friends, and she's asked for my help."

"Doing what?"

"Carlos is Jojo's father. He got Josie pregnant when she was fifteen. They were hot and heavy until a day ago when things changed."

"How is it you know so much about Carlos and Josie's sex life?" J.P. asked.

"She told me," Eddie said.

"For what reason?"

"She wants me to help her make Carlos jealous."

"By doing what?" J.P. asked.

"We're having drinks in the bar. Josie's going to flirt with me."

"People flirt all the time," J.P. said. "It usually doesn't mean much."

"My thoughts exactly," Eddie said. "It seems harmless to me, and I doubt anything will come of it."

"It's getting dark. When is this meeting taking place?"

"She's probably waiting for me in the bar," Eddie said.

"Mind if I tag along?" J.P. asked.

"Why not? The more the merrier."

As Eddie had said, Josie was waiting for him at his table in the bar. She wasn't alone; Toni and Carlos were with her.

Toni crossed her arms, glaring when Eddie said, "Mind if we join you?"

Josie had a half-finished drink in her hand and sounded tipsy when she said, "We've been waiting for you."

"How you doing, Toni?" J.P. said. When her frown was her only response," he said. "Maybe I better go."

Josie was wearing a little piece of nothing black dress whose hemline barely reached her midthigh. Eddie had never seen Josie dressed in anything that even remotely displayed cleavage. His eyes went automatically to the emerald necklace that did as much to highlight her breasts as the expensive gemstone.

Josie was more than pretty, and her gold hoop earrings shouted for people to gaze at her movie star good looks. She wasn't just tipsy. She was already drunk. Eddie noticed, and so did everyone at the table.

"Don't leave, J.P. If Toni's angry, sit by me."

Toni acted as if she were about to leave the table. After thinking about it, she decided to stay. She didn't smile when Eddie sat in the empty chair beside her.

"You look mighty hot tonight, Miss Josie," J.P. said. "What are you celebrating?"

"I'm just happy to be alive," she said.

Meika arrived at the table with fresh drinks and asked, "Anybody hungry?"

"Food only ruins a good drunk," Josie said. "Keep the liquor flowing. We don't need food."

Josie's hand was on J.P.'s leg and maybe a little too close to his private parts. Eddie and Carlos noticed, and so did Toni. J.P. was trying not to react, but the bulge in his jeans informed everyone he was failing miserably. Finally, Toni reacted.

"That's about enough, Josie," she said. "You need to go upstairs and sleep it off."

"It's you who needs to go upstairs," Josie said.

"Give it up," Toni said. "You're not fifteen."

Josie got out of her chair. "What the hell is that supposed to mean?"

Toni had been at the table as long as Josie and wasn't exactly sober.

"You know exactly what it means," she said.

223

Toni reeled when Josie slapped her hard across the face. "You take it back, or I'm kicking your ass right now," Josie said.

Toni slapped her and said, "You're not woman enough to kick my ass."

The fight was on, J.P., Eddie, and Carlos trying to break it up, when Frankie and Adele showed up at the table. Frankie grabbed the two women off the floor and yanked them to their feet.

"What in holy hell do you think you're doing?"

Frankie barely averted a left hook that Toni had thrown. He grabbed Josie's right arm and Toni's left and started toward the door.

"Need my help, baby?" Adele asked.

"I'm taking them to their rooms. I'll be back," Frankie said.

Everyone in the bar was observing the action. Eddie raised his arms and said, "It's over—drinks on the house for thirty minutes."

The bar erupted with applause and cheers as Meika brought drinks to the table and a Mojito for Adele. Eddie, Carlos, and J.P. gave her a look as she sipped the colorful drink through a red straw.

When Adele noticed them looking, she said, "They're sisters. Sisters fight sometimes. They'll kiss and make up tomorrow."

"If they don't kill each other tonight," J.P. said.

The action wasn't over. A handsome, older man approached the table and kissed Adele's hand.

"You must be Adele," he said. "My son Carlos told me you're the most beautiful woman on the island. My condolences for being married to Frankie."

"Who are you?" she asked.

"Fernando Palacio."

Fernando's expensive Italian shoes and sports coat shouted wealth. He had dark eyes and hair;

224

unlike Frankie, he hadn't lost any of his. Fernando
was still holding Adele's hand when Frankie
returned alone to the table.

Chapter 25

Seeing Fernando holding Adele's hand, Frankie's mouth opened in disbelief.

"Why are you here?" he asked.

"To see my grandson," Fernando said.

"Over my dead body."

Fernando's expression remained unchanged when he said, "Don't tempt me."

"Fernando's here because I called him. Have a seat beside Adele. Thanks for coming, Fernando. Sit by me."

Fernando shook Eddie's hand. "It's good seeing your face for the first time," he said.

"Same here," Eddie said. "I'm not with the D.A.'s office any longer. I'm the owner of the Majestic."

"What a beautiful old hotel," Fernando said.

"Eddie has his wires crossed," Frankie said. "The Majestic is mine."

"I thought we had a truce," Eddie said.

"Then why did you file this?"

Frankie had a copy of the pleading Delta had filed in federal court, and he slammed it down on the table.

"Since you all but told me what you intend to do after the ceremony, I decided to get the jump on you."

Frankie grinned and said, Check, though a long way from checkmate. Now why did you invite this asshole to the island?"

"You and Fernando were best friends. Want to tell me what happened?"

"Are you a psychologist now?" Frankie asked.

"I don't have to be a psychologist to know something happened between you two. You're both grandfathers to the same grandson, and you hate each other. What happened?"

When Frankie didn't answer, Fernando said, "Frankie's angry because our wives died the same night. He blamed me for the accident and continues to do so."

"I'm going to my room," Frankie said.

"You've never told me this story," Adele said.

"I don't like talking about it," Frankie said.

"But that's what you need to do," Adele said. "Sit. You're going nowhere until I hear the story."

Frankie returned to his chair and crossed his arms and legs.

Fernando said, "You're a lucky man, Frankie. Adele is as intelligent as she is beautiful."

"Thank you," Adele said. "For both of us."

"I've never told another soul this story," Fernando said. "Not even Carlos. I haven't had a drink since the night of the accident. I need one now."

Meika brought Fernando a brandy, and he drank it as if he were about to be put to death by a firing squad. Eddie could see he was distraught and put his hand on his shoulder.

"You aren't under oath. We'll all understand if you don't continue."

"What I have to say is painful, but I need to get it off my chest," Fernando said.

"Then tell us about the accident?" Eddie said.

"Frankie and I grew up together in New Orleans. We were closer than brothers. We met Laura and Alicin in a bar in the French Quarter. It was love at first sight."

"Laura and Alicin were friends?" Eddie said.

"Best friends. College roommates. Romance ensued, and we were married in a double ceremony."

Fernando smiled when Eddie said, "You're Catholic?"

"I stopped praying the night Laura and Alicin died," Fernando said. "What about you, Frankie?"

Frankie didn't answer.

"How did they die?" Eddie asked.

"The four of us were inseparable. We celebrated our fifth wedding anniversary with a ski trip to Cortina in Italy. We had rented a chalet, though we hadn't checked in."

Fernando's brandy was empty, and he stopped talking. Eddie motioned for Meika to bring him another.

"Please continue," he said.

"We were drinking in Cortina. When it came time to leave, I was drunk and refused to go until we'd had another drink. The chalet complex was up the mountain, and Laura and Alicin took the rental to check us in. Frankie stayed with me. Our wives were killed in an avalanche."

"If we had gone with them, they'd be alive today," Frankie said.

Fernando was sobbing. "Frankie's right. I let everyone down. If it hadn't been for my alcoholism, our wives would be alive."

"You don't know that," Adele said. "If you and Frankie had gone with them, you might also be dead, and there would have been no one to care for Josie, Carlos, and Jojo." Adele looked at Frankie and said, "You can't alter your fate no matter how hard you try."

"Adele's right," Eddie said. "You're as much at fault as Fernando is."

Frankie was also on the verge of tears. After squeezing Adelle's hand, he walked around the table and embraced Fernando.

"I'm not good at forgiving, but so happy you're alive, my old friend," he said. "Let's go upstairs. It's time you met your grandson."

When Carlos stood from the table to go with them, Fernando motioned for him to return to his seat.

"We have issues to discuss, and now isn't the time," he said.

When they were gone, J.P. said, "Your old man is pissed at you."

"He'll get over it," Carlos said.

"I need to apologize," Eddie said.

"For what?" Carlos asked.

"Josie asked me to help her make you jealous. I'm sorry for the brawl it resulted in."

"I'm the one who should apologize," Carlos said. "I'm married and had no right to trifle with Josie's emotions. I flipped out when I learned about the son I didn't know I had."

Carlos nodded when Eddie said, "You're married?"

"With two daughters. I had almost decided to pretend I'd never heard of the boy. Things changed when I saw Jojo with my own eyes. I called my wife earlier, confessed to my discretion, and begged her to forgive me. I intended to confess to Josie tonight and ask her for joint custody of Jojo."

"Her heart's going to be broken again," Eddie said.

"I don't think so," Carlos said. "It looked to me like she has strong feelings for J.P."

"I don't see that," J.P. said.

"Her sister Toni realized it. She has strong feelings for you as well."

"Maybe I better move to Florida," J.P. said.

"It'll work out," Carlos said. "Josie told me you train dogs."

"My partners and I have a canine training facility. We start with exceptionally intelligent dogs and train them to be the best service, police, and specialty dogs worldwide."

"I love dogs," Carlos said. "Is it possible to arrange a tour of the facility?"

"I'll show you now if you don't have other plans," J.P. said.

"Great," Carlos said.

Eddie was soon alone, and the bar began to fill with attractive pagan women. He decided to take a walk on the beach and check on Amani. A light was on in her old Volkswagen van, and she opened the sliding door before he could knock, her black lace dress and the yellow flower on her ear exuding sexuality. She smiled when she saw Eddie and reached for his hand.

"I was hoping to see you tonight," she said.

"And I was hoping to see you."

Amani pulled him into the van, shut the door, and kissed him passionately.

"You left so abruptly the other night I was afraid you were angry with me," he said.

"I wasn't angry. I had things I needed to do."

Amani's cat, Blanco, jumped off the van's front seat and brushed against Eddie's leg. Lightning flashed outside the window as he stroked the big cat.

"Looks as if our little patch of beautiful weather is about to end," he said as distant thunder rumbled.

"We need to go diving again before it does," Amani said.

"Odette and J.P. were duck hunting the day I met you. They saw the ghosts of Lafitte and his pirates burying a treasure chest."

"And?"

"They both swear that you were one of the ghosts," Eddie said.

"You've touched me and held me in your arms. You know I'm not a ghost."

"Is Lafitte's treasure the reason you're on the island?" Eddie asked.

"What I'm looking for is beyond the breakers in the Gulf of Mexico. Why do you ask?"

"Chief and Seraphina bathed in his Magic Fountain and saw the ghost of his grandfather."

"Who is Seraphina?"

"One of the witches on the island to celebrate the life and death of Freya, the woman who performed the séance and was killed in the bombing."

"What did the ghost tell Chief and Seraphina?" Amani asked.

"The rumrunners who built the Majestic and once owned the island had a map to Lafitte's treasure. When they dug it up, their troubles began. Walking Wolf, Chief's grandfather said it was because the treasure is cursed."

"How did the curse affect them?" Amani asked.

"It started with an outbreak of yellow fever."

"The Indian told you this?"

Eddie shook his head. "J.P. and I interviewed a very old Cajun woman who worked for the rumrunners. She told us about the yellow fever outbreak and the accompanying bad luck. The rumrunners reburied the treasure, though it didn't change their luck. They abandoned the island soon after."

"So, what are you trying to tell me?" Amani asked.

"Lafitte's treasure is still on this island and not in the waters of the Gulf of Mexico."

"I don't believe you," Amani said.

"I have the map. I can show you."

"Then let's go now," she said.

"A storm is on the way. Can't it wait until tomorrow?"

Amani wasn't listening and already changing clothes.

"We'll be back before the storm arrives," she said.

"The map is in my office," Eddie said. "We'll have to get it first."

"We don't need the map," Amani said. "Just your ATV."

"We'll need a shovel, assuming we can find the treasure without a map."

Amani had a shovel in her van's floorboard. She showed it to Eddie and said, "Let's go."

The ATV's top was up, and the plastic flaps protected it from the light rain that had begun to fall. The night was damp and gloomy as Eddie followed Amani's directions to the island's backside.

The farther they got from the beach, the more trees and vegetation they encountered. Amani's directions led them to a briny estuary leading to the Gulf of Mexico. Mangrove trees with root systems resembling bony fingers jutted into the water.

"The mangroves are creepy looking in the headlights," Eddie said.

"Because they're alive and sense us coming."

"If you say so," Eddie said. "Hope you know where we're going because I wouldn't want to be lost in the dark."

The electric vehicle made no sound except for the gentle clamor of slipping wheels in the sand.

Sensing Eddie's thoughts, Amani said, "It's winter; the swamp creatures are asleep in their dens."

"What are we looking for?"

"An oak tree," Amani said.

"The forest around the swamp is full of trees. How will you know which is which?"

"There's a trail up ahead," she said.

"I don't see a trail."

"Then slow down, or you'll miss it."

Eddie saw the trail and pointed the nose of the ATV into it.

"This is a trail, all right," Eddie said.

"The swamp has doors," Amani said. "This is one of them."

"How do you know?"

"I know," she said.

Worried about getting stuck, Eddie, guided by ruts in the sandy loam, kept the ATV moving forward.

"If it were summer, the vegetation would mask this tiny trail," Eddie said.

"We're almost there," Amani said.

The trail led them into a clearing to a giant oak tree.

"The old Indian's tree," Amani said.

"How do you know?" Eddie asked.

"I'll show you," she said.

Eddie parked the ATV and followed her to the base of the oak.

"His initials," she said.

Eddie wondered how Amani knew about the initials as he stared at the letters W.W. carved in the tree.

"Where's the treasure buried?" he asked instead.

"This way," she said.

Eddie followed Amani to a spot where the hardwoods parted, revealing a clump of mangrove trees. Woody roots and a leafy canopy formed a cave-like enclosure.

"I can't see a thing," Eddie said. "The opening is big enough to drive the ATV into. I'll get it."

Headlights soon flooded the interior of the mangrove cave. Eddie was carrying the shovel when he joined Amani, staring at the bottom of an empty hole.

"You don't need the shovel," she said. "The hole is already dug."

The hole was dry, the mangrove canopy having kept it from filling with rainwater. Eddie gave Amani a skeptical glance.

"Where's the treasure?" he asked.

"Not on the island," she said.

"How do you know?"

"Because if it were, everyone on the island would be sick with the plague."

Chapter 26

Blanco was kneading dough on Eddie's chest when he awoke alone in Amani's van. He opened the sliding door and saw her sitting in the sand, staring at the waves breaking into shore. Wrapping himself in her camouflage throw, he joined her on the beach.

Amani smiled when he sat beside her and said, "A penny for your thoughts."

"I'm lost in memories," she said.

"Of what?"

"The waves and the sand remind me of something I had forgotten. This island hasn't changed much in two centuries."

"Probably not," Eddie said. "Were you thinking of someone special?"

"Yes," she said. "Can you get the boat today?"

"Sure," he said.

"The sunken galleon beckons. I want to dive on it."

"You think the treasure is somehow back on La Perla Negra?"

Amani nodded and said, "There is treasure aboard the ship."

"How do you know where it is?" Eddie asked.

"I know," Amani said, pointing to a spit of land protruding into the Gulf. "The current makes an abrupt turn near that distant point. The water's a hundred feet deep there—at least twenty feet deeper than the average water depth."

"And?" Eddie said.

"We'll find the wreck of the Spanish galleon in the deep water just off that point."

"Odette and Chief have found doubloons on the beach. You found one out there in the surf. It makes sense the wreck is nearby."

Amani had yet to answer Eddie's question about how she knew where the galleon went down. He was left with many unanswered questions about the previous night. Amani had directed him to the location of Lafitte's treasure and predicted correctly that the treasure wouldn't be there. How did she know?

"I should return to the hotel, shower, and change clothes. I'm starting to look and feel like a bagman," Eddie said.

"No time for that," Amani said. "We can shower in the public facilities. I have a bathing suit you can wear. You can change clothes when we return."

The sky was gloomy, and the temperature was in the fifties. The water pouring from the shower head was cold. There were no individual stalls and only the proximity to Amani's naked body to keep Eddie warm. It was enough. He dried himself with the towel she tossed him and then pulled on the bathing suit that was at least a size too large.

The hour was early when they boarded the Argo, preparing to motor out of the harbor to the point of land jutting into the Gulf. Eddie had pulled a wetsuit on and was growing warmer, though wondering about Amani's secrecy. After untethering the boat, she joined him in the wheelhouse.

"You're excited about the dive," Eddie said. "I can see it in your smile."

"It's something I've waited a lifetime for," she said.

A cold wind had begun blowing beyond the breakers, the water choppy and frothing with white caps, the old hotel growing smaller in the distance. Amani directed Eddie to cut the engines and drop anchor about two miles from the pass leading into Oyster Bay.

"Below us rests the remains of La Perla Negra, a Spanish treasure ship," Amani said. "She sank shortly after sunset in 1818."

Amani shook her head when Eddie said, "In a hurricane?"

"The seas were choppy, much as they are today. Lafitte's band of plunderers attacked La Perla Negra, boarded, and killed almost everyone aboard," Amani said.

Amani nodded when Eddie said, "Jean Lafitte sank the Spanish galleon? I always heard he concentrated on the slave trade."

"Lafitte did many things that aren't recorded in history books," Amani said.

"Such as?"

"La Perla Negra was one of the last treasure ships to transport treasure from Mexico. Lafitte had spies in all the ports and intelligence about La Perla Negra's cargo, destination, and the course it would take. He and his men lay in wait on Oyster Island for the galleon to appear."

"You're saying Lafitte knew there was treasure on La Perla Negra?" Eddie said.

"Not just the usual treasure. La Perla Negra was transporting a fortune in gems the Spanish had taken from the English and French. The Blue Jewel of Dominica was also onboard."

"Never heard of it," Eddie said. "Why was it so valuable?"

"Larimar is the planet's rarest gemstone, found

only in the Dominican Republic. The Blue Jewel of Dominica bore a curse by its owner."

"How do you know so much about the sunken treasure ship?" Eddie asked.

"I know," Amani said.

"So, Lafitte and his band of pirates ambushed La Perla Negra and stole the treasure. What happened after that?"

"Lafitte spared two people from the ship: a mother and her son."

Why did they bury their treasure on Oyster Island instead of taking it with them when they left?"

"Because of the curse, many of the crew contracted the plague, and some died. The tribe of Indians living on the island was also decimated. The Indians told Lafitte that the treasure was cursed and responsible for causing all the sickness and death. They informed him that he and his pirates would never succeed in removing the treasure from the island."

"They believed him?"

"Lafitte and his pirates were superstitious. The curse was real, and it didn't take much for them to believe it."

"How long were they on the island?" Eddie asked.

"Months," Amani said. "Mysterious things began happening, and there was no explanation except for the curse."

"When did things change to allow them to leave the island?"

"The Indians convinced Lafitte there was no choice except to bury and abandon the treasure. Shortly after doing that, they escaped the island with their lives, leaving only a treasure map with the Indians for anyone to know they were ever there."

"Who were the two survivors from La Perla Negra?"

"The Contessa of Dominica. The owner of the Blue Jewel of Dominica. The pirates murdered everyone else on board except the Contessa and her son."

"Why did they spare them?" Eddie asked.

"The Contessa was beautiful, the granddaughter of slaves and white island royalty. The pirates enslaved her. She saved herself from becoming the pirate's whore by becoming Lafitte's concubine. By doing so, she also saved her son."

"Who cast the spell?" Eddie asked.

"The Contessa. Lafitte never realized she was also a voodoo priestess. Storms had damaged the pirate's ship. After many repairs, so it was seaworthy again, they took her to Port Royal in Jamaica, where she escaped."

"What was the Contessa's name?" Eddie said.

"You ask too many questions. Let's dive."

On deck, they adjusted their tanks and prepared to jump overboard.

Before they did, Amani said, "I need to warn you about something. There's a dangerous current down there."

"I guess there's no need for me to ask how you know," Eddie said.

Amani smiled and said, "Charts of prevailing currents. I checked them out."

"How dangerous?"

"Get sucked up in one of those currents, and your body won't surface until you're halfway to Texas."

"Is it something similar to a rip current?" Eddie asked.

"Rip currents are found at the surface," Amani said. "What we'll be dealing with is a deep-water current. It's just as dangerous if it catches you and harder to escape."

"How will we know where it's at?" Eddie asked.

"Sea creatures avoid it like the plague. Hopefully, we'll see the turbulence."

"And if we don't?"

"Deep currents are narrow, usually no more than twenty meters wide. It's hard but not impossible to escape a current. Sometimes, you must let it take you where it will and conserve your strength until there's a change in energy."

"Doesn't sound encouraging," Eddie said.

"That's why a long rope attaches us. If one of us gets sucked in by the current, our weight should be enough to leverage the other out of it," Amani said.

"And if it isn't?" Eddie asked.

Amani tapped her diving knife. "Cut yourself loose. No use both of us drowning."

"Sounds grim," Eddie said.

"The wreck of La Perla Negra will be out of the current, though close to it," Amani said. "We just need to be cautious. Are you okay?"

"I'm good. What about you?"

"Stay behind me the length of the rope. If we're careful, the current will be no problem."

Amani splashed into the Gulf, Eddie following a few seconds later. Something was roiling the water, the visibility much less than during his first dive. He continued downward, following Amani's bubbles as they floated past him.

Eddie tried not to worry about the current. Amani's directions were good and she had spotted the broken hull of a ship. Even at a distance in the murky water, he could see it wasn't the hulk of a boat built in the last century. It was the wreck of La Perla Negra.

Time and the prevailing currents had combined to damage the old ship's hull. It had become home to many diverse sea creatures, the fish scattering as Amani swam between the crevasses.

Amani was looking for something, probably a way into the ship. The old hull had broken into two halves, revealing what was once the ship's inner hold. Amani disappeared into the dark recesses of one of the halves.

Eddie swam across the ship's ruined wooden deck, waiting for what seemed like forever for Amani to exit the broken hold. He grew impatient and anxious until she exited the old ship's dark recesses. She was putting something into her diving pouch. When she saw him, she pointed toward the surface.

Amani followed her bubbles as they rose around her in the murky water, ignoring the tug on her rope until she reached the Argo's metal ladder when a sudden yank left no doubt Eddie had swum into a current.

Eddie had lost sight of Amani because of a sudden lack of visibility. When he realized no fish or sea creatures were around, he remembered what Amani had told him about the current's location."

It was too late. The current had him. Amani felt it when the rope almost pulled her back under the water. She clutched the handrails, removed her fins, and threw them on the deck of the Argo. Climbing aboard, she attached the rope to the ship's hoist and flipped the switch.

Eddie's body was lifeless when it floated to the surface. With some difficulty, Amani finally got him onto the deck of the Argo, not knowing if he was alive when she pulled the top of his wetsuit off of him.

She yanked the regulator out of Eddie's mouth and performed mouth-to-mouth resuscitation. She was searching for a pulse when he started belching seawater. In a moment, his eyes popped open. After a five-minute coughing jag, Amani put an oxygen mask on him, leaving it there until his ashen complexion became normal. When he removed the mask, Amani kissed him.

"I thought I was a goner," he said.

"I wouldn't let you die," she said. "I'm so glad you're safe."

"Me too," he said. "There was no treasure on the ship. Why did you risk our lives to dive on it?"

"I found what I was looking for," Amani said.

"I saw you put something into your diver's pouch," Eddie said.

Amani pulled a floral heart locket from the pouch on her belt and handed it to him.

"A mother's treasure," she said.

The locket was beautiful, intricately engraved with roses, a person's name, and untarnished by more than two centuries below the waters of the Gulf of Mexico. Eddie opened the locket and gazed at the lock of hair as dark as Amani's. The name Diego was engraved on the locket.

"Who was Diego?" Eddie asked.

"The Contessa's son," she said.

She shook her head when Eddie asked, "Did he make it to Jamaica with his mother?"

"He died of yellow fever on the ship. The pirates tossed his body into the sea."

Chapter 27

It was past noon when Eddie returned to the Majestic. Amani had things on her mind, so he left her to them. Fearful of Meika seeing him wearing the same clothes as the previous day, he snuck up to his room, showered, and changed clothes before returning to the bar. Meika had a silly expression when she appeared at his table with a glass of scotch.

"What are you grinning about?" he asked.

"Nothing. Want something to eat?"

"What's on the menu?"

"Isaac's jambalaya. The best I've ever tasted."

"Sounds great," he said. "Anything happening I should know about?"

"Odette interviewed the girl you sent over and hired her on the spot."

"Martha Sonnier's granddaughter?"

Meika nodded. "Her name is Narcisse Denis, and she's one hot mama. I may have to make a play for her."

"Don't let J.P. see her first."

"After last night, J.P. has more problems than he can handle," Meika said.

Meika nodded again when Eddie said, "Toni and Josie?"

"Odette and I told her not to get mixed up with J.P. He avoids permanent relationships like the plague."

When Adele approached his table, Eddie had finished eating and was working on his second scotch.

"May I join you?" she asked.

"Of course," he said.

Eddie helped Adele with her chair and motioned for Meika to bring her a glass of chardonnay.

After sipping her wine, Adele said, "I have another problem."

"Tell me," Eddie said.

"What will Frankie and I do about Josie and Carlos?"

"Didn't Fernando tell you?"

"Tell us what?"

"Carlos is married, has two daughters, and has no intention of divorcing his wife."

"Then he. . ."

Eddie nodded. "He cheated on his wife. He got nailed when he and Grandpa Fernando learned he had an illegitimate son."

"What are his intentions?" Adele asked.

"Tell Josie and confess to his wife. He hopes to work out some joint custody arrangement with Josie."

"Won't work," Adele said. "Jojo hates him."

"Why?"

"He feels Carlos abandoned him and his mom."

"Carlos was only sixteen when he moved to Miami and didn't know Josie was pregnant. She never told him about Jojo. An abandonment charge wouldn't hold up in a court of law."

"Jojo's only eight and doesn't understand the law. He likes J.P. So does Josie and Toni. What am I going to do?"

"Josie is a beautiful woman and hard for any man to resist. I know because we almost married," Eddie said.

"That's why Frankie and I held out hope of a reconciliation," Adele said.

"It was never fated to happen because of two things."

"What things?" Adele asked.

"I couldn't go through with the wedding because I realized I didn't love Josie. I finally forgave myself when I understood she didn't love me either."

Eddie shook his head when Adele said, "Of course she loved you."

"Josie's all woman. We both had powerful physical attractions. That's all it was."

"You can't be serious," Adele said.

"Josie knew how much Frankie and Jojo wanted her to marry me. We almost went through with it."

"I don't believe that," Adele said. "You would have had an ideal marriage."

Eddie shook his head again. "It was Nothing more than a marriage of convenience. We'd have ended up in divorce court and hating each other."

Adele sipped her wine and patted Eddie's hand. "None of that matters now."

"Yes, it does. Josie and I are now good friends. I understand her better than I ever did."

"You and Josie are friends now?" Adele asked.

"At her request, I arranged last night's meeting. It was me she was supposed to make a play on to incite Carlos's jealousy. Even in her drunken state, she realized she didn't want to go there. Instead, J.P. became the target of her affection. It ended up pissing off no one except for Toni."

"You're right about that," Adele said. "I've never seen Toni act that way. It doesn't help with Josie's feelings toward Carlos."

"Josie isn't in love with Carlos. She threw herself at him because they are strongly attracted and sensed marriage would please Frankie and Jojo."

"Then who does she love?" Adele said.

"No one. Josie's a strongminded woman who doesn't need a man."

"If what you say is true, I don't believe she realizes it," Adele said.

"Subconsciously, she does," Eddie said. "I have a plan that might solve all your problems. Can you have Josie meet me here around four?"

"Sure. What's your plan?"

"It's freeform. Each part of the plan is predicated on the preceding step. I can't explain it to you because I want to be free to adjust as I go."

"Okay," Adele said. "What else?"

"Have Toni here around six," Eddie said.

"She'll want to know why. What reason will I give her?"

"Tell her Pancho misses her and will be here."

"Is that it?" Adele asked.

"No. I need you, Frankie, Fernando, and Jojo to arrive at six-thirty."

"I don't know," she said.

"Try hard. This is important."

"Anything else?"

"That's it," Eddie said. "Wish us luck. It'll work if everything goes just right."

"And if it doesn't?"

"Then it's back to square one," Eddie said. "Keep your fingers crossed."

Adele had barely left the table when Eddie called J.P.

"How did Carlos's tour of the Canine Training Facility work out?"

"He loved it and made us a cash offer that was too good to pass up," J.P. said.

"You sold the training center?" Eddie asked.

"Jack, Chief, Odette, and I discussed it. We all agreed we needed an infusion of cash, but Carlos wanted all or nothing. We turned him down."

"Good for you," Eddie said. "Can you join me at my table around sixish?"

"What about Chief and Jack?"

"I need you to come alone. Are the puppies you told me about weaned yet?"

"Yes," J.P. said.

"Want to sell one?"

"No one's going to pay much for an untrained, half-breed mutt," J.P. said.

"Leave it to me," Eddie said.

Eddie dialed Carlos's room. "Carlos Palacio," he said.

"This is Eddie. Have you explained to Josie what you told me last night?"

"Not yet," Carlos said. "I know how much Jojo loves dogs and offered J.P. and his partners a fair price for the training center. They rejected my offer."

"I heard. There may be another way." After explaining, Eddie said, "Josie will be at my table at four. Can you give us ten minutes and then join us?"

"I'll be there," Carlos said.

Eddie had shirked his office duties for several days. After Meika gave him a to-go cup of scotch, he followed the short hall to his office. His feet were propped on his desk when Delta joined him.

"Where have you been?" she asked. "I've worried about Frankie's reaction when he learned of our suit."

"He wasn't happy," Eddie said.

"You spoke with him?" Delta asked.

"He's pissed," Eddie said.

"What do you think he'll do?"

"I haven't a clue," Eddie said. "Frankie's one of the savviest persons I've ever met. I promise we won't like his response."

Eddie's cell phone rang. It was Basil Doles."

"I have bad news," he said.

"Tell me," Eddie said.

"Frankie's having you and Delta disbarred."

"Excuse me."

"The Louisiana State Bar Association is disbarring you and Delta."

"We haven't been notified. What's the cause?"

"You don't need a cause when you're passing money under the table," Basil said.

"The Supreme Court will realize that bribery is involved and see beyond that ruse."

"Don't bank on it," Basil said. "Dad's office and I will help all we can."

"You know I trust your opinion. What do you think?"

"You're the smartest attorney I've ever met. Even if Frankie uses every trick in the book to steamroll you, I'm confident you will prevail."

"Thanks, Basil," Eddie said. "I wish I was as confident as you."

"What?" Delta asked.

"Frankie's trying to get us disbarred."

"On what grounds?" Delta asked.

"A crooked administrator and a fat bribe," Eddie said.

"You're scaring me," Delta said.

Eddie glanced at the clock on the wall and saw it was nearing four.

"I'll think of something. Meet me for a drink in the bar around seven?"

"If I don't slit my wrist first," she said.

Josie was at Eddie's table when he returned. "I'm sorry I made such a fool of myself," she said. "When I saw J.P., I thought using him as the target of my affections might be more realistic. I didn't know he and Toni were dating."

"There's something else you don't know. Carlos is married and has two daughters."

Josie didn't immediately reply. After thinking about what Eddie had told her, she said, "Makes sense. What we once had was little more than teenage hormones."

"You were looking for a father for Jojo," Eddie said.

"Maybe I'll never find him."

"The world is filled with single parents who do a perfectly good job raising their kids alone."

"He needs a father figure," Josie said.

"Let him spend some time with Carlos. He'll come around. All they need to start things off is something in common."

"Such as?" Josie said.

"They both like dogs. Toni takes Jojo to visit the facility every day. J.P. has been showing him how to train dogs. Carlos made J.P. an offer to buy the training facility."

"J.P. and his group would never sell," Josie said.

"No, but they need an influx of money, and some other arrangement might work."

Before Josie could reply, Carlos came around a corner and said, "May I join you."

"Please do," Eddie said. "I'll step away and let you talk in private."

Eddie sat at the bar where Meika met him with a smile and a glass of scotch.

"How much do family counselors make?" he asked.

"No idea," she said. "Why?"

"Because I'm getting good at it."

"Sounds more like a divorce lawyer to me," she said.

"Don't go there," he said. "Have you seen Pancho?"

"In the kitchen helping Isaac," she said. "Want me to get him for you?"

"Not now. Can you have him join us when Toni shows up?"

"If he's still here. Iryna's party is tonight. Pancho, Jack, and Isaac are helping."

"Who does that leave to cook for the Majestic?" Eddie asked.

"Isaac's cousin from Breaux Bridge. He's here now."

"That'll work. If Pancho is still here, have him drop by the table."

"You got it, boss," she said.

When Eddie finished his scotch, he turned to see if Josie and Carlos were arguing. Anything but. They were laughing like old friends. When Josie saw Eddie looking, she motioned him to join them.

"Well?" he said.

"My wife and daughters are on their way here," Carlos said. "I want them to meet Josie and Jojo because we will be partners in the distillery project."

"That's not all," Josie said. "We're partnering in a Canine Training Facility in Miami and buying a franchise from J.P. and the other owners. They'll help us set up, train our personnel, and provide support."

"Wonderful," Eddie said. "What about Toni?"

When Josie glanced over her shoulder to see Toni standing behind her, she exited her chair, embracing her step-sister.

"I'm so sorry about our fight. I have no designs on J.P. and only used him to make Carlos jealous. I didn't know you and J.P. were seeing each other."

"I broke it off with him when I learned he had set up the meeting between Jojo and Carlos."

"Eddie and I planned that little fiasco. We didn't give J.P. the option to say no," Josie said.

Pancho arrived at the table. When he saw Toni and Josie embracing, he joined the embrace.

"A little birdie told me my two favorite granddaughters were fighting. I hope this hug means what I think it does."

"We're cool, Granddad," Toni said. "I couldn't stay mad at Josie for long."

"What about J.P.?" Pancho said. "You know how much I like that boy."

"I'm torn and don't know how I feel about him," Toni said.

"Talking about me?" J.P. said.

Seeing J.P., Josie released Toni and hugged him. "I'm sorry about the other night."

J.P. laughed. "You were a little shit-faced. Don't worry. I've been there and done that."

"What's in the basket?" Eddie asked.

Adele, Frankie, Fernando, and Jojo arrived at the table before J.P. could answer Eddie's question.

Fernando and Frankie's eyes widened when Josie said, "Carlos and I have an announcement to make. Grab a chair."

Fernando eyed his son and said, "You aren't going to embarrass me, are you?"

"Josie and I are becoming partners in a business venture."

"We're putting a distillery on Oyster Island and opening a Canine Training Facility in Miami," Josie said.

"That's not fair," Jojo said. "I can't believe you're going around J.P."

"No one's going around me," J.P. said. "Your mom and dad bought a franchise from us. It's going to make us all bigger and better."

"What's in the basket?" Jojo said.

"Maybe you better come take a look," J.P. said.

Jojo smiled when he peeked into the basket, and a fuzzy puppy jumped into his hands.

"I love him," Jojo said. "What's his name?"

"He's yours to name, though you'll have to share him with your sisters," Carlos said.

"I don't have any sisters," Jojo said.

"You have two of them who are anxious to meet you and a stepmom who will love you. They'll be here tomorrow."

"What about my real mom?"

"Your mom's going nowhere. She'll be with you when you visit Miami."

"And Toni?" Jojo asked.

"We'll need all the help we can get from Toni and J.P.," Carlos said. "No one's leaving your life, only joining it."

Pancho glanced at his watch and said, "I have to go. See you all at Iryna's party"

"Pancho is in heaven," Toni said. "He has a crush on Iryna, and she's teaching him how to cook some Ukrainian dishes."

"Are you going to the party?" J.P. asked.

"Helping Renata decorate. What about you?"

Toni smiled and shook her head when he said, "You aren't still mad at me?"

Everyone left the table except Frankie. "Nothing has changed, Toledo. I'm sinking your ship, and you can take that to the bank."

Chapter 28

Eddie was still smarting from Frankie's threat when Delta arrived.

"How did it go?"

"Perfect right up to the end," Eddie said.

"What happened then?"

"Frankie. Nothing to worry about. He was posturing."

"That's good."

Meika winked at Delta when she arrived with a fresh scotch for Eddie and a lime mojito for her.

When she returned to the bar, Eddie said, "Something you want to tell me?"

"Meika's been flirting with me since I checked in. I think it's cute."

Eddie didn't have time to comment as Chief appeared at the table.

"Pull up a chair," Eddie said. "I heard about your deal with Josie and Carlos."

"Couldn't have come at a better time," Chief said. "We needed money for the improvements we are planning and had run out of ideas about how to raise it."

Delta's face reddened when Meika arrived with a mug of rum for Chief and winked at her again.

"What deal?" she asked.

"Carlos wanted to buy the Canine Training Facility because he knows how much Jojo likes dogs. It was a lot of money, but we turned him down."

"Carlos and Josie came back with another offer," Eddie said.

"We sold them a franchise for a quarter of a million dollars. It was Josie's idea. They are cloning our project in Miami."

"Are you okay with that?" Eddie asked.

"Josie thinks we can make millions. She has lots of other ideas for the island."

"Such as?"

"You need to ask her," Chief said. "If we lose the island, we'll have enough money to relocate elsewhere."

"If you think you'll lose the island, why didn't you simply sell the training center to Carlos?" Delta asked.

"Eddie won't let Mr. Castellano take the island. Now that you're helping him, I'm sure of it. Grandpa Walking Wolf isn't so sure."

"Your grandfather is still alive?" Delta asked.

"His ghost," Chief said.

"Your grandfather is a ghost?"

Chief nodded. "Eddie is one of the few white men Grandpa likes. It doesn't keep him from worrying."

"Why are you here and not at Iryna's party?" Eddie asked.

"Seraphina's going with me. I'm picking her up in my new car," Chief said.

"Your grandfather's Model T was the love of your life," Eddie said. "I can't believe you've replaced it so quickly. What did you get?"

"The perfect car: an all-electric Model T replica. Odette found it online for me. It just arrived an hour ago."

"Good for you," Delta said.

Someone touched Eddie's shoulder. It was Amani. Eddie smiled as he took her hand and helped her into the chair beside him. Meika appeared with fresh drinks and a mug of rum for Amani.

"Delta Becht, this is Amani LeClair."

Eddie had never mentioned Amani to Delta, and she did a doubletake. Seraphina arrived, hugging Delta when she saw her.

"Are we all going to the party?" she asked.

"Eddie and I have something we must do," Amani said.

"What's more important than good food and libations with friends?" Chief asked.

"A talk with your grandfather," Amani said. "Do you mind if Eddie and I use your Magic Fountain?"

"Of course not," Chief said. "I'll give you a ride in my new wheels and drop you off at La Tortue Mountain. You may have to walk back."

"No problem," Eddie said.

Seraphina clutched Delta's hand and said, "Does that mean you're coming to the party with Chief and me?"

"Why not?" Delta said. "Looks like my dance card's empty."

Chief's new car was a replica of his grandfather's Model T, blown up in the explosion that killed Freya. This one was constructed of fiberglass and had all the amenities, even a radio, of a new car.

"Love it," Eddie said.

"Grandpa will be proud," Chief said.

"When I see him tonight, I'll tell him," Eddie said.

The rain had returned to the island, and everyone was happy the top was up on Chief's new car. Amani and Eddie exited the vehicle at the base of La Tortue Mountain.

"It's raining," Chief said.

"We'll be fine," Amani said.

"There are towels in the teepee," Chief said. "If you finish early, join us at Iryna's party."

"Will do," Eddie said.

Eddie seemed perplexed as Chief pointed his new car toward the island's housing development, and Delta worried about him.

"Who is that woman?" she asked.

"You mean Amani?" Chief said.

"She and Eddie seem involved, and until tonight, I didn't know she existed."

"She's from Jamaica. She showed up on the island in an old Volkswagen van. She's camping on the beach," the Chief said.

"What's she doing here?" Delta asked.

"No idea, though she's responsible for Carlos being on the island."

"How does she know Carlos?" Delta said.

Chief shook his head and said, "No idea. Why do you ask?"

"Eddie is the smartest attorney I know," Delta said. "He's an alpha male if there ever was one, though he seems entranced by Amani."

"You're right," Seraphina said. "She seems otherworldly."

"That's what J.P. and Odette think," Chief said. "They both claim they saw the ghosts of Lafitte's pirates burying a treasure. One of the ghosts was Amani, or maybe a woman who looked exactly like her."

"Do you believe them?" Delta asked.

"Oyster Island is haunted," Chief said. "If you don't believe in ghosts when you arrive here, you will before you leave."

"Your mom said as much," Seraphina said. "She called the island magical. I believe it because Chief and I saw his grandfather's ghost the night we bathed in his Magic Fountain."

"Take me back to the hill," Delta said.

"Why?" Chief asked.

"Eddie and I are partners, and I sense he needs my help."

Seraphina said, "It seemed he had things well in hand."

"Either take me back or stop the car and let me out," Delta said.

Chief turned the vehicle around and returned to the base of the hill below the Magic Fountain.

"It's dark, and you have no flashlight," Seraphina said. "Please come with us."

"How do I find the Magic Fountain?" she asked.

"Follow the path up the hill. It continues past the teepee. Keep going. You can't miss it."

Lightning streaked across the darkened sky, and thunder shook the Model T replica. Chief waited until Delta was out of sight before heading for Iryna's party.

Iryna lived with her daughter and granddaughter in an enclave of a dozen houses the Prohibition mobsters had built for the people running Oyster Island. Though identical, Isaac, Odette, and Renata had put their individual touches on their houses.

When Chief and Seraphina arrived, Iryna was in the kitchen with Isaac, Pancho, and Jack. Professor Quinn was also in the kitchen, perturbed Iryna's other suitors were overshadowing him. Iryna's smile indicated she was basking in the adulation. Renata was also having a good time. She and Odette served hors d'oeuvres and filled drink orders as Fernando and Carlos entertained

Sveta with card tricks. The little girl slid off the couch when she saw Jojo's puppy.

"Oh, can I hold him?" she asked. Jojo handed the squirming puppy to her. "What's his name?"

"I haven't named him yet," Jojo said.

"Fernando and Carlos are showing me some card tricks. Want to see?"

Jojo followed her to the couch where the two men were sitting. He grinned when Fernando pulled a card from his ear.

Fernando nodded when Jojo asked, "Are you really my grandfather?"

"Me and Frankie," he said.

"Grandpa Castellano is my grandfather," Jojo said.

"Everyone has two grandfathers," Fernando said.

"Where have you been?"

"Florida. I didn't know you existed. If I had, I'd have come to see you long ago."

"Where is Florida?" Jojo asked.

"It's a southern state on the Gulf of Mexico," Fernando said. "Do you want to learn a card trick?"

"Sure," Jojo said.

Fernando shuffled the deck and dealt them on the coffee table. Soon, Jojo and Sveta were laughing as they enjoyed his sleight of hand.

"Who taught you how to do that?" Jojo asked.

"My papa, your great-grandfather, owned a casino," Fernando said.

"What's a casino?" Jojo asked.

"A place where grownups gamble away their hard-earned money," Fernando said.

"Do you gamble, Grandpa?" Fernando asked.

"No, Jojo. I own the house, and no one ever beats the house."

"Then why do other people gamble?"

"Because they don't have granddads like me to teach them better," Fernando said.

Frankie and Adele sidled up to the couch.

Frankie grinned and said, "Are you teaching my grandson bad habits?"

"I'm teaching our grandson how to avoid bad habits," Fernando said.

"Can you do card tricks, Grandpa?"

"No one can do card tricks like your Grandpa Fernando. He'll teach you, and then you can teach me," Frankie said.

J.P. and Toni had patched things up and were sitting on a swing overlooking the communal garden, the drumming of rain on the tile roof relaxing. Chief and Seraphina were sitting alone, drinking and eating cabbage rolls. Josie could see Jojo was having a good time and noticed Alex sitting alone without a drink. Grabbing two vodkas from Renata's serving tray, she joined him.

"You don't look happy. Are you having second thoughts about our deal?" Josie asked.

"I've never been happier," he said. "I'm just missing Russia?"

"And your friends and family"

"I'm an orphan. I have no family," he said.

"I'm sorry."

Alex smiled and said, "Turns out it's best."

"Will you ever return?"

"Not until the current regime changes. I'm an enemy of the people," he said.

"Want to tell me why?"

"Long story. I was an officer, conscripted a few years after university and starting my own business. Renata, her mother and daughter lived in a town my troops controlled. Renata is a beautiful woman, and two of my men decided to rape her. I intervened."

"You killed them?"

259

"Renata did. Doesn't matter because we were both arrested and faced certain execution," Alex said.

Alex nodded when she said, "You escaped and took Renata with you?"

"Yes," he said.

"You saved her life. She must be grateful."

"She is happy here and functioning again as a human."

"Are you and she a couple?" Josie asked.

"Renata lost her husband. We were separated at the Mexican border, and she suffered through months of sexual and mental abuse. She hasn't yet overcome her grief or repulsion of men."

"Poor woman," Josie said.

"She suffered from traumatic amnesia until J.P., and I returned with her mother and daughter. I can only imagine what she managed to overcome."

"Her mom and daughter were in Ukraine? How did you get them out of the country?"

"Another long story," Alex said.

Josie clutched his hand and said, "I'm sorry for dredging up unpleasant memories."

"Not to worry. The distillery is my dream. I can't remember being so happy."

"What did you do before the army conscripted you?"

"I have a business degree and was a liquor importer."

"Where did you learn so much about distilling and the properties of water?"

"During university, I worked for a man named Alexei. He owned a liquor store. His hobby was distilling, and he had a working model in his basement. He taught me everything he knew and I soaked up his knowledge like a sponge."

"Would you like to see him again?" Josie asked.

"Very much so. Unfortunately, he is dead."

"I'm sorry."

"Don't be sorry. His dream was to distill the world's best Russian vodka. I'm going to live that dream for him," Alex said.

Josie had yet to release Alex's hand. She squeezed it and said, "You're passionate about the distillery. I hear it in your voice."

"Alexei was the father I never had. His dream has become my dream."

"Carlos and I will be good partners," Josie said. "We'll help you achieve your dream."

She laughed when he said, "Do you intend to marry him?"

"Whatever we once had is gone. After experiencing mental lows with Eddie and Carlos, I'm probably destined to die alone."

"You have a wonderful family and will never die alone."

"What about you?" she said.

"I've spent my entire life alone. It's likely how I'll die."

Josie tapped his glass of vodka and said, "Then here's to a long and happy life."

Chapter 29

As if she'd visited La Tortue Mountain many times, Amani led Eddie up the hill, stopping when they reached the teepee.

"Maybe we should feed Chief's cat," she said

"How do you even know he has a cat?"

"Stop asking me how I know things," she said.

"Yes, ma'am," he said.

Eddie followed her into the teepee, where the rain continued to fall. Buttercup, Old Joe, and Coco were asleep on the pallet. They didn't awaken when Eddie stroked the cat.

"Let's don't disturb them," he said. "And no use taking Chief's towels. They'd be drenched by the time we reached the fountain."

"They'll be here when we return," she said. "Plenty of time to dry off then."

"What do you intend to learn by coming here?" Eddie asked.

"The location of the treasure."

"You knew it wasn't in the hole where the mobsters buried it or in the hold of the sunken Spanish ship."

"I know many things," Amani said. "The location of the treasure isn't one of them."

"I'm here; you're here," he said. "I'm ready for a mystical experience."

"Then let's find Chief's Magic Fountain."

Eddie followed Amani through the teepee's flap. Only flashes of lightning lighted their way up the path to the sparkling pool. When they reached it, Amani and Eddie stripped off their drenched clothes and tip-toed into the water.

"Kind of nippy," he said.

"It's January," Amani said. "The rain isn't exactly warm. Hug me. I'll heat you up."

Eddie took her up on her request. They were kissing when the sound of something coming up the trail interrupted them. It was Delta.

"Delta," Eddie said. "What are you doing here?"

"I was worried about you, and now I'm wringing wet," she said.

"I'm good," Eddie said. "Join us."

"All right," she said.

Grinning inanely, she walked into the pool without removing her shoes, blouse, or skirt.

"How much did you have to drink?" Eddie asked.

Delta ignored Eddie's question and said, "I came to protect you."

"I'm in no danger," Eddie said,"

"Let me help you remove your clothes," Amani said. "You won't be comfortable unless you do."

Delta clutched her blouse and pushed away Amani's hands. "No," she said.

"She's tipsy," Eddie said.

Amani laughed and said, "More than tipsy; she's drunk."

Lightning streaked across the sky, followed by a clap of thunder and then an unexpected hazy mist. It was the ghost of Walking Wolf materializing. Delta's eyes opened wide, and she began shivering uncontrollably. Eddie and Amani sandwiched her in an embrace until her shaking subsided.

"It's okay," Eddie said. "It's Chief's grandfather, Walking Wolf. He won't harm us."

"You sure?" Delta asked.

"Promise," he said.

Even normally an impressive figure, the ghost of Walking Wolf was at least ten feet tall, a colorful headdress capping his snowy white hair and face decorated by war paint.

His voice boomed when he said, "Eddie, what are you doing here?"

Eddie had never gotten used to a ghost who knew him by his first name.

"We have questions and hope you have answers," Eddie said.

"First, I have a question for you." Walking Wolf said.

"Ask me," Eddie said.

"Are you going to save the island from the angry white men?"

"Delta and I are giving it our best shot," Eddie said.

"Then keep Delta away from the firewater," Walking Wolf said.

Eddie couldn't help but smile. "She has a mind of her own."

Walking Wolf crossed his arms and said, "What's your question?"

"We have more than one. How did the mobsters get the treasure map?"

"I gave it to them," Walking Wolf said.

"Excuse me?" Eddie said. "Why did you do that?"

"So they would dig it up and be destroyed by the curse."

Walking Wolf nodded when Eddie said, "You knew about the curse?"

"The plague devastated my tribe when the pirates brought it to the island. Our chief finally convinced them the treasure was cursed, and the only way they could escape alive was to bury it and flee the island."

"We know they buried the treasure. Why did they leave the map with your tribe?"

"In their haste, they forgot to take the map. My people found it in their deserted camp."

"And you ended up with it?" Eddie asked.

"I was one of the few Atakapans whose family had survived the plague," he said.

"The mobsters must have been suspicious when you gave them the map," Eddie said.

"I tricked them," Walking Wolf said.

"How?"

"They thought I was an old drunk. I played on their prejudices and had them believing my actions were that of an out-of-control old Indian who'd drunk too much firewater. They never realized my plan was for them to possess the map."

"You're plan worked. They dug up the treasure and released the curse," Eddie said.

"The curse is powerful. The plague struck, and they began to die. When the situation became dire, I told them the treasure was the cause of the curse and that they needed to rebury it in the exact spot where they found it and then leave the island."

"And they did," Eddie said.

"They returned the treasure to the hole in the ground and then left the hotel and everything else as you found it when you moved here."

"Why didn't they rebury the treasure?" Eddie asked.

"I was the one who dug the hole, two men watching me with shotguns as I did. They had just lowered the chest into the hole when it started to rain. It wasn't just any rain. It was as if the Great Spirit was intent on filling the hole with water. The white men ran away, leaving me in the hole to drown."

"Damn!" Eddie said. "How did you escape?"

"The hole filled with water. I floated until I could grab a fallen branch and pull myself out."

"The men didn't return?"

"When the rain stopped, I drove my car to the hotel. Everyone was gone."

"What about the treasure?" Eddie asked.

"I returned to cover it with dirt, but the rain had washed it away. I decided to dump it into the sea."

"The treasure must have been heavy. How did you get it out of the hole?" Eddie asked.

"I had a winch on the front of my car and used it to retrieve the treasure chest. I unloaded the treasure from the chest and transferred it piece by piece into the car."

"You weren't tempted to keep the treasure?"

Walking Wolf scoffed. "I'm not crazy. The treasure was cursed. I wanted to get it off the island for good."

"What did you do with it?" Eddie asked.

"Took it out to sea and dumped it," he said.

"In what?" Eddie asked.

"My pirogue," Walking Wolf said.

"You went out in the Gulf of Mexico in a pirogue?"

"Yes. The waves were high, but the Great Spirit was with me. I took the treasure as far away from the island as I dared, then dumped it overboard."

"Do you remember where you dumped it?"

"I remember," Walking Wolf said.

"Will you tell me?" Amani said.

"Why should I tell a treasure hunter? What good will it do for the island?"

"I only want what is mine, and that is the Blue Jewel of Dominica. That piece of treasure bears the curse. If I recover it, it'll never return to Oyster Island, nor will the curse."

"And the rest of the treasure?" Walking Wolf asked.

"Eddie can have it," Amani said.

"What will he do with it?"

"He's a smart man, and you trust him. The treasure's worth a king's ransom. He will find a way to use it to ensure your heirs become the rightful owners of Oyster Island."

"Can you use the treasure to save the island, Eddie?" Walking Wolf asked.

"I can try," Eddie said.

"Are you sure?" Walking Wolf said.

"Give us a chance," Amani said. "We'll return the island to the Atakapans, which will be theirs forever."

"Do you trust this woman?" Walking Wolf asked.

"Frankie Castellano is breathing down my neck, and the people who sent the man who destroyed your car with the bomb are more dangerous than he is. We have to make it work. Will you tell us where you dumped the treasure?"

"There's a finger of land about two miles from the beach. We Atakapans call it Witch's Finger."

"We know where it is," Eddie said.

"There's a blue hole on the other side of Witch's Finger. The water is deep, so I dumped the treasure there," Walking Wolf said.

"Thanks," Eddie said. "I promise I'll do my best to return the island to Chief and his heirs."

"I trust you, Eddie," Walking Wolf said.

Eddie and Amani realized the storm had intensified when the ghost faded away. Delta was passed out in their arms. Before either could speak, another ghost appeared. It was Freya standing ten feet tall and wearing her long black dress.

"My poor daughter could never hold her liquor," she said. "I love her, though we are so different. I feel as if my real daughter was switched at birth."

"She's your daughter," Eddie said. "You should be proud."

"I am proud, but she's such a prude," Freya said. "She'll probably insist on wearing pajamas on her wedding night."

Eddie laughed. "Walking Wolf told us what we need to know."

"He didn't tell you everything," Freya said.

"What?" Eddie asked.

"There are other killers on the island. They are looking for you and Frankie."

"Frankie's at Iryna's party. It's where I'm supposed to be," Eddie said.

"Watch your back, Eddie, and take care of my beautiful daughter," Freya said.

Freya's ghost disappeared as veins of lightning laced the stormy sky.

"We need to get Delta down the hill," Eddie said. "My cell phone is in Chief's teepee, and I have to give J.P. a head's up."

Eddie and Amani were naked, Delta still unconscious, as they helped her downhill to Chief's teepee. They felt the warmth when they opened the flap and entered the ancient structure. Eddie tossed Amani a towel and then found his cell phone in the jumble of his clothes. He dialed J.P.'s number and waited for his answer.

"J.P. here."

"Another Conexco killer is on the island," Eddie said. "He's looking for me and Frankie. Everyone at the party is in danger."

"We know," J.P. said. They've wired Renata's house to blow. We're trapped, and the front door is the only way out."

"How do you know?" Eddie asked.

"They're demanding we send out you and Frankie in the next fifteen minutes, or they're going to kill all of us."

"Have you called the police?"

"We're on our own. The assassins arrived in a helicopter and blew up the bridge to the island," J.P. said. "No one can get on or off. Where are you?"

"Chief's mountain," Eddie said. "Chief's shotgun is in the teepee. I'll be there as fast as I can."

"There's three of them; two assassins and the pilot. They're trained killers. You wouldn't stand a chance."

"What, then?" Eddie asked.

"If you could make it to Jack's, you could sic Old Joe on them."

"Old Joe is here. Put Chief on the phone." When Chief answered, Eddie said, "Call Old Joe."

Chief was loud when he said, "Danger, danger, danger, Old Joe. We're at Renata's and need your help."

Old Joe went instantly to his feet and out the teepee flap, Coco right behind him. Before starting down the hill, he halted, raised his head to the clouds, and emitted a howl that could be heard across the island. Eddie didn't bother dressing as he grabbed Chief's shotgun, a bandolier of shells, and started down the hill after them.

The dozen houses where Renata lived were about a half mile from the base of La Tortue Mountain. Eddie hadn't gone far when he heard the sound of dogs coming from Jack's house. He was breathless when he reached the house's front yard and saw Old Joe on top of one of the assassins. The man's partner was beating the big dog with his pistol.

"Drop it now and get on the ground," Eddie said.

When the second assassin saw Eddie with a double-barrel shotgun, he pointed his weapon at him and started firing. The bullets miraculously whistled past him as he squeezed both triggers of the shotgun. The man was dead before he hit the ground.

Velvet, Oscar, and Lucky had also reached the melee and ripped into the man beneath Old Joe. Eddie looked up when he heard the helicopter directly overhead.

Eddie loaded two shells from the bandolier into the shotgun, blowing off one of the rotors when he pulled the triggers. The crippled chopper lurched forward and crashed about a hundred feet away. When the pilot climbed out of the wreckage, two dozen snarling dogs from the Canine Training Center surrounded him.

Seeing what was happening, J.P. hurried out the front door, pulled Old Joe, Velvet, and Lucky off the man on the ground, and then knocked him unconscious with the barrel of his forty-five.

Eddie wasn't an athlete and had never played any sport in high school or college. It didn't matter. He was soon piled on by everyone pouring out of Renata's as if he'd just landed a ninety-yard hail Mary to win the year's biggest game.

Chapter 30

When everyone unpiled from the scrum, Renata handed Eddie a bathrobe. He could barely get it over his arms because everyone wanted to high-five him.

"Where did you learn to shoot like that?" Chief asked.

"No idea," Eddie said. "That was the first time I've ever shot a weapon."

"You have to be kidding," Jack said. "How did you know how to release the safety?"

"I was a prosecutor and dealt with weapons my entire career. What I don't understand is how the assassin missed me. He unloaded on me at almost point-blank range," Eddie said.

"Grandpa," Chief said.

"Or Freya," Jack said.

Jojo clutched Eddie's hand and said, "You're a hero."

"Old Joe's the hero," Eddie said. "He saved your lives, not me."

Jojo had his arms around Velvet's neck. "My dog helped," he said.

"She sure did," Eddie said. "How did the other dogs get loose?"

"Don't know," Chief said. "Maybe Grandpa again.

"Your dogs are amazing," Carlos said. "Please don't back out of our franchise deal."

"We're good," J.P. said. "No one's backing out of anything."

Frankie and Adele approached Eddie. "We need to talk," Frankie said.

"Tomorrow," Eddie said. "Amani's waiting for me on La Tortue Mountain."

"I'd take you, but I have to help Jack and J.P. get the dogs back to the training center," Chief said.

"I can walk," Eddie said. "It's not that far."

As he returned to the hill, he realized for the first time that the rain had ceased. The almost full moon was shining behind damp clouds that had begun parting. The path was still damp as he climbed the hill to Chief's teepee. He found Amani beneath a blanket, and he snuggled in beside her. She wasn't asleep.

"It's important for us to be on the water by dawn," Amani said.

"We don't have much time," Eddie said.

Amani pulled him close and said, "Then let's don't waste any of it."

Time began flying, and Eddie didn't want the moment to end. He felt an intense loss when Amani finally pushed him away, got up from the pallet, and began putting on her clothes.

"Get dressed," she said. "We have work to do."

"What about Delta?" he asked.

"She's dry, warm, and in no imminent danger. Just like you promised her mother. We aren't so lucky. The blue hole is a dangerous dive."

The clouds had cleared in the early morning sky as Eddie and Amani descended La Tortue Mountain and trekked on foot toward the Majestic Hotel. When they reached the Argo at dawn, Eddie cranked the old diesel engines and began motoring out of the bay.

"Are you okay?" Amani asked.

"Scared shitless, but not for me," he said.

"Don't be frightened."

Eddie touched Amani's shoulder and said, "You told Walking Wolf that the Blue Jewel of Dominica is yours. Want to explain?"

"I'm out of answers," she said.

"Sorry," he said.

"I have a task to complete, and I can't do it without you. I need you."

"And I'm here," he said.

The storm had passed, leaving the Gulf's surface as still and colorful as a watercolor painting. Gulls flying overhead dotted the sky's perfect azure hue. Eddie could still feel the warmth and softness of Amani's body as they motored past Witch's Finger. His joyful thoughts became feelings of dread as the water changed to dark blue.

"Here," Amani said.

Eddie didn't ask how Amani knew where to stop as he cut the engine and dropped anchor.

"This is it?" he said.

Amani smiled when she said, "Yes."

The water was still, and there was no wind blowing as Eddie and Amani pulled on their wetsuits on the Argo's deck.

"The treasure will be heavy," Eddie said. "How will we get it on the boat?"

"The Argo has a winch. We'll lower the line, cover the treasure with the net, and then hoist it to the surface."

"The blue hole is large," Eddie said. "How do you know the treasure is directly below us?"

"Because we're so close, I can feel it," she said.

"Then let's get started."

273

Eddie's hand moved to the winch controls, his fingers tracing grooves that somehow felt familiar. The mechanism came alive when he flicked the starter switch.

An electrical hum reverberated through the morning's stillness. They watched as the net disappeared into the dark blue water, Eddie's grip tightening on the controls as he guided the cable ever deeper, and the echo of bubbles rising to the surface the only sound. Minutes passed before the cable slackened.

"Is the net on the bottom?" Amani asked.

"A hundred and fifty feet down," Eddie said. "I've never dived that deep."

The air was salty, a slight breeze beginning to blow, and the sun shining brightly. Eddie helped Amani with her heavy SCUBA gear. She sat backward on the boat's hull, waiting to enter the water as Eddie tightened the buckle of his weight belt. Shortly after hearing her splash, he followed her into the blue hole.

The visibility was amazing as Eddie followed the cable and Amani's bubbles to the bottom of the blue hole. He'd taken all the courses necessary to qualify as a competent recreational diver. The hundred feet he and Amani had reached on their previous dive was the deepest he'd ever gone.

Only proficient technical divers should attempt a depth of one hundred fifty feet. He understood this but was anxious and struggled to remember the diving rules as he followed Amani to the bottom.

Eddie didn't want to burst an eardrum and remembered to equalize as he descended. He could only hope Amani was doing the same. They had little time to spend on the bottom because they needed to decompress as they returned to the surface. If Lafitte's treasure weren't directly beneath the net, they would have almost no chance of success.

When he reached the bottom, Amani was waiting for him. When he saw the chest protruding from the mud, he gave her a thumbs-up. Though he couldn't tell because of her mask, he knew she was smiling. They had work to do, and his happiness didn't last long.

The treasure chest was stuck in the mud, Eddie's enthusiasm waning when he realized he couldn't lift the heavy chest enough to slip the netting under it. Time was running out, and he searched his brain for an alternate plan.

The recovery net was attached to the cable with a ball and locking hook. After detaching the net from the cable, he passed it through the chest's two handles and hooked it on itself. With little time to spare, he looked at Amani and pointed toward the surface.

Eddie and Amani surfaced slowly, following their bubbles. The cable was still taut, and the sun shone brightly when their heads popped out of the water. Amani tossed her swim fins onto the deck of the Argo and then climbed aboard. Eddie followed her out of the water.

"How do you feel?" she asked.

Eddie said," I'm exhilarated. I never thought I'd ever make a dive that deep."

"You may have to do it again if we aren't able to pull the chest out of the mud," she said.

"The cable is strong, and so is the lifting engine," he said. "We'll get it."

When Eddie switched on the winch and started the pulley, he began to doubt his optimism. The Argo rocked, and the cable drew taut, but the treasure chest refused to budge.

"The chest is heavy, though not heavier than much of the cargo the Argo used to load in its hold," Amani said.

"It isn't the weight," Eddie said. "It's the suction. If we can break the suction, the chest will come to the surface easily."

"How do we do that?"

"Rock the chest until it burps. The trick is to do it without parting the cable," he said.

Eddie began applying momentary power to the cable and releasing it until he'd established a rhythm. After ten minutes, he switched off the powerful electric engine and began stripping away his wetsuit.

"Please don't give up," Amani said.

"No way," he said. "Rubber suits are too hot to wear when you're sweating. I'll pass out if I don't get this off."

Amani nodded and stripped off her wetsuit as Eddie began working the cable again.

"Amen to that," she said.

Amani's revealing red bikini did little to cover her voluptuous body and soon riveted Eddie's attention.

"You're going to cause me to have an accident," he said.

She was smiling when she said, "Then look the other way. I'm not putting the wetsuit back on."

"Sorry, but I'm having difficulty concentrating on the treasure chest."

Amani found a white shirt Jack or Chief had left on the boat, put it over the bikini, and buttoned it."

"Spoil sport," Eddie said.

"Your own fault," she said. "I won't be responsible for an accident."

When something popped, Eddie continued working the clutch as the cable went momentarily slack.

"It's either pulled loose from the mud, or the cable just broke," he said.

"Please tell me that didn't happen," she said.

Eddie reversed the mechanism until he was satisfied the cable hadn't parted, and the treasure chest had pulled loose from the mud.

"I think we're good," he said. "Let's try to get it out of the water."

Eddie and Amani cheered when the chest broke the water's surface fifty minutes later. He was anything but an experienced crane operator, but it didn't matter. The old treasure chest was soon on the deck of the Argo; Amani and Eddie were ecstatic.

Eddie used a shovel to break off the corroded old lock from the chest's hasp. When he opened the top of the chest, he wasn't prepared for the splendor and magnificence of the jewels and gold.

A crown of solid gold was dominated by diamonds the size of chestnuts, beautiful rubies, and at least one emerald. Tiaras sparkled with magnificent jewels, and priceless bracelets and bejeweled anklets were common. Among the jewels were Spanish, English, and French coins and even large nuggets of solid gold.

"Oh my God!" Eddie said. "Seeing a treasure like this is another thing I never even dreamed of. It has to be worth a fortune."

Too busy unloading the chest onto the deck, Amani didn't reply. The last piece she removed from the chest was the Blue Jewel of Dominica. Even Eddie was stunned by its beauty.

"I can't believe it," Amani said. "I've found it?"

Amani was beaming when Eddie put the golden necklace with the royal blue stone around her neck and fastened it.

"What now?" he asked.

"I promised Walking Wolf I wouldn't return the Blue Jewel of Dominica to Oyster Island. Take me to shore just off the island."

"And then what?" he asked.

"I'll hide the Blue Jewel of Dominica and then hike back to the island," Amani said.

"Then why do I have the feeling that I'll never see you again?" he asked.

"What would you have me do?" she asked.

"Let's drive the Argo until we run out of gas," Eddie said.

"And then what?" Amani said.

"Build a hut on the beach and never get out of bed," he said.

"Oyster Island is your destiny," she said. "You spent your entire life getting there. It's where you need to be."

Amani didn't answer when Eddie said, "What about you?"

Eddie pointed the Argo toward the nearest land. The water was too shallow to reach shore. Dressed in only her bikini, Amani kissed him and prepared to dive overboard and swim to shore.

"This seems like goodbye. Will I ever see you again?" Eddie asked.

"You'll see me," Amani said. "I promise, and I keep my promises."

"What will I do with the rest of the treasure?" he said.

"It's yours," she said. "Do with it what you will. I must go now."

Eddie reached for her, but she dived overboard and swam to shore. He watched her climb out of the surf, waiting for her to turn and wave. Maybe to blow him a kiss. She never did.

Eddie followed the shoreline until he reached the breach in the breakers leading to Oyster Bay. It was mid-afternoon when he moored the Argo. Jack and Chief were waiting on the dock.

"We were heading to the Majestic for lunch when we saw you cruising through the breakers," Chief said. "Where have you been?"

"Treasure hunting," Eddie said.

"Any luck?" Jack asked.

"Amani and I found Lafitte's treasure, if that's what you mean," Eddie said. "It's behind me on the deck."

"You returned the curse to the island?" Chief said.

"That's a negative. The Blue Jewel of Dominica carried the curse. Amani took it, and it isn't on the island. Come aboard. I'll show you the treasure."

After viewing the ancient treasure chest's contents, Jack and Chief were impressed.

"What are you going to do with it?" Chief asked.

"Use it to settle our differences with Frankie once and for all," Eddie said. "Right now, I'm too tired to worry about it. I'm going to bed."

"We'll take it to your office," Jack said.

Eddie grinned and said, "It's heavy."

"We can handle it," Chief said. "Get some sleep."

Eddie was exhausted, both spiritually and mentally. The Hotel lobby was alive with activity, but it didn't matter. He snuck up to his room, pulled down the sheets, climbed into bed, and closed his eyes.

Chapter 31

Eddie didn't awaken until darkness had fallen on Oyster Island. After fifteen minutes in the shower, his blurry eyes and groggy mind disappeared, and he felt almost human again as he walked down the stairs in clean clothes. The bar was crowded, its occupants active and animated. Odette met him at the foot of the stairs before he had a chance to wonder why.

"Where have you been?" she asked.

"Last night zapped me. I had to get some sleep. What's going on?"

"The full moon and Freya's celebration of life and death. It begins at midnight."

"Glad I got some sleep," Eddie said. "What else is up?"

"Frankie Castellano. He's waiting for you in your office."

"Oh, Lord!" Eddie said. "I don't know if I'm ready for this."

"Well, he's ready for you," Odette said.

"I need a drink first," Eddie said.

"Better make it a double," she said. "Frankie looked fit to chew nails."

Meika was grinning when Eddie grabbed a stool at the bar.

"Scotch?" she said.

"Frankie's waiting for me in my office. Better give me a bottle and two glasses. Why are you grinning?" he said.

"Everyone on the island's talking about you," she said.

"Oh yeah? What are they saying?" he asked.

"That you put on quite a show last night. Sorry I missed it."

"I checked out shortly after the chopper crash. What happened after that?"

"The Army Corp of Engineers installed a temporary pontoon bridge, and the police arrested the two surviving assassins," Meika said.

"They probably need to talk to me."

"J.P. covered for you."

"Are you attending Freya's celebration?" Eddie asked.

"You kidding? Wouldn't miss it for the world," she said. "You?"

"If I survive my meeting with Frankie."

Eddie found Frankie and Delta in his office when he arrived with the scotch. Surprisingly, they were both smiling. Eddie poured Frankie a drink and then grabbed the chair beside him.

"Thanks, amigo," Frankie said.

"Amigo? Has something changed?" Eddie asked.

"You kidding? You saved the lives of everyone in my family last night. I'm in your debt."

"Then we're good concerning the Majestic and Oyster Island?"

"Let's don't go that far," Frankie said.

"What, then?" Eddie said.

"I paid lots of money for the island and the Majestic," Frankie said. "I can't just let it go for nothing."

"What do you suggest?" Eddie asked.

"I bought Oyster Island because of the Majestic, but Josie and Carlos have convinced me there's more value there. I want it," Frankie said.

"Where does that leave the rest of us?" Eddie said.

"Still here, but as minority partners."

"What about the Canine Training Center?"

"J.P. and his partners can keep it, but I'm the controlling partner," Frankie said.

Frankie had finished his drink so Eddie poured him another.

"Sweet," he said. "For you, that is, seeing as you have invested nothing in it."

"What do you mean nothing? They built the facility on my land with my building materials. I'd say that's something."

"You know, Frankie, you're far from owning the Majestic, Oyster Island and everything on it. After reading Delta's pleading, I think you realize that."

"You have no chance in court," Frankie said.

"Maybe," Eddie said. "One thing I know for sure."

"What?"

"If you take the island, you risk your entire family turning on you."

"What do you mean by that?"

"Josie, Carlos, Alex, and J.P.'s crew have already agreed on deals. Josie won't stand for you ruining the deal, and I doubt Carlos and your best friend Fernando will either."

"This is business," Frankie said.

"I don't need to remind you who came to your rescue last night. Even if you've forgotten, Adele, Jojo, Pancho, and Toni haven't."

"I can't just let you have the Majestic and Oyster Island," Frankie said. "It's not in my DNA."

"How much do you want for the island and the Majestic?" Eddie asked. "Give me a price."

"A million bucks," Frankie said.

"Deal," Eddie said.

"No one will lend you a million bucks. Show me the money."

Eddie topped up their drinks again. "Come see," he said.

Frankie and Delta followed Eddie to the old chest in the corner of his large office. Their expressions when Eddie opened the lid showed their shock.

"If that's Lafitte's treasure it's mine," Frankie said.

"How do you figure that?" Eddie asked.

"I own everything on the island."

"You don't, and even if you did, I didn't find the treasure on the island. I salvaged it in the Gulf of Mexico and have video evidence to prove it."

"The treasure's worth lots more than a million bucks," Frankie said.

"You haven't spent a million dollars on this island. You're set to make a fat profit on your investment, and as a bonus, you get to keep your family."

Frankie smiled and said, "You drive a hard bargain, Toledo. I was prepared to let you have the Majestic and Oyster Island for half a million bucks."

"That's Good to hear," Eddie said. "I was prepared to raise my offer to two million dollars."

"Then we have a deal?" Frankie said.

Eddie extended his hand and said, "Let's shake on it."

They were soon shaking hands, laughing, and drinking more scotch.

"I still need a trusted consigliere," Frankie said.

"Put Delta and I on retainer," Eddie said. "We're all the legal team you'll ever need."

Frankie finished his drink and said, "You got a deal. Right now, I got to go. I'm having drinks with my beautiful wife and our family."

"One more thing," Eddie said. "I don't want anything like what happened last night ever to occur again. We need to talk about Conexco."

"When the police and I finish with Conexco, they'll never bother anyone again. I promise."

"Thanks, Frankie. That's good enough for me."

Eddie waited until Frankie was gone and then poured himself another scotch. When he glanced up, he saw Delta's frown and tightly crossed arms.

"What?" he said.

"You were rude," she said. "I would have liked a drink."

Eddie grinned and said, "You kidding? I didn't forget you. You can't hold your alcohol, partner of mine."

"Doesn't matter," she said. "You should have offered me a drink. I didn't have to drink it, you know."

"I apologize," he said. "I won't let it happen again."

"Do you actually have video proof of finding the treasure in the Gulf?"

"Little white lawyer's lie," Eddie said.

"What if he'd called you on it?"

"He didn't.

"A good thing. I heard about your heroics last night," she said.

"Chief said it was the ghost of his grandfather that protected me from harm. Jack said it was the ghost of your mom," Eddie said.

"It was neither," Delta said.

"Excuse me?"

"Amani protected you."

"What are you talking about?" Eddie asked.

"I was awake and heard you when you took Chief's shotgun and charged down the hill. I heard something else."

"What?" Eddie said.

"A growl. I peeked out from the blanket to see Amani transform into a monster."

"A monster? What kind of monster?"

"A hairy beast with sharp claws and long teeth. As I watched, the beast disappeared."

"You were dreaming," Eddie said.

"I wasn't," Delta said. "The creature returned to the teepee just before you did and transformed into Amani. When she saw me looking, she said, 'Don't worry, Eddie's safe.'"

"You were drunk," Eddie said.

"Amani is a shape-shifting supernatural being with special powers. She saved you and everyone trapped inside Renata's."

Eddie opened his mouth to speak, thought better of it, and asked something else.

"Are you going to your mother's celebration tonight?"

"I'll be there," she said.

"How long will the ceremony last?" he asked.

"Until dawn," she said.

Delta smiled when Eddie poured her a drink and said, "You may need this."

Delta made a face and said, "I hate scotch. Let's go to the bar. Meika can make me a mojito."

Meika brought Eddie a scotch when he and Delta sat at the bar.

"Can I get you a lime mojito, Miss Cutie?" she asked.

"Please," Delta said. "I need to steel myself for the ceremony."

"Are there more people in the bar than usual?" Eddie said.

"At least three times more," Meika said. "I called Odette to help me. She's bringing Narcisse."

"You need three bartenders?" Eddie asked.

"There must be a thousand extra people on the island. All here for Delta's mom's celebration."

"How many witches are there in south Louisiana?" Eddie asked.

"Not just Louisiana," Meika said. "Texas, Arkansas, Mississippi, and even some from Oklahoma."

"Oklahoma has witches?" Eddie asked.

"You kidding?" Delta said. "Many pagans believe that Spiro Oklahoma is the center of the universe."

Delta shook her head when Meika said, "Are you making this up? Tell me more about this ceremony."

Odette, accompanied by an attractive young woman, entered the bar from the kitchen. They joined Meika at the counter.

"Eddie and Delta, this is Narcisse Denis, the Majestic's newest employee," Odette said.

Like Odette and Meika, Narcisse wore faded jeans and cowboy boots. Her dark hair draped to the shoulders of her blue flowered western shirt. Eddie shook her hand.

"Welcome to the Majestic," he said. "Is everyone treating you well?"

"Very well, thank you," she said. "I love it."

"Good," Eddie said.

"People are waiting for drinks on the other side of the bar," Odette said. "We'll handle it, and I can start teaching Narcisse how to mix drinks."

"Don't let Odette work you too hard," Eddie said.

"You kidding?" Narcisse said. "We're already like sisters."

When they moved away, Meika said, "You were going to tell me more about the ceremony."

"Of course," Delta said. "The celebration begins at midnight with the lighting of a large bonfire. The pagans begin dancing in everchanging circles. The ceremony ends at dawn."

"No one can dance for six straight hours, can they?" Meika asked.

"Have you ever seen a person possessed?" Delta asked.

"Not really," Meika said.

"It's truly both a religious and mystical experience," Delta said. "It happens when someone reaches the limits of their physical endurance."

"I don't believe you," Meika said. "Sorry if I'm skeptical."

"You've heard of a runner's high. It happens when other runners have 'hit the wall.' Some runners don't hit the wall. Instead, the sense of exhaustion is replaced by exhilaration. It also happens when individuals are overcome by religious fervor and come under the control of someone or something unexplainable."

Delta nodded when Meika asked, "Have you ever been possessed?"

"It's like nothing you've ever experienced," Delta said. "You have no control over your actions, though you're sensitive to everything. You tap into the collective consciousness of the universe. The experience fills you with magical knowledge lost to the human race for centuries. It will truly transform your life."

"Wow!" Meika said. "You're scaring me. Is there a sermon or invocation that goes along with the ceremony?"

"Seraphina will sing the pagan song of death accompanied by an ancient wooden flute," Delta said.

"That's it? How will everyone know what to do?" Meika asked.

"The participants will become one with the universe as the ceremony progresses. The dance has great meaning."

"Such as?" Meika said.

"The circle is an unbroken symbol of life and death. It mimics the movement of our solar system and the entire universe. Blood circulation, the seasons, gestation, everything."

"Do you believe in ghosts?" Meika asked.

"Eddie and I saw the ghost of my mom last night," Meika said.

"J.P. calls it an induced trance," Meika said.

"We can't always see what we believe and don't always believe what we see."

"I don't believe in ghosts," Meika said.

"Do you believe in science?" Delta asked. "The first law of thermodynamics says energy can neither be created nor destroyed. When a person dies, their energy isn't destroyed; it simply takes a different form."

"You're confusing me," Meika said.

"Dance with us tonight," Delta said. "Tomorrow, you'll have a different outlook on life and death."

"Why not?" Meika said. "Once the ceremony begins, no one will be left in the bar to serve.

Chapter 32

Meika's prediction proved correct. By quarter of midnight, no one was left in the bar; everyone was outside waiting for Freya's celebration of life and death to begin. Eddie, Odette, and Meika were with them.

More men and women crowded the island than Eddie had ever seen. They were moving toward the beach, where a tall wood pile awaited burning.

A full moon lighted the sky over the beach as people began arranging themselves in an unbroken line wrapping across the beach in a human chain. At exactly midnight, a lone man appeared from the darkness. It was Chief, dressed in only a breechcloth and the full headdress regalia of his grandfather, Walking Wolf.

Chief was an imposing man standing six foot six and with the impressive physique of a professional wrestler. His long gray hair brushed his large shoulders as he approached the wood pile with a lighted torch. When he lit it, flames licked the sky.

Everyone except Eddie and the people from the hotel were dressed in black. The crowd gasped when a short-haired blond woman dressed in nothing more than a diaphanous white gown approached the burning pyre. Eddie also had to gasp because the woman was Delta. Only the crackling of the fire and the sound of the surf breaking against the beach could be heard as she began to speak.

"I am here bearing a damaged soul as I call to my familiar, my mother, my heart. She has left our world and I need her to return."

Eddie didn't know that Chief could play the flute. He was surprised when the big Indian began a haunting melody on an ancient wooden instrument. Someone in a dark robe with a cowl over their head joined Delta. When the person removed the cowl, Eddie saw it was Seraphina. She spoke, responding to Delta's lament.

"Gather us now in the moon's haze, as whispers weave a mystic maze, with petals strewn and incense aswirl. We find new beginnings in life's fleeting breath, and death's soft sigh, in the silence of endings, broken images, and mother of pearl."

Delta responded. "Oh, Mother. Don't leave me alone. I need you. Don't go."

Seraphina answered. "Through cycles of life and circles of death, through winter's snow and spring's soft rain, we leave for now but return again. So let the flute play a whispered, tender, and true melody as you leave this world but start anew."

"Don't leave me," Delta said. "I'm begging on my knees. I need you."

The sound of Chief's flute was poignant as Seraphina said, "Mother Luna, cast your spell. Sing a song and ring a bell as flames flicker where spirits dwell. We celebrate life's melody."

Delta bowed and wept as the pagans began moving in everchanging circles. Hypnotized by the music of Chief's flute and suddenly possessed by some unknown fervor, Eddie joined them. So did Odette, Meika, Jack, J.P. and Toni.

The pagans and those who had joined them moved in circles that Eddie soon felt painted a moving picture of profound symbolism he somehow understood. Though on only a natural high, he felt more intoxicated and invincible than he'd ever been. Whatever was gripping his mind and body had released him from pain, stress, and fatigue.

Eddie was no longer an individual but an instrumental part of a moving entity acting out a group ritual as old as time. As Delta had said, the experience was exhilarating.

When dawn broke the eastern sky, the pagans stopped dancing. Those not already naked cast off their robes and entered the waves of the Gulf of Mexico to complete their healing.

Eddie wandered to the spot where Amani's old Volkswagen van had sat. It was gone, as was Amani. Because of Freya's ceremony, he was able to handle it.

A big white cat was wandering the beach alone. It was Blanco. When he saw Eddie, he jumped into his arms. Eddie hugged the big cat.

"Guess you're mine now, and I am yours," Eddie said.

Chapter 33

The hundreds of people who had attended Freya's celebration of life and death began leaving Oyster Island shortly after dawn. The same went for Seraphina and her Covington witch's coven. By noon, all the witches had checked out of the Majestic and gone home. When Eddie made it downstairs, he found only the regulars. Meika was mixing drinks at the bar as Narcisse and Odette brought him a scotch.

"I'm happy to see your first day at the Majestic wasn't your last," he said.

"I went home early," Narcisse said.

"I returned to my room and caught a few hours of sleep after the ceremony," Eddie said. "What's that wonderful aroma coming from the kitchen?"

"Isaac's famous duck gumbo," Odette said.

"You didn't break the law and buy the ducks from other hunters?"

"I was pumped following Freya's celebration," Odette said. "So were J.P. and Toni. We went hunting and bagged our limit."

"Good for you. If it tastes as good as it smells, we're all in for a treat."

"It does," Toni said. "Isaac gave me a taste."

J.P. and Toni were holding hands. "Guess you two have kissed and made up," Eddie said.

"Last night was the most awesome experience I've ever had," Toni said.

Toni and J.P. reddened when Eddie said, "And dancing naked for six hours likely hastened things along."

Before J.P. or Toni could answer, Professor Quinn, Jack, and Chief joined the group.

"Are you enjoying your stay on Oyster Island, Professor Quinn?" Eddie asked.

"Immensely, though all good things must end," Professor Quinn said. "I'm returning to Goose Island, but not until I've had a bowl of Isaac's duck gumbo."

"You're a migratory bird researcher, Professor," Eddie said. "I wouldn't have thought you would condone duck hunting."

"On the contrary," Professor Quinn said. "It's all about conservation. Predators of all sorts serve to keep a population healthy. Regulation is the key."

"Will you return for a visit?" Eddie asked.

"Next Thursday. I have a date with Iryna if she hasn't succumbed to the advances of Jack, Isaac, or Pancho by then. Seems I'm the only one who can't cook."

"Sounds like Iryna is living her dream," Eddie said.

"Where's Amani?" J.P. asked.

"Gone," Eddie said.

"Back to Jamaica?" Chief asked.

"Or wherever she was from," Eddie said.

"Did you two have a thing?" J.P. said.

"I helped her find Lafitte's treasure if that's what you mean," Eddie said.

"Toss me the keys to your office," Chief said. "Jack and I will get it and show everybody."

They soon returned with the treasure and set the chest on the floor beside the table.

When they opened the top, Toni said, "Oh, my God! Is this for real?"

"As real as it gets," Eddie said. "I'm using part of it to settle with Frankie once and for all. As we agreed, the island is yours, Chief, and the Majestic is mine."

Eddie nodded when Chief said, "Free and clear?"

"Forever and ever," Eddie said. "Frankie has promised to ensure that Conexco never bothers us again."

"I'd still like to know who or what killed the first bomber," J.P. said.

J.P.'s mouth dropped when Eddie said, "Amani killed him."

"Get out of here!" he said. "How do you figure that?"

"Chief told me he heard a creature the night you found the body?" Eddie said.

"A bear, maybe," J.P. said.

"Not a bear," Eddie said. "Chief called it a wendigo, and I think he's correct."

"That's crazy," J.P. said.

"What's crazy was my failure to include Amani as a suspect in the bomber's death. As a longtime prosecutor, I should have known better."

"You'd better explain," J.P. said.

"A clue is a clue, and I shouldn't have disregarded the flower and the larimar we found at the murder scene. Amani left them there for us to find. Your instincts were right all along."

"Who killed the bomber? Amani or this wendigo creature of yours?" J.P. said.

"Amani killed him. Sort of," Eddie said.

"What do you mean sort of?" J.P. asked.

"The wendigo, a supernatural monster, killed the bomber. Delta was drunk the night I spent on La Tortue Mountain with Amani and followed us to the Magic Fountain. She was asleep under one of Chief's blankets when I called, and you told me about the bombers wiring Renata's house."

"So?" J.P. said.

"After I followed Old Joe down the hill, Delta saw Amani transform into a horrible beast. She called her a shapeshifter."

"We Indians call such beings Skinwalkers," Chief said.

Eddie nodded. "Amani was of Spanish, African, and Caribbean Indian descent. She practiced voodoo, and God only knows what else."

"So, Amani, in the form of a shapeshifting monster, killed the bomber and left the cerasee flower and polished larimar as clues," J.P. said.

Eddie nodded. "We incorrectly thought the larimar was from Freya's necklace. It wasn't. Amani left them so we'd know she had been there."

"The police need to know," J.P. said.

"She was only protecting us," Eddie said. "The police have closed the case and don't want to hear a mythical monster killed the bomber."

"Damn!" J.P. said. "It will take me a while to wrap my head around this one."

Delta had approached the table and overheard the conversation about Amani.

"Amani's from another place and time and only came here to reclaim what was hers. She really was the ghost of the woman you and Odette saw while duck hunting."

"Delta's correct," Eddie said. "The person we knew as Amani LeClair was the Countess of Dominica. She accomplished what she came to the island to do and now has returned to where she belongs."

"So, she cast the curse as the Countess of Dominica some two centuries ago and removed it yesterday as Amani LeClair," Chief said.

"That's right," Eddie said.

"And she left the treasure to ensure the island went to the rightful owners," Jack said.

"After last night's ceremony, there's not much I don't believe. Let's break out the rum and celebrate," Chief said.

The booze and duck gumbo were flowing freely when Josie and Alex came downstairs holding hands.

"Do you two have something to tell us?" Eddie said.

"Is it wrong for partners to hold hands?" Josie said.

"Not at all," Eddie said. "I'm glad you're over Carlos and moving forward."

"Very much so. Carlos's family didn't make it to the island, so Jojo, Alex, and I are flying to Miami next week," Josie said. "Jojo can meet his sisters, and Alex, Carlos, and I can finalize our distillery plans."

"What about you, Chief? How do you feel about Seraphina leaving?" Eddie asked.

"Covington isn't far away. I'll visit her, and she can visit me," Chief said.

Eddie and Delta were the only ones left at the table sometime later.

Next week, J.P., Chief and Jack will help me move my belongings from Covington. The house in the complex you've offered me may prove too big," Delta said.

"You'll like it better than living in the Majestic," Eddie said.

Delta clutched Eddie's hand and said, "Are you okay?"

"I'm good."

"I mean about Amani?"

"Amani promised I'd see her again. She has already kept her promise," he said.

Eddie shook his head when Delta said, "Is she back on the island?"

"Though I never knew it, I learned this morning that dreams are where different realms of reality converge. Amani came to me in a dream when I returned to my room and fell asleep."

Delta squeezed Eddie's hand and said, "It was only a dream. Lives intersect for reasons only known by the cosmos. You helped her, and she helped you. Sometimes, that's all there is."

"Maybe," Eddie said. "When I awoke, I found something on my pillow that suggests otherwise."

"What?" Delta said.

Eddie opened his hand and showed her.

"A cerasee flower and a piece of larimar."

End

Book Notes

In other books I've written, time-traveling characters travel from the future into the past. Amani LeClair is my first character who travels from the past to the future. As an author, I often ponder the motivations of these characters who seem to take on a life of their own. Amani LeClair is one of these individuals.

In Oyster Bay Limbo, Amani returns to Oyster Island ostensibly to recover a valuable necklace that likely had significant meaning to her. Perhaps she really returned for the locket containing a lock of her son Diego's hair.

I spent many hours tapping into the collective consciousness to determine Amani LeClair's motivations. What I finally realized is something I already know: life is a forgotten language and fiction a way to translate it.

I hope you enjoyed reading *Oyster Bay Limbo* as much as I enjoyed writing it and that you liked all the eccentric characters. If you did, please leave a review.

You may also like my *French Quarter Mystery Series* with moody private detective Wyatt Thomas and the *Paranormal Cowboy Series* featuring Buck

McDivit, my modern-day cowboy detective who likes horses, cowgirls, and Australian sheepdogs.

Thanks for being a fan. My stories would be little more than morning fog wafting across a forgotten lawn without beautiful readers like you. Thank you

About the Author

Eric Wilder is an American author known for his gripping mystery novels set in New Orleans. He was born and raised in Louisiana, where he discovered his love for storytelling at a young age. After completing his education, Wilder spent several years in the oil and gas industry before pursuing a career as a writer.

Wilder's breakthrough came with the publication of Big Easy, which introduced readers to his signature blend of suspense, action, and local color. The book instantly succeeded, drawing critical acclaim and a devoted following. Wilder followed up with a collection of thrillers set in the heart of New Orleans.

Wilder's writing is characterized by his deep knowledge of the city and its unique culture and his skillful use of suspense and plot twists to keep readers on the edge of their seats. His books have been praised for their authenticity, vivid descriptions, and compelling characters.

Today, Eric Wilder is a respected author with a loyal fan base and a reputation for delivering top-notch thrillers that transport readers to the heart of New Orleans.

Wilder is the author of twenty novels, several cookbooks, many short stories, and Murder Etouffee, a book that defies classification. His series features characters who often find themselves involved in the paranormal.

Eric Wilder lives in Oklahoma near historic Route 66 with his wife, Marilyn, a gorgeous pit bull named Moebius, and two remarkable cats, Buttercup and Blanco.